That Old Cape Magic

That Old Cape Magic

Richard Russo

ALFRED A. KNOPF
New York

THIS IS A BORZOI BOOK
PUBLISHED BY ALFRED A. KNOPF

Knopf, Borzoi Books and the colophon are registered
trademarks of Random House, Inc.

ISBN 978-1-61664-173-3

Manufactured in the United States of America

For Barbara, always

PART ONE

Cape Cod

(First Wedding)

I

A Finer Place

Though the digital clock on the bedside table in his hotel room read 5:17, Jack Griffin, suddenly wide awake, knew he wouldn't be able to get back to sleep. He'd allowed himself to drift off too early the night before. On the heels of wakefulness came an unpleasant realization, that what he hadn't wanted to admit yesterday, even to himself, was now all too clear in the solitary, predawn dark. He should have swallowed his petulance and waited the extra day for Joy.

It had been their long-established habit to flee the campus as soon as Griffin taught his last class. Usually, they hopped on the Freedom Trail (his term for I-95), drove to New York and treated themselves by checking into a good hotel. During the day he would evaluate his small mountain of student portfolios while Joy shopped or otherwise amused herself, and then, evenings, they'd catch up on movies and go to restaurants. The whole thing reminded him of the early years of their marriage back in L.A. It cost a small fortune, but there was something about spending money they didn't really have that made him optimistic about more coming in—which was how it had worked in L.A.—and it got him through the portfolios.

This year Kelsey's Cape Cod wedding had royally screwed up their plans, making New York impractical, though he'd been willing to substitute Boston. But Joy, assuming that thanks to the wedding all the usual bets were off, had messed things up further by scheduling meetings on the day after his last class. "Just *go*," she said when he expressed his annoyance at the way things were working out. "Have a boys' night out in Boston and I'll meet you on the Cape." He'd squinted at this proposal. Didn't you need more than one to have a boys' night out? Or had Joy meant it to be singular, one boy celebrating his boyness? Was that how she'd understood the phrase all her life, as singular? Joy's relationship to the English language was not without glitches. She was forever mixing metaphors, claiming that something was "a tough line to hoe." Row to hoe? Line to walk? Her sisters, Jane and June, were even worse, and when corrected all three would narrow their eyes dangerously and identically. If they'd had a family motto, it would have been You Know Perfectly Well What I Mean.

In any event, his wife's suggestion that he go on without her had seemed less than sincere, which was why he decided to call her bluff. "All right," he said, "that's what I'll do," expecting her to say, *Fine, if it means that much to you, I'll reschedule the meetings.* But she hadn't said that, even when she saw him packing his bag, and so he'd discovered a truth that other men probably knew already—that once you'd packed a bag in front of a woman there was no possibility of unpacking, or of *not* going and taking the damn bag with you.

Worse, Joy, who preferred to watch movies on DVD rather than in a theater, as they were meant to be seen, had given him a list of films he was forbidden to see without her, and of course these were the only ones worth seeing. He'd spent an hour looking through the restaurant guides provided by the hotel, but couldn't decide on one, or even on what kind of food he wanted. Griffin had no trouble making these sorts of decisions when she was around, but for some reason, when he had only himself to please, he often couldn't make up his mind. He told himself this was just the result of being married for thirty-four years, that part of the decision-making process was imagining what his wife would enjoy. Okay, but more and more he found himself stalled, in the middle of whatever room he happened to be standing in, and he realized that this had been, of course, his father's classic pose. In the end Griffin had ordered room service and watched a crappy made-for-TV movie, the kind he and Tommy, his old partner, had been reduced to writing that last year or two in L.A. before he'd gotten his teaching gig and moved back East with Joy and their daughter, Laura. He'd fallen asleep before the first commercial, confident he could predict not only the movie's outcome but also half its dialogue.

In order not to dwell on yesterday's mistakes, he decided to put today in motion by calling down to the bell captain for his car. Twenty minutes later, dressed and showered, he'd checked out of his Back Bay hotel. The whole of Boston fit neatly into the rectangle of his rearview mirror, and by the time the Sagamore Bridge, one of two that spanned the Cape Cod Canal, hove into view, the sky was silver in the east, and he felt the last remnants of yesterday's prevarications begin to lift like the patchy fog he'd been in and out of since leaving the city. The Sagamore arched dramatically upward in the middle, helping to pull the sun over the horizon, and though the air was far too cool, Griffin pulled off onto the shoulder of the road and put the convertible's top down, feeling truly off the reservation for the first time since leaving home in Connecticut. There was something vaguely thrilling about not being where his wife thought he was. She liked to know what people were up to, and not just him. She called Laura most mornings, her brain still lazy with sleep, to ask, "So . . . what's on the agenda for you today?" She also phoned both of her sisters several times a week and knew that June was having her hair done tomorrow morning and that Jane had put on five pounds and was starting a diet. She even knew what new folly her idiot twin brothers, Jared and Jason, were engaged in. To Griffin, an only child, such behavior was well over the line that separated the merely inexplicable from the truly perverse.

Zipping along Route 6, Griffin realized he was humming "That Old Black Magic," the song his parents had sung ironically—both university English professors, that's how they did most things— every time they crossed the Sagamore, substituting *Cape* for *black*. When he was growing up, they'd spent part of every summer on the Cape. He could always tell what kind of year it had been, money-wise, by where and when they stayed. One particularly prosperous year they'd rented a small house in Chatham for the month of August. Another year, when faculty salaries were frozen, all they could afford was Sandwich in June. His parents had been less wed to each other than to a shared sense of grievance over being exiled eleven months of every year to the "Mid-fucking-west," a phrase they didn't say so much as spit. They had good academic careers, though perhaps not the stellar ones that might have been predicted, given their Ivy League pedigree. Both had grown up in the Rust Belt of western New York State, his mother in suburban Rochester, his father in Buffalo, the children of lower-middle-class, white-collar parents. At Cornell, where they'd both gone on scholarship, they'd met not only each other but also the kind of friends who'd invited them home for holidays in Wellesley and Westchester and for summer vacations in the Hamptons or on the Cape. They told their parents they could earn more money there, which was true, but in fact they'd have done anything to avoid returning to their parents' depressing upstate homes. At Yale, where they did their graduate work, they came to believe they were destined for research positions at one of the other Ivys, at least until the market for academics headed south and they had to take what they could get—the pickings even slimmer for a couple—and that turned out to be a huge state university in Indiana.

Betrayed. That was how they felt. Why *go* to Cornell, to Yale, if

Indiana was your reward? But they'd had little choice but to hunker down and make the best of their wretched timing, so they dove into teaching and research and committee work, hoping to bolster their vitae so that when the academic winds changed they'd be ready. They feared the Princeton and Dartmouth ships had probably sailed for good, but that still left the Swarthmores and Vassars of the world as safe if not terribly exciting havens. This much, at least, was surely their due. And before going up for promotion and tenure (or "promotion and tether," in their parlance) in the Mid-fucking-west, they'd each had opportunities—she at Amherst, he at Bowdoin—but never together. So they stayed put in their jobs and their marriage, each terrified, Griffin now suspected, that the other, unshackled, would succeed and escape to the kind of academic post (an endowed chair!) that would complete the misery of the one left behind. To make their unhappy circumstances more tolerable, they had affairs and pretended to be deeply wounded when these came to light. His father had been a genuine serial adulterer, whereas his mother simply refused to lag behind in this or anything else.

Of course all of this was adult understanding. As a boy, the reluctant witness to his parents' myriad quarrels and recrimina-tions, Griffin had imagined that he must be the one keeping them together. It was his mother who eventually disabused him of this bizarre notion. At his and Joy's wedding reception, actually. But by then they had finally divorced—even spite, apparently, was not eternal—and she'd narrowly won the race to remarry. In an ecu-menical mood, she ventured outside the English department for her second husband, a philosopher named Bart, whom she'd quickly dubbed "Bartleby." At the reception, half in her cups, she'd assured Griffin, "Good heavens, no, it wasn't *you*. What kept us together was 'That Old Cape Magic.' Remember how we used to sing it every year on the Sagamore?" She then turned to Bartleby. "One glorious month, each summer," she explained. "Sun. Sand. Water. Gin. Followed by eleven months of misery." Then back to

Griffin. "But that's about par for most marriages, I think you'll find." The *I think you'll find,* he understood, was of course meant to suggest that in her view, his own marital arithmetic was likely to be much the same. For a moment it seemed as if Bartleby might offer an observation of his own, but he apparently preferred not to, though he did sigh meaningfully.

Griffin was about to respond when his father reappeared with Claudia, his former graduate student and new wife. They'd disappeared briefly after the ceremony, to quarrel or make love, he had no idea. "I swear to God," his mother said, "if he buys that child a house on the Cape—and I do mean *anywhere* on the Cape—I may have to murder him." Her face brightened at a pleasant thought. "You might actually prove useful," she told Bartleby, then turned back to Griffin. "Your stepfather collects locked-room murder mysteries. Death by curare, that sort of thing. You can figure something out, can't you? Just make sure I'm in full view of everyone in the drawing room when the fat cow hits the deck, writhing in excruciating pain." She knew perfectly well, of course, that Griffin's father didn't have the money to buy Claudia (who was more zaftig than fat) or anyone else a house on the Cape, of course. She'd made sure of that by beggaring him in the divorce settlement, but the possibility—what of, that he might purchase a winning Lotto ticket?—still clearly worried her.

To Griffin, now fifty-seven, roughly the same age his parents had been when he and Joy married, the Cape place-names were still magical: Falmouth, Woods Hole, Barnstable, Dennis, Orleans, Harwich. They made a boy of him again and put him in the backseat of his parents' car, where he'd spent much of his boyhood, unbelted, resting his arms on the front seat, trying to hear what they, who never made any attempt to include him in their conversations, were talking about. It wasn't so much that he was interested in their front-seat conversations as aware that decisions that impacted him were being made up there, and if privy to these hatching plans he might offer an opinion. Unfortunately, the fact that his chin was resting on the seat back seemed to preclude this. Most of what he overheard wasn't really worth the effort anyway. "Wellfleet," his mother might say, studying the road atlas. "Why haven't we ever tried Wellfleet?" By the time Griffin was a high school freshman, which marked the last of their Cape vacations, they'd rented just about everywhere. Each summer, when they handed over the keys at the end of their stay, the rental agent always asked if they wanted to book it for next year, but they always said no, which made Griffin wonder if the perfect spot they were searching for really existed. Perhaps, he concluded, just looking was sufficient in and of itself.

While he roamed the beach unattended, full of youthful energy and freedom, his parents spent sunny afternoons lying on the sand with their "guilty pleasures," books they'd have been embarrassed to admit to their colleagues they'd ever heard of. They were on vacation, they claimed, not just from the Mid-fucking-west but also from the literary canon they'd sworn to uphold. His mother's taste ran to dark, disturbing thrillers and cynical spy novels. "That," she would say, turning the book's last page with evident satisfaction, "was truly twisted." His father alternated between literary pornography and P. G. Wodehouse, enjoying both thoroughly, as if *Naked Lunch* and *Bertie Wooster Sees It Through* were intended as companion pieces.

The only thing they both read—indeed, studied as intently as each year's Modern Language Association job listings—was the real-estate guide. Unwilling to give the other a first look, they always picked up two copies as soon as they arrived and wrote their names on the covers so they'd know which was which and whose fault it was if one got lost. A house here was part of their long-range, two-part plan to escape the Mid-fucking-west. First they would find real jobs back East, where they'd locate a suitable apartment to rent. This would allow them to save money for a house on the Cape, where they'd spend summers and holidays and the occasional long weekend, until of course they retired—early if they could swing it—and lived on there full-time, reading and writing op-eds and, who knew, maybe even trying their hand at a novel.

A single day was usually all it took for each of them to plow through the hundreds of listings in the fat real-estate guide and place each into one of two categories—Can't Afford It or Wouldn't Have It As a Gift—before tossing the booklet aside in disgust, because everything was more expensive this year than last. But the very next day his father would set Jeeves aside and take another look. "Page twenty-seven," he'd say, and Griffin's mother would set down her Ripley and rummage for her copy in the beach bag. "Bear with me, now," he'd continue. Or, "Some things would have to go right"—meaning a big merit raise or a new university-press book contract—"but . . ." And then he'd explain why a couple of the listings they'd quickly dismissed the day before just maybe could be made to work. Later in the month, on a rainy day, they'd go so far as to look at a house or two at the low end of the Can't Afford It category, but the realtors always intuited at a glance that Griffin's parents were just tire kickers. The house they wanted was located in a future only they could see. For people who dealt largely in dreams, his father was fond of observing, realtors were a surprisingly un-romantic bunch, like card counters in a Vegas casino.

The drive back to the Mid-fucking-west was always brutal, his parents barely speaking to each other, as if suddenly recalling last year's infidelities, or maybe contemplating whom they'd settle for this year. Sex, if you went by Griffin's parents, definitely took a backseat to real estate on the passion gauge.

What he'd do, Griffin decided, was take Route 6 all the way to Provincetown, have a late breakfast there, then poke back up the Cape on tacky old 28. He wondered if it would still be lined with flea markets, as it had been when he was a kid. His father, an avid collector of political ephemera and an avowed Democrat, could never pass one without stopping to make sure there wasn't an old Wendell Willkie campaign button its owner didn't know the value of lying at the bottom of a cardboard box. Republican artifacts were another of his guilty pleasures. "All your father's pleasures are guilty," his mother claimed, "and deserve to be." Of course Route 28 would take twice as long, but there was no hurry. Joy wouldn't arrive until evening, probably late, and the sooner he got to the B and B where she'd booked a room for the wedding, the sooner he'd feel compelled to open the trunk of the convertible, which contained, in addition to his travel bag and his bulging satchel, the urn bearing his father's ashes, which he'd pledged to scatter over the weekend. He wasn't sure that disposing of cremated midwestern academics in Massachusetts waters was strictly legal, and would have preferred that Joy be there for moral support (and as a lookout). Still, if he happened upon a quiet, serene and deserted spot, he might just do the deed by himself. Hell, maybe he'd dump the portfolios in as well—an idea that made him smile.

Pilgrim Monument had just appeared on the horizon when his cell phone vibrated in the cup holder, and he pulled over to answer it. In the last nine months, since his father's death, he'd been in several minor but costly fender benders, so this seemed safer than talking and driving at the same time, though there wasn't as much room on the shoulder as he would've hoped for. A truck roared by, too close for comfort, but no one else was coming. He'd just have to make it quick.

He assumed the caller, at this hour, had to be Joy, but it wasn't. "Where *are* you?" his mother wanted to know. Lately, she didn't bother saying hello or identifying herself. In her opinion he was supposed to know who it was, and thanks to her tone of perpetual annoyance and aversion to preamble, he usually did.

"Mom," he said, not all that anxious to testify to his present whereabouts. "I was just thinking about you." A lone gull, perhaps concluding that he'd pulled over to eat something cheesy, circled directly overhead and let out a sharp screech. "You and Dad both, actually."

"Oh," she said. "Him."

"I'm not supposed to think about Dad?"

"Think about whomever you want," she said. "When did I ever pry into your thoughts? Your father and I may not have agreed on much, but we respected your intellectual and emotional privacy."

Griffin sighed. Anymore, even his most benign comments set his mother off, and once she was on a roll it was best just to let her finish. Their respect for his privacy had been, he knew all too well, mostly disinterest, but it wasn't worth arguing over.

"I have my *own* thoughts, thank you very much," she continued, implying, unless he was mistaken, that he wouldn't want to know what these were, either. "And they are full and sufficient. I can't imagine why your father should be occupying yours, but if he is, don't let me interfere."

The circling gull cried out again, even louder this time, and Griffin briefly covered the phone with his hand. "Did you call for a reason, Mom?"

But she must've heard the idiot bird, because she said, her voice rich with resentment and accusation, "Are you on *the Cape*?"

"Yes, Mom," he admitted. "We're attending a wedding here tomorrow. Why, should I have alerted you? Asked permission?"

"Where?" she said. "What part?"

"Near Falmouth," he was happy to report. The upper Cape, in her view, was strictly for people who didn't know any better. You might as well live in Buzzards Bay, drive go-carts, play miniature golf, eat clam chowder thickened with flour, wear a Red Sox hat.

"Marriage," she sneered, what he'd told her apparently now registering. "What folly."

"You were married twice yourself, Mom."

When Bartleby died several years back, she'd hoped there might be a little something in it for her, at least enough to buy a small cottage near one of the Dennises, maybe. But an irrevocable trust let his rapacious children take everything, and they'd been unrepentant in their greed. "You made our father's final years a living hell," one of them had had the gall to tell her. "Did you ever hear such nonsense?" she'd asked Griffin. "Did they even *know* the man? Could they imagine he'd *ever* been happy? Was there ever a philosopher who *wasn't* morose and depressed?"

"The bride's Kelsey," Griffin told her. "From L.A., remember?"

"Why would I know your California friends?" This was no innocent question. Though she wouldn't admit it, his mother was still resentful of the years he and Joy and then Laura had spent out West, out of her orbit. And she'd always considered his screenwriting a betrayal of his genetic gifts.

"Not *our* friend. Laura's." Though it was entirely possible, now that he thought about it, they'd never met. It had always been Griffin's policy not to inflict his parents on his wife and daughter, who'd really gotten to know her grandmother only after they moved back East.

"How does it look?"

"How does what look?"

"The Cape. You just told me you were on the Cape, so I'm asking how it looks to you."

"Like always, I guess," he said, not about to confess that his heart had started racing on the Sagamore Bridge, that he still loved something that she and her hated husband also loved.

"They say it's too crowded now. I guess we had the best of it. You, me, the man occupying your thoughts."

"Again, what were you calling about, Mom?"

"Fine," she said. "Change the subject. I need you to bring me some books, and I'll e-mail you the titles. I assume you'll be visiting at some point? Or have I seen the last of you?"

"Are these books I'll be able to find? For instance, are they in print, or is this yet another fool's errand you've designed for me?" Since Bartleby's death, Griffin had become the man in his mother's life, and she enjoyed nothing more than setting him the sort of impossible task, especially of the academic variety, that would've been easy if he'd done with his life what she'd intended instead of what he himself had preferred.

"Just because you can't find what I ask for doesn't mean it's a fool's errand. You belong to a generation that never learned basic research skills, who can't even negotiate a card catalog."

"They don't have those anymore," he said, for the pleasure of hearing her shudder.

Which she denied him. "You think typing a word into Google and pressing *Go* is research."

There was, he had to admit, some truth to this. Back in his screenwriting days, he'd always happily delegated research to Tommy, who was genuinely curious if easily distractible. Confronted with his own ignorance, Griffin preferred to just make something up and move forward, whereas his partner, not unreasonably, preferred making sure their narrative had a sturdy, factual foundation. "You *do* know that when the cameras roll they're going to be pointing at something in the real world, right?" he'd asked. To which Griffin would reply that the cameras were never going to roll if they kept getting bogged down in background.

"The things I require are all at Sterling," his mother continued. "I still have privileges there, you know."

It was entirely possible, Griffin knew, this was the real reason she'd called: to remind him of who she was, who she'd been, that she still had privileges at the Yale library. She might not actually need any books.

"There are some journal articles, too. Those you can just photocopy. The library offered to provide that service, but it would be cheaper for you to do it. I'm not made of money, as you know."

As he had excellent reason to. Her TIAA-CREF retirement and university insurance covered a good chunk of her assisted-living facility, but Griffin made up the difference.

"You can pick them up on your way here. Are we talking June, this impending visit?" she wondered. And clearly they'd better be.

"I can come for a couple of days near the end of the month, if you need me to."

"Not until then?"

"I haven't even turned in my final grades yet. The trunk of my car's full of student portfolios." *Not to mention Dad's ashes,* he almost added.

"You actually read them?"

"Didn't you read yours?"

"We had no *portfolios,* your father and I," she reminded him. "We had exams. Our students wrote papers with footnotes. We taught real courses with real content." Their metaphorical cameras had also been pointed, in other words, at something that actually existed. "Assigned readings. Rigor, it was called."

A car blew by, its Dopplering horn loud enough to startle him. "Are you sure I'm qualified to do your photocopying? What if I screw up?"

"So, what were you thinking . . . about your father and me?"

For a moment he considered telling her he feared he was becoming his father, that this was what his recent bouts of indecision, not to mention the fender benders, might be about. But of course it would anger his mother, and prolong the conversation, if he suggested he was more like his father than her. "I thought you didn't want to pry, Mom. Isn't that what you just said, that my thoughts are my own?"

"They are, of course. Still, as a personal favor, couldn't you arrange to think about your father and me separately?"

"I was remembering how happy you both got on the Sagamore

Bridge, how you sang 'That Old Cape Magic'?" *And how miserable you both were in the same spot going the other direction.* "As if happiness were a place."

But she wasn't interested in this particular stroll down memory lane. "Speaking of unhappy places, when you visit, I want you to look at this new one I'm at." Her third assisted-living facility in as many years. The first was connected to the university and full of the very people she'd been trying to escape. The second was home to mid-fucking-western farmwives who read Agatha Christie and couldn't understand why she turned up her nose at the Miss Marples they thrust at her, saying, "You'll like this one. It's a corker!"

"I mean *really* look at it," his mother continued. "It's certainly not what we imagined."

"What did we imagine, Mom?"

"Nice," she said. "We imagined it would be nice."

Then she was gone, the line dead. The whole conversation had been, he knew from experience, a warning shot across his bow. And his mother was, after her own fashion, considerate. She never badgered him during the last month of the semester. A lifelong academic, she knew what those final weeks were like and gave him a pass. But after that, all bets were off. The timing of today's call suggested she'd been on his college's Web site again and knew he'd taught his last class. He knew it was a mistake to get her a laptop for her birthday even as he bought it, but in her previous facility she'd been accused of hogging the computer in the common room. Also of hogging the attentions of the few old men there, a charge she waved away. "Look at them," she snorted. "There isn't enough Viagra in all of Canada." Though she did admit, as if to foreshorten ruthless interrogation on this subject, that there *was* more sex in these retirement homes than you might imagine. A *lot* more.

He supposed it was possible she really did need the books from Sterling. At eighty-five, her physical health failing, she was still mentally sharp and claimed to be researching a book on one of the

Brontës ("You remember books, right? Bound objects? Lots and lots of pages? Print that goes all the way out to the margins?"). But he made a mental note to check her list to make sure he couldn't find them in his own college library.

When a semi roared by, he noticed a foul odor and wondered what in the world the trucker was hauling. Only when he turned the key in the ignition did he see the viscous white glob on his shirt-sleeve. The gull had shit on him!

His mother had made him a stationary target, and this was the result.

2

Slippery Slope

By the time Griffin's parents got divorced, each claiming they should've cut the cord sooner, that they'd made each other miserable for too long, he was in film school out West, and he'd thought it was probably for the best. But neither had prospered in their second marriages, and their careers suffered, too. Together, or at least voting together, they'd been a force to reckon with in English department politics. Singly, often voting against each other, they could be safely ignored, and the worst of their enemies now sniped at both with impunity. Of the two, his mother seemed to fare better at first. Openly contemptuous of the young literary theorists and culture critics when she was married to Griffin's father, she'd reinvented herself as a gender-studies specialist and became for a time their darling. One of her old "guilty pleasures," Patricia Highsmith, had become respectable, and his mother published several well-placed articles on her and two or three other gay/lesbian novelists. Panels on gender were suddenly all the rage, and she found herself chairing several of these at regional conferences, where she hinted to her large and largely lesbian audiences that she herself had always been open, in both theory and practice, as regards her own sexuality. And perhaps, he supposed, she was. Bartleby, who'd begun their marriage preferring not to argue and ended it preferring not to speak at all, remained philosophical when these innuendos were reported back to him. Griffin had assumed his mother was exaggerating his withdrawal from speech, but a few months before his unexpected death (going to the doctor was something else he preferred not to do), he'd paid them a quick visit and they'd all gone out to dinner and the man hadn't spoken a word. He didn't seem to be in a bad mood and would occasionally smile ruefully at something his wife or Griffin said, but the closest he came to utterance was when a piece of meat lodged in his windpipe, turning his face the color of a grape until a passing waiter saw his distress and Heimliched him on the spot.

But his mother's self-reinvention, a bold and for a time successful stroke, had ultimately failed. When the university, mostly at her suggestion and direction, created the Gender Studies Program, she of course expected to be named as its chair, but instead they'd recruited a transgendered scholar from, of all places, Utah, and that had been the last straw. From then on she taught her classes but quit attending meetings or having anything to do with departmental politics. Unless Griffin was mistaken, her secret hope was that her colleagues, noticing her absence, would try to lure her back into full academic life, but that hadn't happened. Even Bartleby's passing had elicited little sympathy. While she continued to publish, run panels and apply for chairperson positions at various English departments, her file by this time contained several letters suggesting that while she was a good teacher and a distinguished scholar, she was also divisive and quarrelsome. A bitch, really.

Despite deep misgivings, Griffin had accepted the university's invitation to attend his mother's retirement dinner. (Joy had volunteered to go as well, but he insisted on sparing her.) There happened to be a bumper crop of retirees that year, and each was given the opportunity to reflect on his or her many years of service to the institution. He found it particularly disconcerting that his mother was the last speaker on the program. He supposed it was possible the planners were saving the best, most distinguished retirees for last, though more likely they shared his misgivings about what might transpire, and putting her last represented damage control. When it was finally her turn, his mother rose to a smattering of polite applause and went to the podium. That she was wearing an expensive, well-tailored suit only deepened apprehension. "Unlike my colleagues," she said directly into the microphone, the only speaker of the evening to recognize that fundamental necessity, "I'll be brief and honest. I wish I could think of something nice to say about you people and this university, I really do. But the truth we dare not utter is that ours is a distinctly second-rate institution, as are the vast majority of our students, as are we." Then she returned to her seat and patted Griffin's hand, as if to say, *There, now; that wasn't so bad, was it?* What she actually said in the stunned silence was, "Here's something strange. For the first time in over a decade, I wish your father were here. He'd have enjoyed that."

His father had fared even worse after the divorce. He, too, had attempted reinvention by attaching himself to the new American Studies major. He'd always been at least as interested in politics and history as literature, and the university had been willing to lend half of him to American Studies provided his colleagues in English had no objections (they certainly didn't). His new office was one floor down in the Modern and Classical Languages Building, and Claudia, a big strapping graduate student, had offered to help him move his seventy or so boxes of books and periodicals. A lot of bending over was required and she wasn't wearing a bra. Though he hadn't really noticed her before, he did now, and his colleagues noticed him notice, remarking that it was clear which half of him was moving down to American Studies and which was remaining behind in English. Griffin was pretty sure his father had little desire to remarry and probably wouldn't have but for the university ban on faculty-student fraternizing. Which was absurd. It wasn't like Claudia was an undergraduate. She was twenty-nine, a grown-up (even by American university standards) who didn't need any institutional protection, though several of her male professors wanted to know who would protect them from *her*. What Claudia did need, according to many in the department, was help, a lot of it, in completing her degree. She'd narrowly passed her doctoral prelims on the second and final attempt, one of her examiners abstaining, after which it took her a full academic year to come up with an acceptable dissertation topic, and like a prize heifer at a county fair, she had to be led (by his father) every step of the way. To Griffin, she indeed had a bovine quality. A full head taller than his father, she had wide hips and full breasts that always seemed to be in motion beneath the loose blouses she favored.

And so it was that this distinguished senior professor woke up one morning to the realization that while his wife had retooled herself as an adventurous gender specialist, he'd reinvented himself as a fool. *Naked Lunch,* Griffin's mother remarked, had finally won the day, showing poor Jeeves the door. Which may have been why, when an old graduate-school friend, who was now a dean at the University of Massachusetts, called to ask if he'd consider a one-year appointment replacing a professor who'd fallen ill, he eagerly accepted. Griffin's mother, of course, had been apoplectic with fury when she heard. Amherst, after all, was—what—two hours from the Cape? He and the fat cow would be able to spend weekends there, or even on the Vineyard or Nantucket, while she was stuck in the Mid-fucking-west with a mute for company. But there wasn't a damn thing she could do about it, which she determined, according to Griffin's father, by trying *really, really* hard.

He and Claudia were gone a full year, returning to the university only at the last possible moment, on Labor Day weekend. Griffin, just then between scripts, had flown to Indiana for a couple days. He hadn't seen his father once during his Amherst stint, and he looked as if he must've spent the whole time in a TB ward. He'd aged a good ten years. Always slender and concave chested, he was now rail thin, with shrunken cheeks, and his hair had receded. Apparently to compensate, he wore what strands remained long on the back and sides, making him look like a Dickensian gravedigger. By contrast, Claudia had become even more zaftig. During Griffin's brief visit, she found numerous opportunities to insinuate her lush body near his, pillowing her unfettered breast against his arm or, if he happened to be sitting, the back of his head, gestures his father appeared not to notice.

They'd returned with excellent news, his father said. Claudia had finished her dissertation, and to celebrate they'd gotten married. He smiled bravely in relating this, while Claudia's bovine version was of a different sort altogether. Their marriage had to remain a secret for now, he explained, until she'd defended her dissertation and she had her degree in hand. Griffin wasn't sure he followed the logic of all this, but it wasn't any of his business, so he agreed not to breathe a word to anyone, especially his mother. Which was why he was surprised when he met her and Bart for lunch in the faculty dining room and the first words out of her mouth were: "So, did your father tell you he's married?"

In fact, she was full of information. No, his father wasn't ill, though she agreed he did look like death warmed over. What he was, she claimed, was exhausted, and why wouldn't he be? During his year at UMass, he'd not only taught all his classes but also researched and—get this—actually *written* Claudia's dissertation. When Griffin asked her how she could possibly know this, since neither his father nor Claudia was likely to have confided it to anyone, she just gave him a look. "And that's not even the best part," she continued. "She wasn't even *with* your father." When his mother dropped this bomb, Griffin glanced over at Bartleby.

Though he hadn't yet gone completely mute, he shrugged, as if to say, *Don't look at me; I just live here.*

Claudia, his mother went on, had gone with his father to Amherst, that much was true. But she hadn't stayed long. The tiny house they'd rented was almost twenty miles from the university, and since they only had one car, Claudia either had to go in to campus or else be stranded there in the boonies until he got home. "Work on your dissertation," his father had suggested. Indeed, he may have rented this particular house in order to give her little alternative but to buckle down. Her response, apparently, delivered in her thick-as-molasses, blasé fashion, was *"All day long?"*

In mid-October there'd been a cold snap, and after several days of frigid drizzle she'd announced to Griffin's father one morning that she meant to go to Atlanta to visit a friend for a while. Even her pussy was frostbit, she claimed, to which he replied he'd have no way of knowing. Why didn't they discuss things later that evening when he returned? But by then she was gone.

His mother admitted to being a bit vague about exactly when he discovered this "friend" wasn't in fact a woman and also that he (and now Claudia) wasn't in Atlanta but in Charleston. Apparently she'd been trying to throw him off track—and here Griffin's mother chortled—as if he came from a long line of tough cops and private eyes and was the sort of guy who'd give immediate chase and never give up, whereas in actuality what he'd done was sigh deeply and say to himself, *So . . . she's gone, then.*

That Claudia planned to remain gone for a good long while was obvious since she'd taken all her clothes, not just enough for a short trip. She took everything, in fact, except the materials she'd assembled, with his help, for her dissertation. These she left stacked impressively in the center of the dining room table, along with a sparse outline he briefly studied before wadding it up. In another man this gesture might have suggested he was through with her, that he'd seen and understood both the muddled writing on the page and the clearer writing on the wall. Unfortunately, all Griffin's father had seen was a more sensible approach to the research and writing of his fiancée's dissertation, so he took out a legal pad and started sketching out how things would proceed if the project were his and not Claudia's. That way, he reasoned, when she returned in a week or two (he still hadn't drawn the necessary inference from the empty clothes closet), she'd find that instead of having fallen behind, she was actually ahead. The once murky, bloated purpose statement was now a detailed, workable template, thoughtfully divided into manageable segments and subdivided into bite-sized pieces that required only mastication, a series of cuds that even the bovine Claudia could chew. Granted, this was something she should've been able to do for herself, but so what? It could be their secret. She'd be so grateful her frozen pussy would thaw.

This, according to Griffin's mother, was how the whole nightmare had begun, as an intellectual exercise in avoidance. That first night, when he'd come home, found her gone and substituted his own outline for hers, he'd have been mortified if anyone had suggested he might actually write any part of his fiancée's dissertation. But a week went by and she hadn't returned, and then another, and the materials still sat there on the table (though he'd moved them to one side to make room for his take-out meals), and he just *hated* for her to fall further and further behind. Of course Claudia, again according to Griffin's mother, had predicted all of this. She might be dumb as a plastic Jesus, but she was shrewd. After all, how smart did a woman have to be to get the best of a man so ruled by his pecker? Anyone with an ounce of self-respect would have tossed her dissertation stuff right into the fireplace, or at least shoved it into a dark closet. Instead Griffin's father had allowed it to sit there accusingly—yes, accusing *him*, not her—until one day, over mu shu pork eaten directly from the carton, a thought occurred to him, as of course it would: *Maybe just a short intro. Where's the harm?*

Because he'd been complicit, if only subconsciously, from the start. Hadn't he made sure that the subject of Claudia's dissertation was one that also greatly interested him? Hadn't he known all along that he'd have to hold her hand through every last page? How different was actually writing the thing? Wasn't it really just a question of efficiency? "Don't tell me I don't know how your father's mind works, how he rationalizes," his mother warned when Griffin objected. She understood all too well. Once he'd started down that slippery slope, he was a lost man. Writing the intro, he reconnected to the source material, making long, excited notes on cards for the body of the essay, its principal thrust and supporting arguments, until sometime during the holidays he slipped a fresh piece of paper into his IBM Selectric and typed: *Chapter One.*

Then an interesting thing happened. Whereas before he'd been anxiously awaiting Claudia's return, he now hoped she'd stay away. He'd always believed this would be—what?—a collaboration, in the best sense. She'd do the actual writing, of course, but he'd be right there to share notes and ideas, to make sure she didn't lose her focus. And wasn't that what all dissertations really were, collaborations? Otherwise, why *have* an adviser? But now he thought, *Fuck it.* He was making good progress, staying up late at night, neglecting, truth be told, his own teaching responsibilities. He'd hit his scholarly stride, and Claudia's return would break it. Maybe he'd surprise her in Atlanta during spring break, he told himself. But when the break came he decided to work through it (just as well, Griffin's mother said, since Claudia wasn't in Atlanta anyway and never had been), figuring that if all went well, he'd have a draft before the end-of-semester crunch. She could help him revise it while familiarizing herself with his conclusions and methods, because of course she was the one who'd have to defend them (though he'd be there to throw her a rope if she needed one).

All might have been well, except in April he'd come down with a toxic dose of the flu. At one point he awakened shivering and curled up in a ball on the bathroom floor with no memory of how he'd gotten there, though the commode testified eloquently as to why he'd needed to. Was he hallucinating or had Claudia called the day before, wondering how the dissertation was coming along? Had she laughed at him when he reported it was almost done?

Eventually the flu ran its course, but he never fully recovered his strength or the weight he'd lost as a result of vomiting and skipping meals, but guess what? He'd finished, and *wasn't he proud*? Only when Claudia actually returned in late August, just when he'd concluded she was gone for good, did the enormity of what he'd done come down on him like an anvil. Not so much the dishonesty of it, but rather that this could have been *his book*. It was quite possibly the best thing he'd ever written. Any good university press would be happy to have it, maybe even a mainstream trade publisher. It was possible that real money, as opposed to the bogus scrip universities routinely printed, redeemable only in the academic commissary, might change hands. But there was an obvious problem. How could he claim the work as his own when it was supposed to be Claudia's? He could argue she hadn't written any of it, and everyone who'd ever taught her would believe him, but that would mean he'd stolen her idea. He'd already signed off on the fact that it was *her* idea when he and two other colleagues approved the proposal.

"Mom," Griffin had protested at this point, "you can't know all this. And don't tell me Dad confided it, either. They aren't the kind of things he'd admit to anybody, especially not you." After all, he'd just spent the last twenty-four hours with his father, who hadn't dropped a single hint, even an oblique one, about any of this.

Another woman might have taken umbrage at his *especially not you*, but his mother didn't even slow down. "Pipe down," she said gleefully. "I haven't even gotten to the best part yet. Claudia was *blackmailing* him.

"Well, not in the conventional sense," she conceded. "It's more like emotional blackmail." Since they'd returned from Amherst,

Claudia had taken to wondering out loud what his colleagues would think if they knew what he'd done. Had he always been so dishonest, she wanted to know, or was this something new? Was what he'd done a firing offense? Would the scandal make the front page of the *Chronicle of Higher Education*?

"But that's an absurd threat," Griffin felt compelled to inject. "She couldn't expose him without exposing herself."

"True," she said, "but he's terrified anyway."

"He didn't look scared to me."

"Trust me."

"But Mom, the story doesn't track. Any undergraduate fiction workshop would tear it apart." Well, okay, maybe not completely. It was more disjointed and inconsistent than unbelievable, and Griffin suspected he knew why. The academy was a small world, and his mother had friends, and friends of friends, everywhere. She'd no doubt been following her ex-husband's year at UMass, or trying to, through half a dozen spies. She'd glean small bits of information from a wide variety of sources and stitch these into a single narrative as best she could, drawing inferences, pretending, as she always did, to be privy to everything.

Nor did she appreciate him suggesting she wasn't. "Undergraduate workshop," she snorted. "Right. Now *there's* a test."

"Okay," Griffin conceded. "I'm not saying there's no truth to what you're saying. I'm just—"

But she waved him off. "Do you want to hear the best part or not?"

"The blackmail wasn't the best part? There's more?"

She arched a sculpted eyebrow. "Get this. The whole time he was in Amherst?"

He waited until it was clear she had no intention of going on without a specific invitation. He had to go on record as wanting to know what she had to tell him, which, unfortunately, he did.

"What, Mom? The whole time in Amherst what?"

"The *whole time* your father was in Amherst," she said triumphantly, "he never even made it to the Cape. Not once."

In retrospect, his mother had been right about at least one thing. She'd given his father's marriage another year. Not a full year, either, she insisted, an academic year. And that's exactly how long it had lasted. The following May, Claudia had departed for good, and shortly after that his father had left the university to take a position as acting department chair at a small branch of the state university of Illinois. "He's in a downward spiral," his mother had reported. "In fact he's circling the drain." From there he'd become the dean of faculty at a small Christian college in Oklahoma, where he served until failing health forced him to retire.

And now, Griffin thought ruefully, he was in the trunk of his car.

3

The Great Truro Accord

By the time Griffin arrived in Provincetown it had warmed up, so he went to a café with an outdoor patio. In the foyer he noticed a stack of real-estate guides, so he grabbed one and leafed through it while he waited for his eggs. The listings, he quickly determined, were either mind-bogglingly expensive or little more than shacks. Can't Afford It and Wouldn't Have It As a Gift. The old categories apparently still applied. Which begged a question. If he hadn't given up screenwriting to move back East and become a college professor, would *they* have had the money? Hard to say. He'd made a lot more money in L.A., but they'd spent a lot more, too. It had been one of the great mysteries of his parents' marriage that nothing they did or didn't do seemed to change their overall economic outlook all that much. Near the back of the guide, looking completely out of place, was a full-page ad for a high-end assisted-living community near Hyannis, which sent a chill up his spine. His mother knew he was on the Cape. Was it possible their conversation had awakened the old dormant passion? He could easily imagine her Googling the assisted-living options here (like hell Google wasn't research). It was even possible that out in Indiana she was at that very moment looking at the same image that he was studying here in Provincetown. A creepy scenario, and so utterly plausible that when his cell phone rang, he was surprised to see it was Joy and not his mother.

"Where are you?" his wife demanded, sounding almost as annoyed as his mother had been earlier, though to her credit she'd at least said hello before wanting to know just how far he'd strayed from her expectation.

"Provincetown," he informed her. "I woke up early."

"If you don't start sleeping soon, I want you to see somebody."

There was real concern in her voice now, for which he was grateful. It was true he hadn't been sleeping well, waking up for no apparent reason in the middle of the night and unable to get back to sleep. The usual end-of-semester pressure, no doubt. He'd already had his standard academic-anxiety dream, the one where he arrived at his classroom only to find a note on the door saying his class was now meeting in another building across campus. When he arrived there, same deal. And no matter how he hurried to catch up, his students were always receding at the end of an impossibly long corridor. All of it would probably disappear when he turned in his grades.

"Guess who I'm having breakfast with?" he said, anxious to change the subject.

"Who?"

"Al Fresco," he said. It was an old joke, no doubt summoned to the front of his brain by being on the Cape and eating outdoors. His parents always made sure their summer rental had either a patio or porch so they could have breakfast outside and read the paper "with Al," ignoring Griffin's pleas to finish so they could go to the beach. He and Joy had used Al Fresco back in their L.A. days, but it wasn't that great a joke and had naturally fallen into disuse.

Still, he was a little hurt when Joy said, "Al who?"

"I don't know about yours," he told her, "but my day's begun poorly."

"I know," Joy said, sounding exhausted now. "She called here, too. The semester's officially over, I guess."

Griffin had put off introducing Joy to his parents for as long as possible, explaining that they were involved in a particularly acrimonious divorce. "But I *am* going to meet them, right?" she'd inquired, already suspicious. "I mean, they *are* your parents." He suggested, "How about at the wedding?" and she'd laughed, thinking he was joking. Down the years she'd gotten on well enough with his father, though he could never quite seem to place her, even when she was standing next to his son. Living two thousand miles apart, they saw each other infrequently, of course, but each time they met, his father acted more delighted and charmed than seemed natural. "Is it my imagination," Joy said after their second meeting, "or had he forgotten me entirely?" Griffin told her not to take it personally. At the end of each semester his father still didn't know his students' names, except the two or three prettiest girls.

His mother was a different story. Though polite, she'd never made a secret of her low opinion of Griffin's choice of a mate. "Where did she do her graduate work?" was the first thing she'd wanted to know when Griffin called to say he was engaged. For her there was no greater barometer of personal worth. Moreover, when she asked people this question, they generally asked her back, and she got to say her doctorate was from Yale; if they didn't ask, she told them anyway. In Joy's case, she'd been expecting UCLA or Southern Cal. Griffin had anticipated this question, of course, and reminded himself there was no reason to be embarrassed to answer it, though naturally he was. He'd taken a deep breath and explained that Joy had gone directly to work after getting her undergraduate degree and that she had a good job, one she enjoyed. "Yes, but what sort of person doesn't do graduate work?" His mother inflected the word *person* ever so slightly, as if to suggest that anyone who didn't go to graduate school might belong to neither gender, or perhaps to both. Poor Joy had spent the first decade of their marriage trying to get her mother-in-law to think better of her, the next trying to fathom why that wasn't happening and the one after that pretending it didn't matter. Of late she seemed to favor getting an unlisted phone number.

On their honeymoon, she'd paid him an unintentional compliment by asking if there was any chance he'd been adopted. Back then he bore little physical resemblance to either parent, though over the last two decades that had changed. His hair had thinned in the exact same pattern as his father's, and his nose, delicate when he was a younger man, had started to dominate his face as well. He'd kept in reasonably good shape by jogging and playing tennis, and he didn't weigh much more than he had when they married, but the weight had subtly begun redistributing itself, his torso becoming noticeably concave (again like his father's), as if he'd been kicked in the chest by a horse. With the exception of the small mole that bisected her left eyebrow and had appeared on his own in his thirties, his mother's genetic gifts were more temperamental, if no less disturbing for that, and Joy had conceded long ago that there was no chance he'd been adopted. "That's your mother talking," she was fond of observing whenever he was unkind or snobbish, especially about someone in her own family.

"She wants me to visit," Griffin told her now.

"Of course she does."

"She doesn't like her new place."

"Of course she doesn't."

"She's going to live forever."

"No, but she'll make it seem like forever."

The first thing he'd done when arriving at the restaurant was to wash his shirtsleeve in the men's room. Though he thought he'd done a good, thorough job, he could smell it again. "When she called, I pulled over onto the shoulder, and a gull took a shit on me."

But Joy had lost interest in the subject, just as she often did with stories at what he considered their most vivid and interesting point. "Have you called your daughter yet?"

Your daughter, rather than *our*, usually meant that in Joy's opinion he was shirking some important parental duty. "She doesn't get here until this afternoon, right?"

"She's been on the Cape since yesterday. She's in the wedding party, remember?"

Well, now that he thought about it, he did. "I'll call her when I get to the B and B," he promised.

"Good. She could use some reassuring."

"About what?"

"She can't understand why we're arriving in separate cars. Explain that to her, will you? Then she can explain it to me."

Griffin sighed. He'd succeeded in deflecting Joy from her purpose by complaining about his mother, but now they'd circled back. Best to get it over with and apologize. "I should've waited for you," he admitted, pausing a beat before adding, "Boston wasn't much fun without you." And, when she still didn't say anything, "I meant to spite you and ended up spiting myself . . . Are you still there?"

"I'm here."

"I hope you aren't waiting for me to humble myself further, because that's all I've got for you."

"No," she said. "That should do it."

By the time Griffin drove back down the Cape and checked into the B and B, it was nearly noon. He brought his travel bag and satchel up to the room, leaving the trunk empty except for his father's ashes. He'd passed a couple of peaceful, secluded spots, but there'd been a brisk breeze, and he feared that when he opened the urn a strong gust might come up and he'd be wearing his father. Also, he'd feel less self-conscious saying a few words in his memory if there was someone besides himself to hear them, so he decided to wait for Joy.

His father had died of a massive embolism the previous September, and the circumstances were nothing if not peculiar. He'd been found in his car in a plaza on the Mass Pike. Like most rest stops, this one had a huge parking lot, and his father's car was on the very perimeter, far from other vehicles. It was unclear how long it had been there before someone noticed him slumped over in the passenger seat, his head resting against the window. Except for the trickle of blood, dried and crusty, below his left nostril, he might have been taking a nap. But why wasn't he behind the wheel? The glove box was open. Had he been rummaging around in it, looking for something? On the backseat the road atlas was open to Massachusetts, with Griffin's phone number scrawled on the top of the page. The key was in the ignition in the ON position. The car had apparently run out of gas there in the lot.

"Must've been coming to see you," the young cop said when Griffin arrived on the scene to identify his father.

"It's possible," Griffin told him.

"He didn't mention it, though? Coming to visit?"

Griffin said no, that it'd been a good six months since he'd seen him and almost as long since they'd spoken on the phone.

"That normal?"

He wasn't sure what this fellow was getting at. Normal for them, or normal for other adult fathers and sons?

"I mean, you didn't get along?" the cop said. He seemed less suspicious than saddened to consider the possibility that over time his relationship with his own dad might similarly devolve.

"We got along fine."

"It just seems . . . I don't know. What do you make of the fact that he was in the passenger seat?"

"I have no idea," Griffin said, though that wasn't true. The inference to be drawn was inescapable. He'd been in the passenger seat because someone else had been driving. All his life he'd stopped for pretty hitchhikers, a habit that had infuriated Griffin's mother. "Better me than somebody else," he always argued, lamely. "The next guy might be a pervert." (At this she'd roll her eyes. "Yeah, right. The *next* guy.") The other possible explanation was that he'd talked one of his coeds into making the trip with him. Though he'd retired the year before, the university still allowed him to teach one seminar each fall. More than once he'd let on to Griffin that girls at Christian schools like this one were often interested in exploring a more secular approach to life and love, if this could be done discreetly. Boys their own age offered neither experience nor discretion. It *had* been a woman, possibly a young woman, Griffin learned from the cop, who'd made the anonymous call to the state police about the man slumped over in his car in the rest-stop parking lot.

It was unconscionable he'd waited so long to dispose of his father's ashes, Griffin thought as he unpacked, hanging his suit in the closet and placing his shaving kit in the tiny bathroom. He should have made a special trip to the Cape last fall. His father had left a will but no instructions on where he wished to spend eternity. But on the drive back home from the turnpike plaza, Griffin had come to what had seemed an obvious conclusion. His father hadn't been on his way to see him and Joy, since if he'd meant to pay them an unannounced visit he would've gotten off the pike at the previous exit. No, he was headed for the Cape. Griffin advanced that theory to his mother when he called to tell her what had happened. "His suitcase was packed with summer clothes," he told her. "He had two big tubes of sunblock."

She hadn't answered right away, which made him wonder if she was trying to compose herself. "I could have told him he'd never make it" was all she said before hanging up.

The B and B had a large wraparound porch, so Griffin brought his satchel full of student papers down and set up shop in a rocking chair in the sun, where he sat trying to remember how that famous Shakespeare sonnet about death went. "Fear no more the heat o' th' sun . . ." was as far as he'd gotten when his cell vibrated, Joy calling him back.

"I forgot to ask," she said. "Did Sid get ahold of you?"

"No," he said, sitting up straight. Sid was his agent back in L.A., in his late eighties and still a legend in the business, despite his shrinking client list. Griffin sincerely hoped he was calling about a job. Money had been worrying him of late. Joy, who kept the books and wrote the checks, insisted they were fine, but if Laura got engaged, as she'd been warning them might happen soon, maybe even this weekend, there'd be a wedding to pay for, and a quick studio rewrite would be just what the doctor ordered. "When did he call?"

"Last night. He wanted to know if you'd turned your grades in yet. It sounded like he meant for you to drop everything, hop on a plane and drop into the Universal lot by parachute."

Joy, since they moved to Connecticut, had little patience with Sid, whose ongoing, albeit sporadic presence in their lives she considered vestigial, an appendix that was liable one day to rupture. He was also one of those Angelenos who never took time zones into account when telephoning. Four in the afternoon—seven back East, about the time Griffin and Joy usually sat down to eat—was when he took the bottle out of his desk drawer, unscrewed the cap and poured, then started calling people. She might have been less peeved, Griffin thought, if Sid was calling with work, but mostly he just wanted to reminisce about old Hollywood—Bogart and Mitchum and Lancaster and Holden—until nostalgia morphed into anger that the town was now overrun by "bitches," his term for the current generation of young male stars, action-movie pretty boys pretending, not very convincingly, to be tough guys. "Not a one of 'em could take Renée Zellweger in a fair fight," he was fond of observing. "You did the right thing getting out when you did, kid. Who needs it?"

Who needed him? was the better question, according to Joy. Why couldn't he understand that they'd moved on?

Toward the end of their conversations Griffin always reminded him that he was still a dues-paying member of the Guild and that if the right gig came along, especially in the summer . . . but before he could finish, Sid always interrupted. "My advice?" he said, as if he'd just extended such an offer. "Don't lower yourself. You've got respectable, grown-up work now." Joy had usually finished eating and was loading the dishwasher by the time Griffin managed to get off the phone.

This sounded different, though, and Griffin immediately felt the adrenaline rush, his mind racing in that old, calculating, savvy L.A. way he'd all but forgotten. If Sid was so worked up, it had to be a feature film, maybe one that had already gone into production with a horseshit script. Wouldn't *that* be sweet. Some A-list actor had probably come on board at the last second and to accommodate this dickhead's busy schedule they'd agreed to start shooting early. That would explain why they were coming to Griffin, who worked faster than anybody.

It took him about a second to invent this scenario and another to check it for holes, of which there were several. The most obvious was that nobody out there remembered whether he was fast or slow, because, face it, nobody remembered *him*. Still, it was a pretty entertaining sequence of events, sort of like imagining a woman totally out of your league falling in love with you. It could happen and, in fact, already had. Back when they met, every man he knew had been in love with Joy, who was not just beautiful but genuine, a quality in short supply everywhere and especially in Southern California.

Okay, so suppose for the moment that Griffin was right. Sid had found him something. A feature film. Everything would immediately go at warp speed. He'd have the fucked-up script in his hands by this evening, Sid would negotiate the deal over the weekend and Griffin would be on a plane to L.A. by Monday. Or to wherever they were shooting. It'd be a laptop gig. Late nights. Chinese (probably Thai, now) ordered in. Early wake-up calls. Pay commensurate. Just like the good old days.

"Universal?" Could that be right? Who did he know at Universal?

"No, I was just using Universal as an example."

"But it's a gig?"

"I don't know, Jack," Joy said, clearly impatient. "It sounded like work. You can find out when you call him back."

"But what did he say, exactly?"

"We didn't talk. He just left a message on the machine. I called back and left *him* a message to call your cell."

"Then why didn't he?" Not that he really needed Joy to explain. He hadn't called back because he had a list of names in front of him and probably had already penciled through Griffin's. At this all-too-plausible explanation Griffin's heart sank, though it, too, was flawed. Why leave an urgent message to call back if you were already moving on?

"You're asking me?"

"No, just thinking out loud."

"Have you called Laura yet?"

"Joy. I will, okay? Right now, in fact."

Hanging up, he scrolled down his phone's contacts list, pausing at LAURA before continuing to SID. Half a dozen times over the last year he'd come close to deleting Sid's entry, but he'd been right not to, he thought, smiling. After four rings his agent's machine picked up, inviting him to leave a message. Strange. Even with the three-hour time difference, he should've been in the office by now, or if not Sid himself, then Darlice, his longtime assistant. Had business slowed to the point where he'd had to let her go? Sid's speed dial had once been a who's who of Hollywood royalty, but one by one, according to Tommy, his important clients had moved on. Still, Sid answering his own phone? Impossible. It then occurred to Griffin that Tommy might know what Sid was offering. His old writing partner always prided himself on knowing whatever was in play. He was tempted to give him a call, except that every time he did the first thing Tommy wanted to know was whether he'd given up on "going straight" yet. To his way of thinking, screenwriting was a lot like stealing, and he'd warned Griffin that moving to Connecticut would be like Butch Cassidy's going to Bolivia. When Griffin argued that he could just as easily write screenplays in New England and deliver them by e-mail attachment, Tommy just laughed and said, "You just keep thinkin', Butch. That's what you're good at."

Before he could make up his mind, he received another incoming call, and MOM was the warning displayed on the screen. What in the world did she want now, he wondered, letting it go to voice mail. There was a roof over the porch where he sat, but he leaned forward and scanned the sky anyway.

Laura answered on the first ring, sounding groggy, though it was nearly one in the afternoon. "Hold on," she said, and he could hear her telling Andy, her boyfriend, to go back to sleep. "There," she said, coming back on the line. "I'm out on the balcony. Last night we all stayed up to watch the sun rise. Alcohol may have been involved."

"You should take it easy," he said, immediately regretting it.

Why on earth should she? She and her friends were still in their twenties, an age when you could both work and play hard, before it all started catching up with you. It would be years, at least a decade or two, before any of them started greeting the sunrise for a whole different set of reasons. "How's Andy?"

"Great. Wonderful." As if the words had not yet been invented to describe just how great, how wonderful. But then her tone immediately became serious. "What's up with you and Mom?"

Laura had spent much of her adolescence terrified that one day he and Joy would split up. Most of her friends' parents had divorced, traumatizing their youth, so, she reasoned, what was to prevent the same thing from happening to her? He and Joy seldom argued, but when they did, the first thing they had to do afterward was console their daughter. Telling her they both loved her, loved her more than anything, wouldn't do the trick. No, what she wanted to hear was how much they loved each other. Nor, at twenty-six, had she outgrown this old anxiety. Just last year she'd confessed to Joy that she still had the occasional nightmare about getting a phone call from one or the other of them to say they were calling it quits.

"Nothing's the matter, sweetheart. Your mother just got tied up with some meetings."

She was quiet for a moment, and he expected further grilling, but instead she said, "Are you still going to Truro after the wedding?"

"Why would I go to Truro?"

"Not you," she said. "The two of you."

"Which two?" Perhaps because his mother had recently established a beachhead in his consciousness, his first thought was that Laura meant him and *her*.

"You and *Mom*, of course," she said. "Is there someone else?"

Griffin assured her there wasn't.

"Well, she said you discussed it."

Griffin scrolled back through the last week's worth of conversations with Joy, many of which, truth be told, *had* been at cross-purposes. But "Truro" did provoke the faintest of recollections, though far too smooth and slippery to grasp. "It's possible," he conceded. "But I might have to fly to L.A. right after the wedding. Sid may have found something for me."

"Sid," she repeated. "That man frightens me to this day. Remember how he used to pretend to be a dog and bark at me?"

Griffin chuckled. He hadn't thought about that in years: Sid, down on his hands and knees, at eye level with a terrified Laura, barking and growling and refusing to quit, even after Griffin had picked her up and turned away from him as you would from an actual dog. And Sid, ignoring him, continued barking up at Laura, too much of a Method actor to stand up.

"Why would a grown man do something like that to a child?" she wanted to know, as if it was one of those childhood riddles that growing up hadn't solved.

"I don't think he knew any other children," Griffin told her. "He was probably as scared of you as you were of him." Which, oddly enough, had been his own parents' clichéd wisdom to him about real dogs.

Laura, still reliving the experience, wasn't interested in explanations. "And after we moved here—did I ever tell you this?—he called one night when you and Mom were at a party somewhere, and he just barked into the phone. I'd have been like fifteen, and it *still* scared the shit out of me."

She giggled then, confusing Griffin until he realized Andy had joined her on the balcony and was making *ruff-ruff* noises. "Sounds like this would be a good time to let you go," he said.

"Why don't you join us for dinner tonight? We're all going to this martini-and-tapas bar in Hyannis."

"What time?"

"Nine."

"I'll be in bed by then. Asleep, probably."

He'd intended this as a joke, half hoping she'd say, "Oh, *Daddy,*" and talk him into coming along, but she apparently took him seriously, maybe even deciding that being asleep by nine was appropriate for a man his age. "Okay, then," she said, "but we'll see you in the morning? You and Mom will be attending the wedding *together*?" She was joking now, he was pretty sure.

"Unless she meets someone along the way."

"Good*bye,* Daddy."

Hanging up, he remembered what the Truro thing was all about. By way of apology for the end-of-semester cock-up, Joy had suggested they drive out to the Cape after the wedding and see if the inn where they'd honeymooned still existed, maybe check in for a day or two. It'd be kind of romantic, she said, threading her fingers through his. There'd been a time when that particular gesture would have meant romance right then. Lately, it had come to mean that she might be amenable to the idea in a week or so, under the right circumstances, if he played his cards right, if he didn't do anything between now and then to fuck things up. Which had made him grumpy enough to go to Boston without her.

The afternoon had grown pleasantly warm and, having slept poorly the night before, Griffin soon nodded off, the first of his student portfolios unread in his lap. A breeze awakened him an hour later, manuscript pages strewn all over the porch. Several had blown up against the railing, one slipping between the slats and impaling itself on a rosebush. After he'd retrieved the scattered pages and put them in order, three were still missing. He found one a block away, stuck to a telephone pole like a flyer for a lost pet. The other two were probably on their way to Nantucket. Jesus, he thought, his resemblance to his father wasn't just physical. He'd been famous for losing student work, whole stacks of research papers going missing at once. "If you don't want to read them, don't assign them," Griffin remembered his mother always saying when yet another batch disappeared without a trace and his father was forced to ask his students to resubmit their work. "I'd set the whole weekend aside to read them," he said, feigning (she was certain) disappointment.

Griffin's mother loathed grading papers, too, of course. Who didn't? But she was meticulous about correcting errors, offering style and content suggestions in the margins, asking pointed, often insulting, questions (*How long did you work on this?*) and then answering them herself (*Not long, one hopes, given the result*). But such industry was possible, his father always countered, only because her courses were about a third the size of his own. Only the bravest, most ambitious English majors took her classes, which she explained was evidence of her rigor and he cited as proof that she was a bitch on wheels.

His father's larger, more diverse classes made that laudable attention to detail impractical, or so he claimed. At the end of each paper he would affix a large letter grade and a general reaction like "Good" or "Could be better," unless the student was a pretty young woman, in which case he'd suggest she come see him during office hours. With his male students, many of whom were athletes, he had an unspoken understanding. He would give them one letter grade higher than they deserved, and in exchange they were to leave him alone. His students enjoyed his affable, slightly distracted manner in the classroom, as well as his fondness for bad jokes and that he kept up on the issues of campus life, which other professors considered beneath them. He generally liked them, too, though at the end of the semester he wouldn't have been able to pick a single one out of a police lineup, where, according to Griffin's mother, most of them belonged. By contrast, she knew her students well enough to dislike them as individuals, for their intellectual laziness, their slovenly dress, their conventional instincts, their religious upbringing. They mostly disliked her, too, though a few wrote her after they graduated to thank her for the tough discipline she'd instilled. She always shared these notes with his father, remarking how little editing they required by comparison to the moronic screeds (often beginning *Yo, Prof Griff*) his former athletes sometimes sent him.

Griffin, now entering his second decade of teaching, feared that as a teacher he'd inherited the worst attributes of both parents. He was popular, like his father, but then screenwriting courses always were. His students appreciated that he had real experience, that several of his and Tommy's screenplays had been produced and that, if pressed, he could tell them cynical Hollywood stories. He liked them personally far more than he expected to. Except for the scholarship kids, they were the children of entitlement and privilege, but it turned out that just meant lots of books and music around the house, plenty of piano lessons and travel to shape their personalities. Their politics were mostly liberal, like their parents'. All that was fine, but by temperament he was more like his mother than he cared to admit. He offered his students far more comment and advice than they wanted, and the vast majority paid it exactly no attention whatsoever, given that their subsequent efforts were riddled with the same mistakes. Lately, he'd begun to wonder if his father's indolence might in the end be more beneficial. Informed that his work "could be better," a student of his might actually pause to reflect on how, whereas Griffin's detailed analyses of various shortcomings simply caused the heavily edited pages to become airborne. This screenplay with the missing pages (airborne ahead of schedule) was typical. Its narrative, he felt certain, cohered about as well without them. It would take him a good half an hour to explain why, labor that was probably for his own edification anyway.

It was so disheartening to contemplate, especially on such a lovely afternoon, that he stuffed it and all the others back in his satchel. When he redialed Sid's number, it again went directly to voice mail. How disappointed was Joy going to be, he wondered, if there wasn't time to go to Truro before he flew out to L.A.? Probably not very, he decided. It was nice she considered the idea romantic, but Truro, if she actually thought about it, was more likely to expand their recent conflict than to shrink it. Where they would honeymoon had been the first real disagreement of their relationship. She had favored the coast of Maine, where as a girl she'd vacationed with her family. Every summer they rented the same rambling, ramshackle old house, not far from where her mother grew up. It was drafty and creaky, its floors so pitched that if you dropped a Parcheesi marble off the kitchen table, you'd end up chasing it around the living room. But the place was familiar and had scads of room for her parents, the five kids and their weekend visitors. Joy had many fond memories of family dinners and evening excursions to a nearby amusement park, of all-day Monopoly and Clue tournaments when it rained. Even after her father got transferred and the family moved out West, they returned to Maine each July, never mind that its beaches were rocky and its water too frigid to swim in. Joy had even suggested the same house might be available for their honeymoon. Which begged Obvious Question Number One: why had Griffin talked her into the Cape instead? Given the opportunity to imitate a happy marriage—and there was no denying that Joy's parents had one—why choose to follow his own parents' miserable version?

Still, they'd been happy in Truro, hadn't they? It wasn't like he'd bullied her. They discussed, finally agreed, and it had been fine. They spent the whole time making love and excitedly mapping out the rest of their lives. It was there, walking hand in hand among the Truro dunes, that Joy first talked about the sort of house she dreamed of them owning one day. It seemed to be a cross between the Syracuse house she grew up in and the summer rental in Maine: old, inconvenient, graceful, full of character, a house that had a rich history before you showed up and might even harbor a benign ghost or two. That Joy believed in ghosts was one of the more endearing things he'd learned about her on their honeymoon.

She was certain the Syracuse house had been haunted. The whole family—even Jared and Jason, her much younger brothers—had sensed the ghost's presence; it was, they all agreed, a woman. Only her father was immune, but he didn't count, she explained, because he never noticed anything.

The exuberant clarity with which she envisioned not just her dream house but also their futures back East was infectious. Griffin concurred with all of it, and why not? It would be nice to leave Los Angeles eventually, to live a saner, quieter life away from the clogged freeways and the ambient noise of what passed for culture there. He didn't think he'd write screenplays forever, he told her, or maybe even for very much longer. He enjoyed the work, but it was hardly literature he and Tommy were writing. For some time now he'd been thinking he might try his hand at something more serious, a novel or collection of stories. But that, unfortunately, wouldn't be nearly so lucrative, which meant they'd have to start saving; and when they made the break he'd probably have to teach. He'd been talking along these lines for a while when it occurred to him that he was lying. He *hadn't* actually been toying with the idea of writing fiction for "some time," and in fact it hadn't occurred to him until he heard the words coming out of his mouth. Odder still, what he heard himself proposing was a life not all that different from his parents'. What had possessed him? Why give up screenwriting, something he was good at, even if it wasn't serious work they might approve of? And who knew if he could write anything that was. But never mind, he told himself. He wasn't so much lying as dreaming, and what was wrong with that? Wasn't Joy doing the same thing? He'd only meant to suggest there was more to him, or might be more at some future date, than was now apparent, that she needn't fear growing bored with him, because of course he'd change and grow. They both would.

But to Joy his dreaming might have sounded more like a promise. "A professor's house, then," she said, excited, when he mentioned teaching. That meant a library with floor-to-ceiling bookcases and comfortable chairs for reading, a big *OED* on its own stand, a small stereo for quiet, contemplative music. There'd be no "family room," at least not like the one in her parents' house, with its "entertainment center," fake mahogany shelves lined with bric-a-brac purchased on cruises and at gift shops in state parks. The total absence of books in their home was the first thing Griffin had commented on, and he could tell she'd been embarrassed and hurt by the observation, though she'd gotten over it quickly. It reassured him, in Truro, to know that there was room for him in Joy's dream house, that she intended it to be not just hers but theirs, a natural extension of who they were, of their marriage and, one day, of their family. And it thrilled him to know that in the important arena of values, she'd sided with him over her parents.

Griffin didn't dislike them exactly, but they had little in common. Harve had taken early retirement and they'd recently moved from Orange County to a gated community in a suburb of Sacramento, where they filled their lazy days with golf and tennis and bridge and visits from Jane and June—who lived nearby, on purpose, if you could imagine that—and their children. Jill (Jilly-Billy, Harve called her) had never had any interest in working outside the home. Ever since Griffin and Joy announced their engagement, her parents were forever badgering them to visit more, saying that even the twins, Jared and Jason, both in the service, got home more often. They seemed not to understand that Sacramento wasn't a suburb of L.A., that Griffin often wrote under deadline, that writing was a job like any other. Even more inexplicable to Harve was Griffin's aversion to golf, which Harve insisted was the sport of kings. "The prosecution rests," Griffin told him, but it went right over his head. Griffin would love the game, Harve insisted, if he'd just give it a chance. After they were married, Joy's first big gift to Griffin—at the suggestion of her father, who helped her pick them out, Griffin later learned—was an expensive set of clubs. The idea, she explained, was that the two of them could bond, and perhaps even find other commonalities, on the golf course. For a while Griffin dutifully took lessons, but he was a halfhearted student who never could master what Harve referred to as "the first damn rule of golf," which was to keep your head down when you swung. "I'll watch where it goes," he barked every time Griffin topped the ball off the tee. "Just remind yourself in your backswing . . . *If I look up, all I'm going to see is a bad shot.*" The problem was that on those rare occasions Griffin did manage to keep his head down through impact, when he finally looked up, he always saw his father-in-law, two big paws shading his eyes, squinting down the fairway and saying, "Now where the hell did *that* go?"

But they weren't bad people and did try to establish a relationship. Unlike Griffin's parents, Harve and Jill were duly impressed that he worked in the movies, though the former had a hard time grasping precisely what had to be written before filming started. Once, all four had gone to see a movie he and Tommy had written. Harve, who was hard of hearing, sat next to Griffin and asked loud questions throughout, ignoring his wife's attempts to shush him. Every time one of the characters got off a good line, Harve said, "You *wrote* that?" as if he'd always assumed actors provided their own dialogue, much like a carpenter might be expected to bring his own hammer. Griffin replied that, yes, he'd written the line, or Tommy had. "How about that boat?" Harve said when one roared by, pulling a water-skier, in the background of the shot. "You didn't write that part? Then what's it doing there?" In other words, how could a real boat appear, unintended, in what Griffin insisted was a product of the imagination?

His own parents at least understood that films were scripted. Unfortunately, to their way of thinking, this didn't qualify as "real writing," an odd opinion, he thought, to be advanced by people who wrote academic criticism. Once, he'd made the mistake of telling them how much he and Tommy stood to make on a quick rewrite of a horror movie, which prompted a lengthy discourse on America's skewed values, whereby critical-care nurses were paid less than supermarket butchers. Griffin agreed about the nurses, but his parents also seemed to imply that the exorbitant fees he and Tommy earned for writing crappy movies were what prevented scholars from being paid fairly for their jargon-riddled articles and university-press books. Which begged Obvious Question Number Two: why was he more resentful of Harve and Jill, who really wanted to understand how he made his living, than his own parents, who had never, to his knowledge, seen a single film he had anything to do with? Was pigheaded disinterest grounded in quasi-morality somehow more admirable than rapt thickheadedness?

The Great Truro Accord. That was how, in the years to come, Griffin jokingly referred to the future he and Joy mapped out on their honeymoon. At the time, deeply in love and drunk on sex, it had seemed they agreed about everything, as if they'd spend the rest of their lives excitedly finishing each other's sentences. Still, it wasn't just the love and sex. They really *had* agreed. They both wanted a family—okay, maybe not immediately, but someday. And when they had a family, of course they'd need a house, and there was nothing wrong with the one Joy dreamed of. And so what if Griffin had surprised himself by floating that trial balloon of one day turning his talents to something more worthy and real? Maybe it felt like a lie at first, but the more he thought about it, the more he wondered if the lie hadn't tapped into some deeper, subconscious truth. After all, he'd gotten into screenwriting, at least in part, to thumb his nose at his parents and their insufferable pretensions. But what about him? What did Griffin himself really want? After telling Joy he might want to write a novel one day, he'd discovered he actually did. Moving back East made sense, too. Why live in L.A. if you weren't working in the industry?

Okay, maybe it should have been the Great Coastal Maine Accord, and perhaps, early in their marriage, he'd used his superior rhetorical skills to gain an advantage when he might have been more generous, more considerate of her desires. Sure, the time line had always been a bone of contention, and you couldn't say Joy hadn't been a model of patience. But when you looked at the original accord, as he'd been doing lately, the thing that jumped out at you was that Joy didn't have much to complain about. She'd gotten everything she wanted, hadn't she? They had Laura. He'd quit screenwriting. They'd moved back East. She'd gotten her house.

But he had to admit there *was* something they *hadn't* agreed on, something the Great Truro Accord hadn't even addressed. With respect to their families, Griffin had hoped to invoke a simple, equitable policy: a plague on both their houses. Have as little to do with Harve and Jill, and with William and Mary, as decency permitted. And he was more than willing to make the first gesture. He had no intention of inflicting his parents on Joy or, when the time came, on their children. Was a little reciprocity too much to hope for?

What he'd failed to comprehend in Truro was stark in its simplicity. *Joy loved her family.* Maybe she didn't share their politics or their values, but she loved them still. Whenever they visited Harve and Jill in Sacramento, which he only did under protest, she slipped effortlessly into the old family routines, doing the complex ballet of kitchen and dining room with her mother and sisters, with children always underfoot, not to mention singing along with the songs on the oldies station that they made fun of back in L.A., banishing him to the family room to watch sports he didn't care about with Harve and the idiot twins.

Perhaps because Jason and Jared were both marines and because their father was so full of bellow and bluster, it had taken Griffin a while to understand the gender dynamic that ran just under the surface at these family gatherings: it was the women who charted every course, who made every decision. As military cops, the twins were enforcers of rules, but in civilian life they were trained to await instructions, and so was their father. When the dining room table was cleared, the dishes and pans washed and stacked, the dreadful board games came out—Monopoly, Clue and Life; Scrabble they refused to play because Griffin always won— and they were called back to the table whether or not the sporting broadcast had finished. They grumbled, of course, as men do, wanting to know why they couldn't be left in peace, but it wouldn't have occurred to them to decline the invitation, which, to their credit, they recognized as a command. It was over these ratty, faded board games, many of them held together with Scotch tape along the center fold, that all the old family stories, many of which originated in that old Maine summer rental, got trotted out and told at a decibel level that sent only-child Griffin out onto the patio in search of quiet, though he knew full well that this made him seem standoffish.

At the conclusion of these endless visits, he always found a jazz station on the car radio for the trip back to L.A., during which he and Joy seldom spoke. It wasn't the silence of argument so much as simple reentry. The drive was a long one, and just as well, too. Griffin could feel her exchanging—reluctantly, he sometimes felt— one suit of emotional clothes for another, one life for another. But the silence could and sometimes did morph into argument. One Thanksgiving at Harve and Jill's, not long after they were married, having exhausted all the board games, they'd played Twenty Questions, and Joy's sister Jane had stumped everyone at the table for the better part of an hour, Harve stubbornly refusing to give up. Finally, though, everyone else pleaded with her to surrender her fictional identity, which turned out to be Princess Grace of "Morocco."

That evening, when they pulled into the garage of their rented condo in Brentwood, Joy was still fuming because Griffin, instead of laughing along with the rest of the family at Jane's goof, shook his head in disbelief, got up from the table and left the room, as if her mistake had been intentional or malicious and such bizarre mistakes could be assigned a moral value. Now, four hours later, when he turned off the ignition and started to get out of the car, Joy remained seated. When he asked if she meant to stay the night in the garage, she said, "I hate jazz."

"Apropos of?" he asked.

"Apropos of I want you to know I hate jazz."

She later told him it wasn't really true. She liked jazz. She just for some reason felt the need to tell him she didn't. Something had gotten into her, she said. She had no idea what.

4

The Summer of the Brownings

In addition to his students' work, Griffin's satchel also contained a long, unfinished story, "The Summer of the Brownings," its precomputer pages yellowed and curled. A couple
years after they were married, it had been his first attempt to imple-
ment that provision of the Great Truro Accord by trying to write
something other than a screenplay. He'd come across the story
when he was cleaning out his filing cabinets at the college in order
to make room for the few things of his father's that he wanted
to keep. His father's last years were spent in a small, cramped,
university-owned flat, and most of the furnishings weren't even his.
There were lots of scholarly journals and books, including a pris-
tine copy of Claudia's dissertation, published by a good university
press, that she'd proudly signed. Griffin found his father listed on
the acknowledgments page, along with the other members of her
doctoral committee. The book's stiff spine suggested that the book
hadn't been opened, much less read. Of course if his father had
written it, as his mother alleged, there would've been no need to.
In a token gesture of revenge Griffin had given it away with the rest
of his father's library, keeping as mementos only a few of the
P. G. Wodehouse and Henry Miller books he remembered him

reading on Cape Cod beaches. He'd almost missed, in the recesses of a dark closet, the dozen shoe boxes full of campaign buttons and other political trinkets his father had continued to collect down the years, and he kept these as well. "Scoff all you want," he remembered him telling his mother when he stopped at flea markets. "You won't be laughing when we sell the whole collection and use it for a down payment on a house."

Was it worth anything now? Griffin supposed it might be and made a mental note to inventory the items and have them valued, but then he'd shoved the shoe boxes into the back of the filing cabinet and hadn't thought about them since. The only real surprises among his father's effects were a couple VHS tapes of movies Griffin and Tommy had written. He couldn't remember sending them himself, so had his father bought them? Or had a colleague, noticing the screenplay credit, given them to him as a gift? They had been viewed, but by whom?

"The Summer of the Brownings" had an interesting provenance. The writers had gone on strike that year, as they were forever doing, and he'd used the work stoppage to write it. "You're shitting me," Tommy said when Griffin explained what he was doing. Why not write a spec script, he argued, which every other screenwriter would be doing, because then they'd have something they could sell once the strike was over. Be in the driver's seat for once, instead of having to take the first horseshit assignment they got offered. Griffin told him to go ahead and start something if he wanted, but he knew Tommy wouldn't. He relied on Griffin for direction and wouldn't even know where to begin.

The story was about the summer he was—what—twelve? He and his parents had gone to the Cape, as usual. He couldn't remember exactly where, only that it was pretty remote and they'd stayed only two weeks, which meant they weren't flush. Their tiny, shingled cottage (Wouldn't Have It As a Gift!) was set back from the highway in a stand of scrub pines along with eight or ten others arranged in a horseshoe around a brown, hard-packed children's play area. To get to the water you had to cross the macadam road, then walk down a winding dirt road past million-dollar beach homes (Can't Afford It!), between rolling, grassy dunes for a good half mile. Only one other cottage was occupied, so it must have been early in the season, probably the last half of June, because he recalled it had been warm.

"At least they're over on the other side," his father said, indicating the two children playing outside that cottage. His parents never made any secret of the fact that they loathed children, and that the whole compound was organized around a rusty swing set and jungle gym they took as an evil omen indeed. Even before they were finished unpacking the car, Griffin, changing into his bathing suit in the tiny upstairs bedroom under the eaves, heard his mother say, "Good God, here they come." And sure enough, the whole family from across the way was trooping through the playground, clearly intending to welcome the newcomers. Griffin hurried down to meet them.

They were the Brownings, they said; the mother and father were both teachers from somewhere in western Massachusetts and roughly the same age as Griffin's parents. The kids were a boy, Peter, and also a little girl. Mr. Browning wondered if they were thinking about buying the cottage, indicating the FOR SALE sign leaning up against the porch. "God, no!" Griffin's father replied with a shudder. While the cottages were identical, the Brownings apparently took no offense, even though they themselves were part owners of the one they occupied, they explained, along with two other couples that taught at their school. The cottages were all individually owned, looked after in the off-season by a local caretaker, but most were rented for at least a month or two in the summer, and there was always a nice mix of people.

"You must be teachers, too," Mr. Browning said, indicating the institutional decal on the rear window of the Griffins' car.

"University professors, actually," his mother said, clearly anxious to set them straight on this score.

Mrs. Browning, a tall, beautiful, olive-skinned woman, touched her husband's elbow then, saying they were heading to the beach, and since their boys were about the same age, would Griffin like to come?

"Go on," his parents said in unison.

That was the beginning. By the end of the day he and Peter Browning had become fast friends. Every morning, when his parents were reading the newspaper (his father drove into town early to pick it up, along with fresh pastries, though he kept forgetting he was supposed to get a box of Griffin's favorite cereal, too) and having breakfast with Al Fresco, they'd hear the Brownings' screen door creak open on its unoiled hinge and Peter would shout across the playground, "Can you come over?"

"Have fun," his parents said, by which they meant, *Leave us in peace.*

Except, wait, that wasn't true, at least not at the beginning. On their second day, when Griffin was again invited, midmorning, to go to the beach, his mother had said no, that he should stay with them. They'd be going to the beach themselves, right after lunch. So off the Brownings had trudged, a big cooler swinging between the adults, the little girl (why couldn't he remember her name?) skipping on ahead, Peter shouldering a big mesh laundry bag full of towels and colorful beach toys and looking devastated as he waved goodbye. When Griffin wanted to know why he hadn't been allowed to go along, his mother explained that people like that always wanted something in return for kindnesses, and she had no intention of playing *that* game.

Two interminable hours later, Griffin and his parents, not nearly so well provisioned, emerged from among the dunes, and he glimpsed the Brownings a hundred yards down the beach to the left. "Go right, go right, go right," his father said, nudging him forcefully in the other direction and pretending not to notice the entire family standing up and waving. "They teach *junior high*," his mother explained when Griffin asked why they weren't being more friendly. "Do you know what that means?" He didn't, but understood he was supposed to. Was it that people who taught, say, kindergarten didn't associate with people who taught seventh grade, who didn't socialize with people who taught high school, who didn't mix with college professors? It had to be something like that, he decided.

Fortunately, though he had no idea why, his parents changed their minds about the Brownings wanting something, and the next day he was allowed, indeed encouraged, to go with them while his parents finished breakfast with Al. They never budged until after lunch (they hated eating on the beach, and his father's pale skin was susceptible to sunburn), by which time most families with bratty kids were packing up, and they'd have a long stretch of sand to themselves. Without Griffin to nag them, they usually emerged from among the dunes midafternoon with their towels and books and a couple folding beach chairs and not much else. The Brownings typically set up camp to the left, which meant that his parents headed to the right. That embarrassed him, especially the day the Brownings (intentionally?) changed things up by making their camp right where his parents usually sat, so when they arrived at their usual time they took a couple of steps toward them before noticing, then quickly reversed course. Griffin saw the look that passed between Peter's parents and felt himself glow hot with shame.

"Aren't they tired of you yet?" his mother asked over breakfast one morning near the end of their first week, as if to suggest that she couldn't imagine what was taking them so long.

If the Brownings were tired of Griffin, they gave no sign. Mrs.

Browning always had enough sandwiches and Cokes in the cooler for everyone when they went to the beach. Of Italian descent, she introduced him to exotic new foods: fatty, spiced ham and hard salami, marinated mushrooms and artichokes, blistering hot cherry peppers, and a mouthwatering macaroni salad that tasted like nothing that came from the supermarket deli where his mother shopped. And in the evening, back at the cottages, there were always extra hot dogs and hamburgers and chicken on the grill. (Griffin's father never grilled outdoors, not even on vacation, not since the year the flame from the smoking briquettes climbed up the stream of lighter fluid and torched his eyebrows.) Nor did the Brownings seem to mind that his parents took advantage of the free babysitting, driving into town most nights for dinner, just the two of them. "You should let us return the favor some night," Griffin's mother suggested, her insincerity clear even to him. "Give you and your husband a vacation from the kids."

"We think of it as vacation *with* the kids," Mrs. Browning said, and he saw the remark land, but it was only a glancing blow.

"If you pass someplace that sells ice on your way back, you could pick up a bag or two for the cooler," Mr. Browning told Griffin's father. "Save me a trip in the morning." But they must not have passed anyplace that did, and the Brownings didn't ask any other favors.

Griffin had had friends before, but never one all to himself, and never one he liked as much. Peter was good at things. He knew how to bodysurf, something Griffin had long wanted to do but was too afraid to try. His father, who was prone to minor injury, was so afraid of riptides that he refused to even go into the water. His mother liked to swim, but she'd sidle gracefully through the waves until she was out beyond where they broke so she could do her languid crawl. Peter, a wave aficionado, showed Griffin how to get the maximum ride out of the smaller waves and later, when he grew bolder, how to keep the larger ones from bouncing him on his head. Despite being several inches shorter, the boy was a natural athlete and could beat Griffin at anything that involved hand-to-eye coordination, though he generously explained his victories as owing to genetics. "My dad's good at sports"—he shrugged, as if that didn't really amount to much—"so I am, too." The heredity angle, of course, contained a veiled insult, and Griffin was pretty sure Peter and Mr. Browning, after watching his father's daily struggles to unfold his beach chair, had sized him up as physically ungifted. "Your dad's quite a reader, I see," Peter's father remarked one day, perhaps searching for a compliment that would have some basis in reality, and Griffin nodded, again glowing with shame.

By the end of their two weeks together, he and Peter had developed an intimacy that was wholly foreign to his experience and made him wonder if this was what love was like. It wasn't a sexual feeling, though it constricted his heart with a strange, purposeless urgency he didn't comprehend. When he wasn't with Peter, he needed to talk about him and, no surprise, his parents tired of this subject quickly, especially when Griffin began to lobby them about renting one of these same cottages next summer, so he and Peter could be together again. Having already sounded him out about the owners' rotation, he knew that the Brownings would be on the Cape in July. Please, *please,* he begged, couldn't they book a cottage right now? If they couldn't afford the whole month, at least take it for the first two weeks of July, so they'd all arrive together. Otherwise, Peter might develop some new summer friendship before Griffin could get there.

The reason he was so certain his attraction to Peter wasn't sexual was that his feelings for the boy's mother were *precisely* that. When Mrs. Browning wore a two-piece bathing suit, he had to lie on his stomach in the hot sand to conceal his erection. He didn't let on to Peter, of course, not even daring to say something innocent like "Your mom's really pretty," but somehow he seemed to know anyway. Was it possible Peter harbored similar feelings for his own mother? Did that happen? Mr. Browning also noticed Griffin's admiration, but instead of being annoyed or even angry, as Griffin imagined he might be, all he did was smile, as if he understood his wife's charms all too well and couldn't blame the boy for being taken with them. In fact, his kindness so shamed Griffin that for a day or two he tried his best to banish any dirty thoughts (as he'd characterized them) about Mrs. Browning, but it was no use. One afternoon, lying on her stomach in the warm sand, she untied her bathing suit top to take full advantage of the sun and then fell asleep. The waves were perfect that day, but Griffin told Peter he was tired of bodysurfing, whereas in truth he was intoxicated by the possibility that when Peter's mother woke up she might momentarily forget the untying and rise up, bare-breasted. She didn't, of course, but again Griffin felt that his friend knew what he was up to.

Had he ever again felt quite so sick at heart as at the end of their Cape vacation that summer? Not in adult life, surely. During the first of their two weeks he'd fallen in love, however improbably, with the whole Browning family, and every day, even the rainy ones, was radiant. During the second week, though, everything pivoted, as each passing day moved relentlessly toward the conclusion of their stay. The thought of leaving the Cape and never seeing Peter or any of the Brownings again engendered in Griffin a dark, complex emotion every bit as powerful as love. Part of it he recognized as despair, a panicked anxiety that left him breathless and weak, certain that things would never again return to normal or, worse, that normal was no longer enough, that his previous life amounted to starvation. But there was something else that scared him even more than despair: the desire to . . . what? To harm himself. To hurt even worse than he was already hurting. To ensure that whatever had been broken was beyond repair. Though there was a word for it—*perversity*—he didn't know it yet, wouldn't for many years. He knew only the feeling, but that was full and sufficient.

The evening before the Griffins were to leave, the Brownings invited him over for hamburgers and ice cream. Mr. Browning had some sparklers they were saving for their own last night, but since their new friend and his parents were departing, they'd decided to break them out early. Wanting desperately to accept their invitation, he instead told Peter that he and his parents were going out for a fancy dinner at the Blue Martini. It was very expensive, he said, but his parents had promised him he could order whatever he wanted, no matter what it cost, so he'd have to say no to the hamburgers. The look of disappointment on his friend's face provided a kind of bitter satisfaction.

It was true his parents had planned a fancy dinner out, but for just the two of them, and their surprise and annoyance when he told them what he'd done was pleasurable as well. "Why?" his mother said. "It's your last night with Steven. For the last two weeks it's been nothing but Steven this and Steven that."

"*Peter,*" he'd corrected her—shouting at her, really, and not caring if this meant trouble. "His name is *Peter.*"

She studied him for a long beat. "Why are you acting like this?" she said, but her tone suggested that she knew perfectly well, as if she'd been wondering when this side of his personality would reveal itself. "You're only hurting yourself," she told him. "You know that, don't you?"

But of course that part was a bluff. He *wasn't* hurting only himself. He was hurting her and his father, ruining their plans, and also disappointing Peter and the rest of the Brownings. That was the beauty of the thing, indeed its only beauty: the equitable sharing of unendurable loss and disappointment. There was another part of him, of course, that wanted to be talked out of this new, terrifying strategy, to subdue this vengeful, self-defeating emotion, and if his mother had tried harder to persuade him to, she might have succeeded. But she just gave him a wry smile and said, "If that's the way you want to be."

"That's the way I want to be," he said, feeling something rip inside, because it wasn't what he wanted, but rather what he *needed*. Later, he heard his father call the restaurant and cancel their reservation. They went instead to a family seafood place, where they ate at a weathered picnic table, their dinners served in paper boats.

"I loath fried seafood," his mother said, pushing her scallops away.

"This wasn't what I had in mind, either," his father said bitterly.

"We could've gone to the Blue Martini anyway," his mother said.

"Yeah, but what would be the point?"

Two weeks earlier Griffin wouldn't have understood the question, but now he did. Indeed, what was the point of anything? He'd never asked himself such a question before. After dinner, as darkness fell, they took a long drive with no particular destination in mind, as they sometimes did their last night on the Cape, breathing it all in, filling their lungs with the salt air, as if they could carry it back with them to breathe in the Mid-fucking-west. No one spoke. By the time they returned to the cottages it was pitch-dark except for the dancing sparklers in front of the Brownings' cottage. Griffin paused when he climbed out of the car, waiting for Peter's disembodied voice to call him over, so he once more could say no and derive that same perverse satisfaction, but no invitation came.

Upstairs—in his tiny bedroom under the eaves—he undressed in the dark and crawled into bed. From his window he saw five distinct sparkler tracks writing their ghostly script, but how could that be, with only four Brownings? Was one of them waving two sparklers at once? In the last twenty-four hours several other cottages had become occupied. Had the Brownings already found someone to replace him? Feeling his throat constrict at this cruel possibility, he pulled the shade down. But even with his eyes clamped tightly shut, he could still see the Brownings' joyous sparklers etching their collective happiness on the night.

It had been the stuff of good fiction, Griffin knew, but he'd somehow managed to mess it up in the telling, and when the writers' strike ended sooner than expected he'd pretended disappointment when in truth he was relieved. The story was already too long, but he had no idea how to end it, to resolve the conflict he'd never managed to clearly articulate. He'd hoped to capture what it felt like to be impossibly happy and miserable at the same time, to be held in the grip of powerful new emotions you couldn't understand. But when he read over what he'd written, it all felt wrong. He wanted readers to fall in love with the Brownings, as he had, but as written they felt like a TV sitcom family, especially Peter. In the story, the two friends had taken long walks on the beach, just as Griffin and Peter had done in real life, straying so far that their parents became tiny specks among the dunes before disappearing altogether, leaving them alone and content in the world, talking about everything under the Cape Cod sun. Unfortunately, Griffin couldn't for the life of him remember a single conversation they'd had, and when he tried to invent one it sounded, well, invented, an adult writer giving adolescence either too much credit or too little. He'd discovered that his memories of that summer were like bad movie montages—young lovers tossing a Frisbee in the park, sharing a melting ice-cream cone, bicycling along the river, laughing, talking, kissing, a sappy score drowning out the dialogue because the screenwriter had no idea what these two people might say to each other.

Nor was it just the details of this friendship that he couldn't bring to mind. Peter's sister . . . there'd been something wrong with her, hadn't there? Griffin vaguely remembered the little girl having episodes of some sort when she got tired or overexcited, but episodes of what? Not being able to breathe? Somehow that didn't seem right, but there'd been something. He remembered seeing the child feverish and curled in her mother's lap, and a look passing between her parents that contained both fear and sadness, a detail that hadn't made it into the story. Nor had Peter's father. In real life the man had been ambiguously fascinating. He'd had a very large head, Griffin recalled, and while he wasn't exactly ugly—Griffin's own father was better looking—he wondered how Mr. Browning possibly could've won a woman as beautiful as Peter's mother. But he did have a kind of physical grace, a sureness of movement. There seemed to be a connection between what he meant to do and what he did. Griffin couldn't imagine him ever standing in the center of a room unsure of his next step, his own father's signature gesture. Peter hadn't been scared of him, but was always respectful, as if he knew all too well that his father, for all his kindness, wasn't someone to cross. How, then, had he become so two-dimensional in Griffin's story, a surrogate for Wisdom, the voice of adult Truth?

Even more embarrassing, he wasn't even sure he'd gotten himself right. Griffin kept imagining studio notes: *Who is this kid? What does he want?* Or worse, the ubiquitous *Why are we "rooting" for him?*

"The kid's gay, right?" Tommy said. "That's where you're heading?"

Griffin hadn't wanted to show him the story, but Tommy was insistent.

"And at the end he'll commit suicide?"

"No," Griffin told him, dispirited, "nothing like that."

"Because that's where it seems like you're going, unless the little fucker's going to get unreal lucky and bang the other kid's mother."

"No," Griffin admitted, "not that, either."

Of course it was possible that Tommy was still pissed at him for working on this piece of shit when they could have been writing a spec script. Because now the strike was over, and they were broke, they'd have to take the first crappy assignment they could get, just as he'd predicted. But he did seem genuinely puzzled by the story. "You gotta feel sorry for the poor fucking kid, though," he admitted. "I mean, those asshole parents . . ."

That, Griffin felt, was the most dispiriting thing about it. Tommy hadn't said it in so many words, but he didn't have to. The only characters in the story that rang true, felt real, were the kid's parents. Griffin hadn't really intended to include them, except as devices. They were only there because a kid that age wouldn't be alone. Parents of some sort were necessary, and generic ones would've done just fine. Instead, it had all gushed out, the stuff he'd only half understood at the time—how glad the fictional parents were that their son had been temporarily adopted by this other family. Not glad for *him*, not pleased that he'd found a friend, but for themselves. Because now they could have a leisurely breakfast on the deck with Al (yes, he'd used Al Fresco), spend their long afternoons reading on the beach without being pestered to come into the water and then, in the evening, go someplace nice for dinner.

Curious to revisit the story after so long, Griffin had stuck it in the satchel with his students' work. Who knew? Maybe it wasn't as bad as he remembered. Actually being on the Cape as he reread it might help him see the ending that had eluded him in L.A. If so, and if Sid wasn't calling about a script, he'd revise it over the summer. Unfortunately, in the lazy afternoon warmth on the B and B's porch, Griffin found it difficult to fully enter its fictional world. Part of the problem was that his earlier assessment seemed to be correct: the story just wasn't very good. But what puzzled him even more was why he'd tried to write it in the first place. Would he have done so but for the Great Truro Accord? He doubted it. Some stories, even ones buried deep in memory and the subconscious, had a way of burrowing up into the light, of demanding conscious attention, until you had little choice but to write them. But "The Summer of the Brownings" hadn't been like that. He'd remembered them only when the strike loomed and he was casting about for something he might work into a story or novella. But why write either? Why had he been so willing, even anxious, to concede there was something wrong with the life he and Joy were living? What was so wrong with being young and free? With running off to Mexico on impulse? With turning their cars over to an endless parade of envious valets? That's what living in L.A. was, if you could afford it, and they could. It was unfair to blame Joy, of course. It wasn't like she'd tricked him. If anything, he'd tricked himself. In a moment of weakness, besotted by love, he'd imagined himself a different sort of writer from the one he knew himself to be. Joy had simply reacted to his enthusiasm. All she'd done was love him, the man he was, the man he'd been fool enough to believe he might become.

Maybe nobody was to blame, but the end result of the exuberant, love-inspired Great Truro Accord was that he and Joy were now out of plumb. *Plumb.* Griffin couldn't help smiling. He hadn't thought of that term in years. One summer he'd worked as a carpenter's assistant on a road-construction crew that built concrete footers. That whole July and August, in the blistering Midwest heat, he'd worked with the same two guys, Louie and Albert. Where conversation was concerned, they'd been minimalists. "Are we plumb?" Albert would ask after a good hour of silence. "We were a minute ago," Louie would respond, placing his level on the two-by-four in question, cocking his head to look at the bubble. "We're plumb some," he'd tell his partner, shrugging, which Griffin understood meant *close enough.* "We're not building a skyscraper." As they explained it to Griffin, a half bubble off in a foundation was no big deal unless you were going up thirty stories. Of course, half a bubble, factored over thirty floors, was no small thing. That, he now realized, was how he'd been feeling two days ago when he'd packed that bag and headed to Boston alone—thirty floors up and half a bubble off. Plumb the last time they checked, but now, suddenly, *plumb some.*

Stories worked much the same way, Griffin thought, shoving "The Summer of the Brownings" back into his satchel. A false note at the beginning was much more costly than one nearer the end because early errors were part of the foundation. That was the problem with most of the scripts in his satchel. Griffin knew that much without even reading them. They would end unconvincingly because of some critical misstep at or near the beginning. Over the next few days, despite his lack of enthusiasm for the task, he'd carefully examine every one of his students' rickety narratives, figure out exactly where they went wrong and how to go about fixing them, should their authors want to. They wouldn't, though. He knew this because he himself didn't want to revise "The Summer of the Brownings." As far as he was concerned, if the error was somewhere in the foundation, in some awkward place you couldn't get at with the tools at hand, it could just *stay* a half bubble off. Better to forget it and start something new.

He really did hope Sid had something for him.

5

Smirt

That evening Griffin went to a steak house not far from the B and B. The Olde Cape Lounge had a frozen-in-amber fifties feel, but it was mobbed, the line of people waiting for tables stretching out the door. There was, however, a vacant stool at the bar, so he climbed aboard and squinted at the sign above the back bar, which read, in ornate Gothic letters:

> 𝕳eresto pands pen d
> asoci al hourin har
> mles smirt hand funl
> etfri ends hipre ign
> bej usta ndkin dan
> devil spe akof no ne.

The words, somehow foreign and familiar at the same time, sort of reminded him of *The Canterbury Tales*, which he'd read long ago in college. *Pen, hand, ends, devil* and *no* were all recognizable words and should have been helpful in deciphering the whole, but somehow they weren't. Though devoid of meaning, *smirt* par-

ticularly appealed to him. When Laura was a little girl, she com-
piled long lists of words she loved, based purely on how they looked
and sounded, as well as others she hated. On which list, he wondered, would *smirt* have appeared?

"A couple martinis and it'll make sense," the bartender said
when he noticed Griffin studying the sign.

"Promise?"

"Absolutely."

"How about Grey Goosely?"

"Done."

In the mirror that ran the length of the bar Griffin noticed an
Asian man in his mid-to-late twenties. Wearing a well-tailored
three-piece suit and a handsome tie, he also appeared to be studying the sign. When his eyes met Griffin's in the mirror, he smiled
and nodded, as if to say, *Okay, got it. How about you?* Griffin hoped
his own look in return might be interpreted as, *Yeah, sure, me too,*
then feigned interest in his cell phone until his drink arrived,
unwilling to enter into conversation with some lonely tourist
whose English might be marginal. As if on cue, the phone vibrated
with an incoming e-mail, Joy writing to say that her meetings had
run long, but she was finally on the road and she would stop for
something to eat. Expect her around ten. Which was pure, unadul-
terated smirt. No way, on a Friday evening, with I-95 summer traffic heading for the Cape, would she get in before eleven.

And speaking of smirt, he himself had hoped to accomplish
just two things today—get a good start on those portfolios and
scatter his father's ashes—and he'd managed neither. Not scattering the ashes was more disconcerting, and he really should've done
the deed, wind or no wind. Why drive the length of Cape Cod, out
and back, with your old man in the wheel well and *not* do such a
simple thing? He supposed the Cape itself and the memories it had
evoked since he crossed the Sagamore were part of it. And whether

he cared to admit it or not, the unexpected phone call from his mother (and being doused with birdsmirt) had rattled him. But was there some further reluctance, some unconscious, unacknowledged scruple, at work? Some reason *not* to put his father to rest?

He supposed it was possible. Joy noticed his bouts of insomnia had begun right about the time his father was found on the Mass Pike, and claimed the two had to be related, as well as to what she described as his recent funk. He didn't know what to call it, only its name was *not* Professor William Griffin. He had been restless, though, give Joy that much, and Sid's call, together with Griffin's inability to reach him, had intensified that. Trying to reread "The Summer of the Brownings" hadn't helped, either. Suddenly it was as if his dead parent, his living one, his old profession and his boyhood self were all clamoring for attention.

This was profoundly silly. After all, his parents hadn't played a dramatic role in his life since the seventies. That's what heading west instead of east for college, and later going to film school, had been about, and staying in L.A. and marrying a girl who hadn't done graduate work. Like Huck Finn he'd lit out for the Territories at his first real opportunity. The problem seemed to be that you could put a couple thousand miles between yourself and your parents, and make clear to them that in doing so you meant to reject their values, but how did you distance yourself from your own inheritance? You couldn't prevent your hair from thinning or your nose from taking over the center of your face. Even worse, what if he hadn't rejected his parents' values as completely as he'd imagined? Joy maintained, for example, that he was inclined to locate happiness not in the present, as she did, but in some vague future. "And this reminds us of whom?" she often wanted to know. But was this his nature, as she implied, or just nurture? When he was growing up, his family had lived in a different house every year, renting from professors who were away on sabbatical. That was the reason he hadn't ever had a really good friend until Peter Browning. The Griffins were never in one place, nor he in one school, long enough. Often they hadn't completely unpacked their boxes from one move before they had to repack them for the next. University living, his parents called it, as if it were superior in all respects to how other people lived, "trapped" in a single house.

No doubt about it, they were born renters, his parents. And the houses of senior faculty were gracious and the rents cheap, at least until word got around how careless Griffin's parents were with other people's possessions. One professor returning from a European sabbatical would find that her china service for ten had become a service for seven, another that his favorite Queen Anne chair, now missing a leg, had been relocated to the damp basement. "When we left for Paris," they'd say, "there was a blender on the kitchen counter." To which Griffin's mother would reply, "Oh, *that* piece of crap," as if to suggest that its owner owed them a debt of gratitude for putting the offending appliance out of its misery. One year they'd nearly burned down a colleague's house by starting a grease fire in a cast-iron skillet and trying to put it out with cold water. The worst had been the year they'd gotten a beautiful old Victorian rent free. The only thing the elderly professor who owned it had asked of them was to make sure the pipes didn't burst during a cold snap. If it got below zero, she reminded them, they should leave the kitchen faucet running when they went to bed. She seemed fixated on that scenario, actually, calling twice from Italy to make sure the pipes were okay, because she'd heard the winter was brutally cold. "She doesn't even realize she's projecting, the frigid bitch," Griffin's mother remarked after hanging up. "Pipes my ass," his father added. "What she wanted to impress on us was that she's in Tuscany while we're stuck in fucking Indiana." But that very night an arctic clipper had blown in, the pipes burst, and by morning the whole first floor was underwater.

Eventually, people either refused to rent to the Griffins or required huge deposits and locked away anything of value in a closet. That last tactic didn't work, though, because a locked closet was both an affront and a challenge, and his father's one physical skill was as a picker of cheap padlocks. By the time Griffin was in junior high, his parents were reduced to renting damp, drafty, decrepit dumps on fraternity row, and even these they managed to leave the worse for wear. "Houses are nothing but trouble," they told him over and over, every time something went wrong, though even as a boy he understood the more commonly held view was that houses were fine, it was the *Griffins* that meant trouble.

The way his parents saw it, renting allowed them to remain flexible, so if a job came along at Swarthmore or Sarah Lawrence they wouldn't be saddled with an unsellable house in the Mid-fucking-west. And, of course, the money they saved by renting would then be available for a down payment when the right property on the Cape finally came along. Except they never managed to actually save. Indeed, they exhibited the professional humanist's utter cluelessness where money was concerned. They bought on impulse, often things that required assembly, saying, *how hard could it be,* then finding out. Bookshelves invariably had at least one shelf where the unfinished side faced up, its rough edge facing out. When you pulled open the upper-right-hand drawer of a desk, its lower-left-hand one opened in noisy sympathy. They gravitated to failed technologies like eight-track tapes and Beta recorders.

This carelessness was amplified in automobiles. His father specialized in rear-end collisions in the parking lots of grocery stores and shopping malls. The crashes all occurred without warning. The first sign that anything was amiss came with the impact itself, followed by the shriek of metal twisting, the shattering of glass and a moment of deep silence before his father, studying the rearview mirror, would say, "Where the hell did *he* come from?" Griffin, as a kid, had actually been in the car for most of these accidents, never seatbelted that he could remember, and in childhood often had a stiff neck. "Do you realize that sixteen-year-old boys on learner's permits get better rates than we do?" his mother complained to their insurance agent. "Sixteen-year-old boys have fewer collisions," the man told her. The cop who'd talked to him at the turnpike rest stop had noted that his father's dented trunk was secured by a bungee cord, testimony to a recent accident, and Griffin had to explain that it would've been far more unusual if the trunk had *not* been mangled, and also that the accident in question probably hadn't been that recent. His father had been the sort of man who considered the bungee cord a permanent solution, at least as permanent as the car itself. "He was an English professor," he explained.

For the first several years of their marriage, with the Great Truro Accord temporarily on hold, Griffin and Joy had lived almost as nomadically as his parents, moving from apartment to apartment, as people often did in L.A. if they were young and worked in "the industry." Sometimes they changed apartments to be closer to the ocean, other times to be closer to work. Or a new complex offering better amenities—a nicer pool, or Jacuzzi, or tennis courts— would open up. Once they'd even moved to be closer to a favorite restaurant. "This place is so much better," they agreed after each move, settling into their new surroundings. "Why didn't we think to do this sooner?" They didn't have or want a lot of possessions, and friends like Tommy and his wife, Elaine, always helped with the moves, which was sort of fun, and of course they returned the favor. There were no trick knees yet, no stiff lower backs. Every other weekend, it seemed, there'd be a housewarming party somewhere. Back then, Joy also enjoyed feeling footloose and fancy-free, spending their money in restaurants and running off to Mexico when Griffin and Tommy landed a lucrative gig. She and Elaine were good friends, and they loved lounging around the pool while "the boys" banged away toward their deadline at the portable typewriter set up on the balcony above.

But then Tommy and Elaine split up, and overnight things began to change. Little stuff, mostly. For instance, Joy had always worn her hair straight and long, which Griffin loved, but one day he came home and found her shorn and styled. "I can blow it dry," she explained. "Ten minutes and I'm done." He doubted it could possibly take that long. Then, other things. Instead of keeping one or two bras on hand for when they visited her parents, Joy's top drawer was suddenly crammed full of them, and when he asked about this she replied that she couldn't very well go through her whole life braless, could she? A rhetorical question, apparently. Not long after this she told him, "I woke up yesterday morning, and for some reason I was thinking about Truro." Remembered, "for some reason," that the life they were now living wasn't what they'd planned. Okay, it had been fun, she admitted, but was all this moving around and jaunting off to Mexico natural? (Again, rhetorical.) The whole time she was growing up, she reminded him, not counting the place they rented in Maine, her family had lived in just two houses, the one in Syracuse and the other, after her father got transferred, in Orange County. "It's time we stopped pretending to be your parents," she concluded, "and started pretending to be mine."

If this included a gated community in Sacramento, Griffin wasn't so sure. Still, until Joy put it into words, it hadn't occurred to him that this was what they'd been doing. He'd always assumed that the way they lived was, if anything, a repudiation of his parents. Certainly that was how *they* viewed it. Their son *choosing* to live on the West Coast? Who wrote television scripts instead of books? Who'd chosen a profession where you didn't get summers off? Why, he didn't even own a decent tweed jacket. But okay, point taken. Yet, even if their nomadic ways *were* an unconscious reflection of his parents' behavior, did that mean that it was now time to start consciously reflecting Joy's? Worse, he suspected that his wife's just happening to remember the Great Truro Accord "for some reason" wasn't entirely credible. Her whole family loved to interfere in their lives, and he sensed their shadowy presence behind the string of changes. Was it her sisters—one newly overweight, the other newly religious—who'd convinced her it was time to start wearing a bra again, to get a more "grown-up" hairstyle? For years now Jill, whom Joy talked to on the phone every other day or so, had been wondering out loud, "Do you kids think you'll ever settle down?" Or, as her father, who gravitated to sports metaphors, put it, "What's your endgame, is what I'd like to know."

Griffin assumed that the true subject here was children. Joy's sisters had started their families right after they married (or, in Jane's case, according to his arithmetic, a couple months before), whereas he and Joy were pushing thirty without a breeding time line. But maybe it wasn't just about kids. "You aren't a real adult until you have a mortgage you can't afford," Harve liked to observe. "That's when you find out if you can hit the long ball or if you're just hoping to draw a walk."

Harve could speculate and philosophize all he wanted, but in one respect, real estate, the terms of the Great Truro Accord actually worked in Griffin's favor. Joy hadn't forgotten her dream house. Far from it. But that house simply didn't exist, at least not in Southern California, and even if it had, given the breathtaking home prices in and around L.A., they wouldn't be able to afford it. He would've sworn they were in complete agreement about this, but suddenly the whole house issue was on the table in a new and unexpected way. The outrageous cost of real estate here, Joy now argued, was actually a reason to buy something as soon as possible, even if it was a crappy tract house in the Valley (Wouldn't Have It As a Gift!). Harve agreed, not that Griffin cared. Every year they didn't enter the market put them that much farther behind the eight ball (Jesus, now a pool metaphor). It would be different, Joy conceded, if they'd been putting money aside toward a down payment, but here too they'd been imitating Griffin's parents by *meaning* to save rather than actually saving. Maybe money did talk, as people claimed, but all it said to them was goodbye. Her parents, she said, were not only ready to help but anxious to. (They'd discussed this? When?) "They *want* to," Joy said, exasperated, when Griffin categorically refused. "They loaned money to both my sisters, and they want to do the same for us. They don't understand our reluctance."

His own parents understood perfectly. His mother was particularly adamant that borrowing money from Harve and Jill was a bad idea. "Good God," she said. "Imagine owing money to people like them."

"That's a bit harsh, Mom, given that you've only met them once," he chided her, but thinking as he did so how strange it was that he always ended up defending Joy's parents to his own, an impulse he otherwise kept under control. He had, in fact, imagined vividly what indebtedness to her parents would mean. In practical terms, every Thanksgiving, Christmas, Easter and Fourth of July invitation would have to be accepted. Nor would paying back the loan nullify such obligations. Worse was the attendant symbolism, because accepting their money would be a tacit admission that they needed it, and Harve would brag about "helping them out" long into the future. Griffin was pretty sure he made better money than Joy's father ever had, but accepting this loan would cede to him the high economic moral ground. Harve could lay claim to a kind of fiscal virtue, and Griffin himself would become, by implication, the wastrel who needed assistance. This was, of course, an ungenerous view of his in-laws' motives, one he didn't go into with his mother. "They mean well," he told her, damning them with faint praise. Though even this, his mother thought, was overly generous. "Boorish know-nothings" was how she remembered them from that single meeting. "Proud of their ignorance."

"Maybe you just know different things."

"Did you or did you not tell me they belong to a country club, that they live in a gated community?"

Which was his mother in top form. Catch her in one unkindness and she'd quickly hopscotch to another. Attempting to corner her was like trying to put a cat in a bag; there was always an arm left over and, at the end of it, claws.

"Call your father," she advised. "He and I may not agree on much, but I'm certain he'd never want to owe money to anyone who plays golf. Bartleby would agree, too, if he ever said anything."

Actually, he happened to know that his father himself had taken up golf after Claudia left him. His doctor at the time, himself an avid player, had suggested it as a way to relax—strange advice, Griffin thought, since the sport had pretty much the opposite effect on him, though that probably had less to do with the game than that he usually played it with Harve.

In lieu of offering to loan them the money herself—had Griffin actually imagined she might?—his mother continued to explain why he'd be wise to reject the offer of someone who had. "Remember your Thoreau," she counseled. "Simplicity, simplicity, simplicity."

"That's all well and good, Mom, but Joy's talking location, location, location."

"Then save. When you have enough for a down payment on a crappy three-bedroom ranch out there, you'd have enough for a real house back East, maybe even a place on the Cape. I could visit you there. I've missed you."

Now *this* was a surprising admission, and Griffin immediately tested its sincerity. "You could visit us now in L.A."

"That's all right. I can wait."

Save and wait. For a while at least, that's what they decided to do. *Dear God,* he remembered thinking. Was he actually going to follow his mother's advice? But in this case it made sense, didn't it, to scale back and get real? Okay, maybe not *Thoreau* real, but real enough. For instance, there was no law that said screenplays had to be written on the balconies of expensive Mexican hotels (though in Tommy's opinion there should've been). If they could rein in their spendthrift ways (yeah, Harve was right, they did spend too much and get too little for their money), Griffin made more than enough for them to live on. Joy, who worked part-time in the UCLA admissions office, didn't make a fortune, but if they opened a savings account and deposited her earnings automatically and treated the money therein as sacred, in two or three years they'd have a tidy sum. If it wasn't tidy enough, they could revisit the idea of a loan from her parents. By then maybe he'd be ready to quit screenwriting, which was, let's face it, a young man's game. He'd already been at it far longer than they planned in Truro.

If it weren't for Tommy, who'd be lost without him and needed time to get back on his feet after the meltdown of his marriage, he would've already said goodbye to the whole twisted life. Feature-film deals were getting harder and harder to make, and Griffin hated that the deals always seemed more important than the work that resulted from them. He could and often did riff on the subject. The "juice," the creative surge, was all front-loaded. Talking up the deal, you were excited and the producer was excited and the young studio exec was fucking beside himself with excitement. Why? Because nobody had ever *made* a movie like this before. It was beyond quirky, it was fucking unique. It was fucking better than unique, it was one of a kind. Just go away and write it, the exec would tell them, because this was a can't-miss idea. In fact, there was almost no way to fuck it up. After two years, a new producer and fifteen drafts (only three paid for) based on fifteen conflicting sets of notes, what you had, if you were lucky and the whole thing hadn't been put in turnaround, was yet another standard-issue piece of shit that lacked a single compelling reason to shoot it, which was, Tommy was fond of pointing out, the best reason to think it would be. Fuck it, Griffin thought. Another two or three years, and he was out.

Joy accepted his assurance, but for the record she expressed several explicit objections to his (or his mother's?) strategy to save, scale back on spending and patiently bide their time. For one thing it flew directly in the face of human nature in general and their own in particular. The best way to save for the house they wanted back East, she (or her father?) argued, was to buy one here. They wouldn't even *have* to save (something they'd never demonstrated much skill at), because the house itself would do the saving for them. It would appreciate in value, and when the time came to sell, the profit they made would provide the down payment on the house they wanted. Also, it was all well and good for Griffin to rail against the business of screenwriting and claim he was burning out, but there wasn't ever going to be a good time to quit. Ten years from now Tommy would still be lost without him, and they'd always be in the middle of a project, unable to walk away. Even Tommy, ever the cynic, agreed with her. When it came to quitting, to getting the hell out, screenwriters were like stockbrokers. You could hate the job all you wanted but it remained lucrative, which fact hit home when you seriously considered the other options. Plus, he reminded Griffin, deep down, fucked up as it was, you loved it. A Stockholm syndrome kind of love, maybe, but real enough for all that.

And Joy had one further objection, this one more personal than practical. If they followed his plan, it was she, not Griffin, who'd have to explain to her parents why they'd decided not to accept their generous offer of help. She did it, though, calling home over the Fourth, when the family always gathered for a patriotic celebration. This year Jason and Jared were both home on leave, and the family had been especially disappointed when Griffin and Joy had begged off, pleading, as always, a deadline. No, she told them, they weren't ready to take the house plunge quite yet. They appreciated the offer, they'd talked it through, but this was what they'd decided. Maybe next year, or the year after that . . .

Harve, at least, had shrugged it off. Hey, his son-in-law was proud—okay, hardheaded—but, hell, he could understand that, maybe even admire it a little. Just so long as his little girl understood the money wasn't going anywhere. In the end, he assured her, Griffin would come around, and when he did, she could just let him know, and he'd write the check. Jill, though, was more perceptive. "I can't help feeling Jack doesn't like us," she confessed to her daughter. ("Don't be ridiculous," Harve bellowed from the next room. "Why wouldn't he like us?" followed by Jared and Jason, who shared a talent for mimicry and used it to devastating effect on their father, "Why wouldn't he like us?") Griffin had listened in on his wife's half of the conversation and her patient attempt to dispel her mother's misgivings ("No, no, that's not true, Mom. He's just afraid we won't be able . . . I know, I know . . . He doesn't mean anything by it . . . Of course he does, and so do I . . . Of course I'm happy . . ."). After Joy finally hung up, she was quiet, staring out the window at the courtyard below, where a young woman was shrieking with delight as two young men tossed her into the pool. Griffin turned off the radio, which had been playing jazz.

He now had to admit that Joy had been right about all of it. It had taken him close to another decade to quit screenwriting and find a suitable academic position back East at a college that was adding a screenwriting component and a film series to their creative-writing major. He and Joy saved for a while, but not enough, and, just as she'd predicted, they raided the house account in emergencies. So in the end, when Joy got pregnant, he'd had to give in and accept the loan from her parents. He'd hated it even then, but it was the right thing to do. They bought a nice, modest house (though his mother Wouldn't Have It As a Gift) at an immodest price in the Valley, and it was the equity from its eventual sale that paid for Joy's dream house in Connecticut. It had also been the home of Laura's childhood, and whenever she was in Southern California she drove by the old neighborhood to make sure it was still there, still being cared for.

But Griffin couldn't help remembering how, at the closing, as he signed his way through the mountain of paperwork, there'd been a little voice in the back of his head—his mother's? his father's? his own?—noting that he and Joy were no longer "flexible," that if something better came along it'd be tough to pull up stakes and go. But of course *he'd* been right about a few things, too. Even after the loan had been repaid in full, Harve continued to remind them about what had given them their start, that they should've taken the money sooner. Jill scolded him when he went on like this, but Griffin could tell she, too, was proud of the part they'd played in making her daughter and son-in-law home own-ers, and of course she subscribed to Harve's view that Joy and Grif-fin had had to be dragged, kicking and screaming, into adulthood. "These two would still be hippies if it wasn't for us, Jilly-Billy," Harve chortled.

Actually, his father-in-law's boasting and the endless I-told-you-so's had bothered Griffin less than he'd imagined they would, and to Harve's credit, when Griffin repaid the loan, he hadn't wanted to take the money. Jane and June and their husbands had never paid him back, he admitted, not that he'd wanted them to. That Griffin was even offering to was repayment enough. But Grif-fin had insisted, hoping against hope that the absence of debt would buy them some freedom.

"Could we spend Christmas in Baja?" he asked Joy, driving back to L.A. after a particularly brutal Thanksgiving in Sacramento.

Laura, then four, had been sick the whole trip. She'd been running a fever even before they left L.A., but no, even a sick child was no excuse.

"Baja," Joy repeated. "Why would we want to go to Mexico for Christmas?"

"Okay, then you decide. Anywhere but Sacramento. Someplace where nobody will say, 'How's that house of ours? Tell me that's not the best decision you ever made.' "

She stared out the passenger-side window for a good mile before responding. "If we were going to visit *your* parents, mine would understand."

"I don't *want* to visit my parents," he said. "God forbid."

"So?"

"I guess what I don't understand is why we can't have one holiday with just us."

"You mean just the two of us, or could our daughter come, too?"

"Unfair."

It was Laura, her face a thundercloud, who'd spoken next, from the backseat. "You're fighting," she said, and Griffin, whose own backseat memories were still raw and vivid, felt a chill.

So, again, the headline? JOY WAS RIGHT. And nothing that followed in the fine print made that headline less than true. His wife, like Tommy, was a big-picture person. They both saw the whole, the entire structure, while Griffin tinkered with the characters' gestures and dialogue, the smaller moment-to-moment truths of story and daily life, the tiny burrs under the narrative saddle. It was Joy's ability to see the big picture that was responsible, he knew, for the fact she seldom harbored misgivings. She always knew in broad strokes what she wanted. It had been the same when they finally moved back East. Their Connecticut country house was the first place their realtor showed them, ten miles inland from the coast, an easy twenty-minute commute to the college. Large, rambling, inconvenient, full of character, on three acres and surrounded on three sides by woods, it was the house she'd been dreaming of since Truro. It had everything she wanted but the benign ghost. Yes, it had seemed more than they could afford and needed a lot of work, but she took it all in and judged correctly that it could be done, a room at a time if necessary, and so they'd done it, or rather hired it done, finally finishing last spring. Maybe if Griffin had done the work himself—if he'd been that kind of man, the kind Harve was— he might have felt the same sense of pride and accomplishment Joy got from being more involved, studying the magazines, choosing fixtures, riding herd on the contractors.

Why then, especially now, question the wisdom of the Great Truro Accord? Did he believe there was something fundamentally unfair or unwise about it? No, of course not. It wasn't like he'd grown weary of their good life, their good marriage. *That* would be serious. Though he had to admit, despite Joy's best efforts, he sometimes thought of the house as hers, not theirs, almost as if they'd divorced and she'd gotten it in the settlement. It was hers for the simple reason that it made her happy. She had what she wanted. Was it possible that her contentment was the true cause of his funk? Her ability to still want what she wanted so long ago? This was a failing?

It was almost as if his parents, who'd many years ago lost the argument over which set of parents he and Joy would end up imitating, were now whispering to him that they'd been right all along.

By the time Griffin finished his martini and ordered a prime rib, the two bar stools on his right freed up and a middle-aged couple took them. The woman, in her late forties, was all dolled up and taking in the Olde Cape Lounge as if it were just too wonderful for words and she meant to commit its every detail to loving memory. Her dress was cut low in front, revealing a body that, though thickened, remained somehow hopeful. Her companion, who looked a few years older, had a plunging neckline of his own, his maroon, long-sleeved shirt unbuttoned to reveal a vast expanse of gray chest hair. He carried his sizable gut proudly, as if he imagined it might be the very thing that made him irresistible to women like the one he was with. In L.A. he'd have been cast as a lower-echelon mafioso, an expendable foot soldier, second-act fodder. Having arrived at the bar a full five seconds ago, he was annoyed the bartender was still shaking some other patron's drink.

The woman was squinting at the sign above the bar. "What's that say?"

"Beats me. Or it would if I gave a shit."

"What kind of word is *smirt?*" She leaned forward to peer around him at Griffin. "Can you read that?"

Griffin confessed he couldn't.

Her companion met his eye and shrugged, as if to suggest there was no accounting for what interested broads. You wanted a mystery to solve, you could start right there. "It's like a proverb . . . a saying," he told her. "It don't mean nothin'."

"It's got to mean something. It's like in *The Da Vinci Code,*" she said. "Everything means something." She was leaning forward again to speak to Griffin. "He's not a reader," she explained. Then, to her companion, "*I* think it's some kind of spell. Maybe to ward off evil spirits."

"Bartenders is what it wards off," he said. "I'm gonna go find the can. If our friend down there ever heads in this direction, order me a Maker's. Get yourself whatever."

"A cosmopolitan," the woman said, scrunching up her shoulders with pleasure at the idea, the front of her dress gapping as she did. Griffin noticed, and she noticed him notice, with gratitude, unless he was mistaken. Something about her expression gave him to understand that she didn't usually dress so provocatively.

Tonight was special, and she meant for things to go well with the man who'd just abruptly abandoned her. Better than well, in fact. Though as a general rule they didn't. "*We're* going to figure out what that says," she told Griffin, scrunching up her shoulders again. "You and me."

How, he couldn't help wondering, did you get to be this woman's age and still believe, as she apparently did, that everything meant something? She was obviously one of those people who just soldiered on, determined to believe whatever gave them comfort in the face of all contrary evidence. And maybe that wasn't so dumb. The attraction of cynicism was that it so often put you in the right, as if being right led directly to happiness. Probably her companion believed the sign had no meaning because this absolved him from making an effort to decode it and insulated him from failures of both intelligence and imagination. Easier to cleave to the card counter's arithmetic, which meant at least you weren't a sap.

"That prime as good as it looks?" the man said when he returned from the gents. When Griffin said it was, he looked him over frankly, as if trying to decide whether he could be trusted to second a motion that he himself had just made. Apparently so, because when the bartender set down his second Maker's, he said, "You could give us a couple of them prime ribs, I guess."

"We're going to eat here?" the woman said. Clearly, she hadn't gotten all dressed up to eat at the bar.

The man rotated on his stool so he could survey the restaurant. The bar had been set up for diners, but a piano player was noodling show tunes in the main dining room, and that seemed to be what the woman had in mind. "This ain't a bad spot."

"It's not that—"

"You'd rather wait another half hour so you can eat there?" He was indicating the nearest table, five feet away, where an elderly couple looked up from their fish, surprised to find themselves at the end of a large, hairy-chested stranger's index finger, a negative example.

"Could we look at a menu, at least?" the woman said, staring at her cosmo, embarrassed.

He leaned back on his stool so she could have a clear, unobstructed view of Griffin's food. "What about that don't look good to you?"

"Fine," she said without looking.

"Two menus," the man told the bartender. "We don't want to do nothin' rash."

When Griffin glanced in the back-bar mirror, the young Asian man he'd noticed earlier looked away. Had he, too, overheard the bickering couple?

Finishing up quickly, Griffin paid his tab, hoping he could slip away without the woman telling him no, he couldn't leave, not yet, not until they'd figured out what the sign said. But he was lucky. As he slid off his stool, the bartender arrived with their two big slabs of bloody beef. He told himself not to look at her, but did anyway, just a quick glance, enough to see that she was quietly crying.

Outside, it had clouded over, the dark sky low and ugly, and as he unlocked the car door a fat raindrop hit him on the forehead. By the time he got the convertible's top up, cold rain was leaping off the hood. He turned the key in the ignition, then turned it off again, thinking about the woman inside and also about Joy, about a morning, years ago, when he'd come upon her in the shower. He'd driven into campus and was parking in the faculty lot when he remembered he'd left a stack of graded papers on his desk back home. He'd stayed up late to finish them, having foolishly promised to return them today. When he got back, he could hear the upstairs shower from the kitchen. Grabbing the papers, he poked his head in to say goodbye again, in case she'd heard him come in and was wondering why he'd returned.

She stood in the shower stall facing the spray, her forehead resting on the tile beneath the nozzle and most of the water pounding the glass door behind her. Though her shoulders were quaking violently, it wasn't immediately apparent that she was sobbing. To Griffin it seemed impossible that she could be. When he'd left her at the breakfast table less than fifteen minutes before, everything had seemed fine. What could have occurred in the interim to provoke such sorrow? If something had happened to Laura she'd be frantically trying to reach him at the office, so that couldn't be it. The life they'd dreamed of in Truro had finally come to full fruition. What was there to grieve about?

What came to Griffin, standing there, was that he wasn't supposed to be witnessing this. Whatever heartbreak his wife was giving vent to now had been fully present half an hour ago, but she'd waited for him to leave. Nor, after he did, had she broken down there in the kitchen. She'd gone upstairs and taken off her robe and nightgown and gotten into the shower, where the evidence of her sorrow would be washed away immediately. How long did he stand there in the doorway, rooted to the spot, staring in stunned disbelief, before quietly backing out of the room, getting back in the car and returning to campus?

How good it would feel, Griffin thought, to go back inside the Olde Cape Lounge and coldcock the woman's companion, knock him clean off his bar stool, bloody his fucking nose. Here she was, trying valiantly to be happy, and this asshole wouldn't let her.

Instead he took out his cell and dialed Sid's number. He'd called him half a dozen times that afternoon, always getting the answering machine. It was now eight-thirty, only five-thirty on the West Coast, but again the machine picked up. There was no point in leaving another message, so he hung up and scrolled down his contacts list, stopping at Tommy's name. A moment later his old writing partner was on the line.

"Griff," Tommy said, as if he'd been expecting the call. *You through screwing around back there, shoveling snow? You coming back to work?* That's what Griffin expected him to say, not "Jesus, I was so sorry to hear about Sid."

"Hear what about Sid?" But even as he asked, Griffin suddenly knew why today's calls hadn't been answered.

"I almost called you," Tommy told him. "The poor bastard woke up dead, is what I heard. His housekeeper found him."

Griffin looked out across what had been the parking lot and was now a lake. It was astonishing, really, how hard it was raining.

"What the hell's that noise?" Tommy wanted to know. "Are you under attack or something?"

"It's hailing," Griffin said, realizing only as he said so that it was true. Semitranslucent pellets the size and shape of cold capsules were dancing off the hood of the convertible.

"Yeah, but who lives like that?" Tommy demanded. "I mean, voluntarily."

"I can't believe it," Griffin said. "Sid called me yesterday. Left a message on my machine. I've been trying to reach him all day."

"Come out for the service, why don't you? You were one of his favorites. I could be wrong, but I've got this feeling he didn't really have anybody."

Sid had been Tommy's agent, too, but his new partner, the one he'd briefly teamed up with after Griffin left, had been represented by one of the big agencies, and Tommy had moved on.

"Besides, it'd be good to see you. You want, I'll introduce you to my guy. Bring Joy. We'll all do something, go someplace we can't afford and misbehave. Like the old days."

He was tempted to tell Tommy that the old days were long gone, that he and Joy never misbehaved anymore, that the woman he was remembering didn't exist. That day in the shower had been an anomaly, and he was grateful for that. His wife had every single thing she wanted, and he couldn't remember the last time she'd changed her mind. And Griffin himself? If the woman Tommy remembered didn't exist anymore, then probably he didn't, either.

But of course he said none of this. They left it that Tommy would call when he found out details. Griffin hung up, but the phone rang before he could turn the key in the ignition, and Griffin, thinking Tommy must have forgotten to tell him something, picked up.

"I just want you to know you're not fooling anybody," his mother said.

"What are you talking about, Mom?"

"You're going to scatter his ashes there, aren't you? *That's* why you were thinking about him."

"Mom—"

"You always were sneaky. Even as a kid."

And then she was gone, the line dead.

God, Griffin thought, it was raining hard. As if all the grief in the world were coming down from the sky.

6

Laura and Sunny

Griffin was worried that he and Joy would be among the
first to arrive, but dozens of people were already milling
around, drinking mimosas on the hotel's back porch.
From there a vast expanse of manicured lawn sloped a good hundred and fifty yards to the water's edge.

"You made it," Laura said, then she and her mother went into
their customary clinch, hugging as if one of them had been in grave
danger and they'd feared they might never see each other again.
Actually, Joy's journey the evening before *had* been harrowing.
Unbeknownst to Griffin, cloudbursts of the sort he'd experienced
in the parking lot of the Olde Cape Lounge had pummeled the
entire region. Three different times she'd been forced to pull off the
turnpike, and her car was a lunar landscape of hailstone pock-
marks. Farther out the Cape, Laura and her friends had also gotten
pounded. First bird shit, then torrential rain and hail. Suddenly
Griffins everywhere were coming under attack (as Tommy had put
it) from above. What next, frogs? He checked the sky, but it was a
cloudless blue.

"You look—" Joy started to say "great," Griffin could tell.

"—like Snow White," Laura finished.

Which she did. Her bridesmaid's dress might have been on loan from the Magic Kingdom. She also looked as happy as Griffin had ever seen her. His daughter had spent a long time between boyfriends, searching for Mr. Right with no interest at all in Mr. Right Now, which had made Joy proud. Griffin supposed he was proud, too, but he'd also been worried. As a girl she'd once flirted with the idea of a religious vocation, and he'd wondered if her willingness to put off intimacy might be a vestige of that romantic and utterly perverse impulse. But more likely it was exactly what Joy thought it was, a brave refusal to settle that was at long last paying off. She'd gone to a lot of her college friends' weddings, and this was the first where she had someone of her own. She seemed to think she'd soon be engaged, and Griffin couldn't imagine what he'd do, how he and Joy would console her, if that didn't happen.

"Andy actually likes it," she said, rolling her eyes. "Men. No taste and plenty of it."

"Speaking of Andy, where is he?" Joy said.

"Around," their daughter sighed. "He disappears."

Which gave Griffin pause. Was the boy naturally shy, or did he already understand that disappearance would become a necessary survival skill if he married into Laura's family? He hadn't met the rest of them yet but had probably heard stories, and of course he'd already overheard scores of half-hour phone conversations between Laura and her mother. If he turned out to be the one, Griffin would have to take him aside and validate his instincts.

"Tough duty for him," Joy said, with genuine sympathy, since Andy wouldn't know anyone at this particular wedding.

"He's fine," Laura said, turning to Griffin now. "Everybody loves him." The hug she gave him was very different from the one she'd just given her mother. His assumed he was fine, maybe even indestructible, and he was glad if that's how he seemed to her, though he had to admit that it puzzled him, too. "I'm sorry about Sid, Daddy. Will you go out for the funeral?"

"Maybe. Tommy's going to call when he hears—"

"*There's* the boy," Laura said, her face suddenly radiant, all thoughts of mortality evaporating. She'd spied her boyfriend half-way down the lawn, talking to one of the groomsmen under the big tent that had been erected for the reception. The wedding ceremony itself would take place by the water under an ornate arch. A hundred and fifty or so folding chairs had been set up there—yesterday, by the look of it, since several hotel employees were busy wiping them down with towels.

"By the way," Laura said, looking at the card that Joy had picked up in the hotel foyer. "I'm really sorry about table seventeen. I wasn't consulted."

"The leftover table?" Griffin guessed.

She nodded. "You aren't going to know anybody," she said, then was visited by a happy thought. "Actually, that's not true. You'll know Sunny Kim."

"Little Sunny?" Joy said.

"He's about six-two now and very good-looking. Anyway, I should get back to the bridal party. I'll tell A-boy you're here."

They watched her go, tripping down the lawn in her Snow White dress. Joy took Griffin's hand. "Have you ever seen anyone so happy?" There was a certain wistfulness in her expression as she watched her daughter and this new boy she'd chosen, as if she knew all too well he could turn out to be Mr. Wrong and end up breaking Laura's large, generous, trusting heart. Or maybe, Griffin thought, it was the knowledge that what was just now filling that heart to overflowing could in the end leak away, and that in thirty-four years, love's urgency, if not love itself, might have dissipated.

While she studied their daughter, he studied her, trying to decide which it might be.

Then Sunny Kim emerged onto the porch, where he squinted into the bright sunlight. He hadn't looked so tall the night before, but of course at the Olde Cape Lounge he'd been sitting down.

. . .

Kelsey Apple, the bride, had been Laura's best friend through middle school, back in L.A. Laura's had been the more dominant personality, or so it had seemed to Griffin. Wherever she was, that's where Kelsey had to be, and whatever she had was what Kelsey wanted, including Griffin and Joy for her parents. Her own were dour and dull, her father some sort of bean counter for a movie studio, her mother religious. "It's so weird being in your house," Kelsey once told Laura. "Your parents, like, actually talk to each other. You can tell they still have sex."

When Griffin accepted the teaching position back East, they feared Laura would be devastated to leave her L.A. life and friends, but it was Kelsey who'd come unglued at the news. "You can't," she told Laura matter-of-factly as they walked home from school, as if that declaration meant the end of the discussion. That evening after dinner, Mrs. Apple had called the Griffins to say that Kelsey had pitched the mother of all fits and locked herself in her room. Could Laura maybe come over and reassure her that their moving to Connecticut wouldn't mean the end of the girls' friendship, that they could still write and even talk on the phone? Joy had gone along with Laura for moral support and also ended up talking to Kelsey through her locked bedroom door, a conversation that quickly devolved into a negotiation. Of *course* Kelsey and Laura wouldn't lose touch, and of *course* they could talk on the phone each and every week, and of *course* Laura wasn't going to go out and find a new best friend and replace her. And next summer (Joy had to promise this, too, not just Laura) Kelsey could come visit them in their new home and stay as long as she wanted. Leaving no stone unturned, Kelsey then insisted both her parents join them in the crowded hallway, grant their permission and promise they'd somehow find money for the trip. Only then did she open the door and embrace her friend. "I'd still rather you wouldn't," she told Laura, clearly suffering buyer's remorse now that the deal had finally been struck. Walking home Laura confided to Joy that she was just as happy to be moving far away, that Kelsey's friendship, always needy, was becoming impossible.

New England was different, though, and she found it tough sledding in her new high school. The cliques were long established, and since Laura wasn't the type to crash them, she spent most of her free time babysitting and wishing she had a best friend again, even a needy one. Kelsey visited for two weeks that summer, and after that first year's separation both girls seemed profoundly happy together. Kelsey had a boyfriend now, Robbie, but he was from her mother's church and he thought he might become a minister, so in some respects it was a lot like not having a boyfriend. She told Laura she was thinking she'd break up with him as soon as she got back to L.A., though then again maybe she'd wait until she had someone to replace him. The following summer, when she visited again, Kelsey was still with Robbie, who now was pretty sure, at least when they were necking in the backseat of his parents' car, that he didn't have a vocation after all. It wasn't until junior year that Laura got a boyfriend, the son of one of Griffin's colleagues, and this ended her isolation, because being a couple allowed them access into the same social circles where they'd been unwelcome as singles.

That was also the year of college applications, and Kelsey frequently called to ask what schools Laura had visited the weekend before, which had impressed her the most, how she was leaning. She wanted desperately to apply back East herself, but her parents said she had to stay in California, in the state university system. Private schools were out of the question. Which they would have been for Laura but for the generous tuition-reimbursement program offered by Griffin's college.

By the fall of her senior year Laura had settled on Skidmore

College. Jonathan, her boyfriend, applied there as well, though not early admission as Laura had and expected him to. His parents wanted him to keep his options open, he explained, but she was worried there might be more to it, that maybe those options weren't just academic. Worse, what if that wasn't really his parents' idea but his own? Griffin didn't say anything, though he feared she might be right. Jonathan's father struck him as a careerist who was using his present position as a stepping stone to a better one at a research university. He'd even asked him for a letter of recommendation earlier that year, stressing the necessity for secrecy. If Griffin was right—and he was reasonably confident of his ability to recognize academic snobbery and ambition when he saw it—then the apple hadn't fallen very far from the tree. Laura was deeply in love with Jonathan, though, and while he undoubtedly cared for her, she was afraid that maybe he wasn't quite as much in love with her as she with him. The harder she tried to find out, the more elusive and distant he became. When she got the good news about Skidmore, he was happy for her, but she thought maybe he was also relieved to know that her decision had been made, that she wouldn't be able to wait and see where he was going. When he applied to eight schools and got in everywhere except Skidmore, Laura tearfully confessed to her mother that she suspected he'd withdrawn his application there. "You should give Kelsey a call," Joy had suggested, hoping to cheer her up. "See how things are shaping up for her."

Laura said she would but never did. She'd told Kelsey too much about Jonathan and didn't want to confess the extent of her broken heart. In fact, they didn't talk until late that spring, when her friend called with exciting news. She hadn't called earlier, she explained, because she was waiting to hear what kind of financial package her favorite school would offer, but she'd just learned today that she, too, would be enrolling at Skidmore. The *other* reason she hadn't called was that she'd been down in the dumps since Christmas, when she'd spent the holidays wondering whether to break up with Robbie, only to have him break up with her. All that backseat groping had caused him to backslide into the church. He'd confessed to his pastor that he was pretty sure he and Kelsey would have sex soon (she told Laura his optimistic anxiety on that score was entirely unwarranted), and the pastor had said that breaking up was definitely the right thing to do. So for now she was dating a boy who was really more of a friend, someone there was no danger of getting serious about. Laura knew him, actually. Did she remember Sunny Kim? Probably not, but he remembered Laura and was always asking about her.

Of course Laura did remember both Sunny and his family. Mr. Kim was an engineer who'd thrived since arriving in America. Mrs. Kim didn't work outside the home and in fact seldom left it. Griffin remembered Sunny, the oldest of their half-dozen children, as a well-mannered boy, prematurely adult and serious. He wasn't allowed to play sports or join clubs. When school let out Mrs. Kim was always there at the curb with a wagonful of well-behaved little Kims, the two youngest still strapped into car seats. Years before, Joy and Kelsey's mother had invited Mrs. Kim to join their car pool, since the three families lived within a few blocks of one another. But she'd declined, saying in fractured but earnest English that transportation was her duty and her husband wouldn't approve of her sharing it. She wasn't unfriendly, though, and seemed, if not tempted by their offer, at least grateful for it. Determined to raise their children as Koreans, the Kims apparently feared all American influences, as if Southern California culture itself were rooted in decadence and corruption, which—admit it—didn't exactly make them fools. That Sunny also wasn't allowed to ask girls out made Laura guiltily glad, because she knew he had a crush on her.

It was interesting that later, when they finally relaxed a bit and let Sunny date, he chose (or was it his mother?) the daughter of one of the women who'd been kind to Mrs. Kim so long ago. Laura suspected that the real reason he dated Kelsey was that he knew she and Laura were still friends. Sometimes they'd talk for a good half hour on the phone and then, just before hanging up, Kelsey would say, as if in afterthought, "Oh, Sunny says hi," and Laura would realize that he'd been there all along, waiting patiently to be acknowledged, for his name to be introduced into the record, anxious not to be completely forgotten. When Kelsey headed east to join Laura at Skidmore, Sunny enrolled at Stanford, where he'd earned a full scholarship. "Do you think Sunny's gay?" Kelsey inquired idly one day, as if this happy possibility had just occurred to her. They'd dated throughout senior year, and Sunny, though always attentive and eager to please, had never even tried to kiss her. She hadn't wanted him to, exactly, but still. Now, at Stanford, he apparently wasn't dating.

"No," Laura told her, "Sunny's not gay."

What he was, at Stanford, was poor. He had the scholarship, sure, but he also worked two part-time jobs. His father, a stereotypical Asian workaholic, had fallen ill that summer and had to have an operation. Afterward, he'd gone back to his job too soon and gotten sick again, a pattern that was to recur during Sunny's college years. "Is it okay if I give Sunny your e-mail address?" Kelsey asked one day during their spring semester. He'd been writing her every week, long e-mail letters that made her feel guilty about the brief ones she sent in return, so guilty that she'd solved the problem by responding only to every second or third letter, and it would be good to have someone to share the burden. "Besides," she told Laura, "he keeps asking about you."

Laura said that of course it was okay, but for some reason Sunny didn't write. Probably, she decided, he was just as shy as he'd been in middle school, always standing awkwardly off on the periphery of things, never willing to put himself forward. So after a couple weeks she wrote him instead, asking how he was, how his classes were going, whether there was a girl in his life yet. By evening he'd responded—good, fine and no. But he was very happy to hear from her. Yes, Kelsey had given him her address, though he hadn't been sure she'd remember him after so many years. Still, since she'd been so kind, would she mind if he wrote her occasionally and promised not to do it too often? He knew how busy she must be, and of course she wouldn't be under any obligation to reply.

"Excellent!" Kelsey said when Laura told her about all this. "Now he's yours, which is only fair. I dated him. This is the least you can do."

And so the two began a correspondence. Every couple weeks Laura would receive a newsy e-mail and wait a few days before writing back, not wanting to give him the wrong impression, though in fact she did enjoy hearing about his family, his classes, his part-time jobs. Gradually she learned to read between the lines, factoring in Sunny's modesty (he wasn't doing "okay" in his classes, but brilliantly), his optimism (his father's condition wasn't likely to "improve soon," but rather would continue its decline), his stoicism (he was friendly with several of his professors, meaning he had no other friends). His classes had many attractive and intelligent girls, he admitted, but most were spoken for and, besides, his mother was determined that when the time came he should marry a Korean girl and bring her to this country. For this precise purpose she'd kept in touch with friends from the old country who had daughters roughly Sunny's age. He wasn't in favor of this plan, he confessed, but until such time as he should fall in love with a girl who loved him back, he saw no reason to bring his mother unhappiness by refusing to consider the possibility of a Korean wife.

Laura's e-mails to Sunny were far less circumspect. She was enjoying college and doing well, but she confided to him that she and Kelsey were going through a rough patch in their friendship.

Kelsey had originally suggested they room together, and her feelings were hurt when Laura, who was still ambivalent about her being there, said they should probably be meeting new people. To her surprise, though, Kelsey proved more adept at making friends than she was, and by the end of September she had a new boyfriend and had pledged a sorority. Laura began to sense that the shoe of neediness was now inexplicably on the other foot. At the beginning of the spring semester, when Kelsey asked if she wanted to pledge her sorority, Laura said she didn't think so, but the way Kelsey just shrugged and said "Fine" made her wonder if she wasn't relieved.

Laura also confessed to Sunny that she was still in love with Jonathan, who'd gone off to a midwestern university. Worse, his father had published a well-reviewed book that won him a job at an Ivy League school, and the family had moved, which meant she wouldn't be seeing him even on vacations. Most of the boys she'd met at Skidmore were wealthy city brats majoring in alcoholism who saw no reason to waste time on a girl who wasn't going to put out, not when the next girl would. *Kelsey is lucky to have you for a friend,* Sunny wrote back. *And you are right not to give in to social pressure. You're too special.* That made her feel guilty, detailing her own brokenheartedness to a boy who she suspected was himself brokenhearted over her.

Much as Sunny liked to write long e-mails, he had little use for instant messaging. Most of her college friends—Kelsey in particular—were on IM every night with a dozen friends all over the country. Laura, wary of the habit, tried to stay off-line except on weekends. Sunny agreed that it wasted time, but he had another reservation, too. *I like to think about what I say,* he explained. *When I speak impulsively, I sometimes say foolish things.* She'd noted, of course, that his communications were formal to the point of stylistic stiffness, that he never contracted words or used slang or made grammatical errors, but she'd attributed this to the combination of his brilliance and cultural upbringing. Eventually she began to suspect that he not only wrote carefully but also revised again and again. The reason he didn't write more often (as he'd done with Kelsey) was that every letter had to be perfect. It was the *instant* in instant messaging that frightened him, and himself he distrusted. *You need to loosen up,* Laura wrote him. *So what if you say something dumb? It's just me. We're friends. I say dumb things all the time.*

No, he wrote back in his next long letter. *You never say dumb things.*

One Sunday night Laura awoke before dawn, as she often did on days when she had a big exam or presentation. She'd forgotten to turn her computer off the night before, and now noticed that Sunny was online. She'd put him on her IM buddy list, but until that moment he'd never actually used it.

Sunny, is that you? In California it was 2:00 a.m., not so very late for a college student, but still.

Then, after a long beat: *Laura?*

How are you?

An even longer beat, then: *A terrible thing has happened. My brother has been arrested.*

Laura watched the blinking cursor and had just about concluded that he wasn't going to say anything more when words started flying onto the screen in a torrent. His brother and a friend had broken into a house in Beverly Hills. A girl they'd met at a club lived there and told them no one would be home. She was angry with her parents, who'd left for Europe without her, fobbing her off on an aunt in Brentwood for a whole month. She'd given Sunny's brother the security code and told him to take everything. Except it turned out she didn't really live there, that the people who did weren't her parents and weren't in Europe, that the code she'd given them didn't even have the right number of digits. Sunny's parents had had to borrow money against their house to get his brother out of jail. The story had been in the newspaper, the family disgraced.

Sunny was afraid his father, his health precarious as always, might now take his life for the shame of it. His mother was talking about moving back to Korea. She wanted Sunny to leave Stanford immediately and come home.

Your brother has disgraced himself, not you, not your family, Laura wrote. *If you leave Stanford I'll never forgive you.*

Again, she watched the blinking cursor for a long time. Finally, he came back. *You are right, of course. May I tell my mother you said this?*

I hope you will.

Please don't tell Kelsey.

Of course I won't, she promised. *Hey, you know what? I'm proud of you. You wrote a spontaneous message. It contained actual mistakes, a misspelling, even. You can rest easy, though. You didn't say anything foolish.*

He wrote back, *The thing I wanted to write but did not . . . that was the foolish thing.*

Laura didn't have to ask what that thing was.

"I'll tell you, but only if you promise not to judge me too harshly," Sunny told Joy when she asked what he was doing in D.C. The day had turned hot, and Griffin took off his sport coat and loosened his tie. Guests were now gathered on the lawn, waiting for the wedding party to emerge from the hotel. Sunny had walked with them to the last row of folding chairs when Joy waved him over, giving her a graceful kiss on the cheek and shaking Griffin's hand with firm forthrightness, though neither gesture should have been particularly surprising. The kid had graduated from Stanford, after all, then gone to law school at Georgetown, so there was no reason for him to be shy or awkward anymore. "I've become two terrible things," he said with a wry grin. "A lawyer and a lobbyist."

Though not so very terrible, of course. Under cross-examination Sunny confessed that he worked for a liberal law firm that handled public-interest litigation. He himself was one of its immigration specialists.

"I'm sorry I didn't recognize you at the restaurant last night," Griffin said.

"I should've introduced myself," Sunny told him. "I was pretty sure it was you, but when I didn't see Mrs. Griffin . . ."

The last time Griffin had seen him was at Laura's thirteenth birthday party. Joy had had to banish him from the kitchen, where he wanted to be put to work. "You're a guest," she told him. "Join the others and have fun." The one thing the poor boy had no clue how to do.

"I wish it would get dark," Griffin recalled telling Joy. "I can't bear to watch this."

As instructed, Sunny had joined the others on the patio but seemed to have little in common with the other boys, who'd congregated, as boys will, near the food, strutting and joking and pushing and checking out the giggling girls who'd cleverly staked out the punch bowl. Sunny had positioned himself in the middle, as if he represented a third gender, smiling broadly at nothing in particular, his head bobbing arrhythmically to the horrible boy-band music, pretending, Griffin was sure, to enjoy himself.

In fact, watching the kid reminded Griffin of his first boy-girl party at a similar age. He should've known how to behave, since his parents were forever throwing parties back then, though of course those were for adults only. He was expected to make a brief appearance after the guests started arriving and then to disappear, which was why, he supposed, he never learned the requisite skills. His first junior-high party had been a nightmare. Not only did all the other kids know one another, it also seemed like they'd been going to parties like this for years. Griffin remembered positioning himself where he could see the clock and will it to move. At one point, after

he and the others had filled their paper plates with food at the buf-
fet table and eaten standing up, a few parents hovering around,
everyone, it seemed, began trooping downstairs into the rec room,
where music was playing on a portable record player. Griffin was
still on the stairs when the lights went out. It had taken his eyes a
minute or two to adjust, and when they finally did he discovered, to
his mortification, that all the other kids were couples necking in the
dark. One boy he knew had his hand under a girl's shirt. "What are
you doing down here?" came a voice in the dark, and he'd known
with terrible certainty that he was the one being addressed.

"I didn't know . . . ," he'd stammered.

"Yeah, well, now you do."

And there'd been snickers, lots of them, to help propel him
back up the stairs.

Poor kid, Griffin remembered thinking as he regarded Sunny.
He must be suffering just like that.

"Why don't you go somewhere, then," Joy told him. "You're
making me more nervous than he is."

He'd gladly taken her advice and gone out for a drink with
Tommy, returning just as the party was breaking up. Sunny Kim,
still smiling, was among the last to leave, and he shook Griffin's
hand solemnly. "It was a wonderful party," he said. "You have a
lovely home."

"What kind of thirteen-year-old says, 'You have a lovely home'?"
he asked Joy later, as they were cleaning up. In his mind's eye he
could see the poor kid practicing the line until his parents were sure
he'd got it right.

"We *do* have a lovely home," Joy pointed out. "And he *did* have a
good time. Quit worrying. They're just kids. They have to figure
these things out."

"That's the problem," he said. "They already have it all figured
out. Who's cool, who's not, who's in, who's out. Nobody had to
teach them, either."

Sunny's parents lived in a modest stucco ranch on the other side of Shoreham Drive, in a mixed-race neighborhood where single-level houses, wedged in tightly together, were cheaper and sported carports rather than garages. On the Griffins' side of Shoreham, the homes, while not extravagant, were more likely to be larger split-levels with attached garages, with real lawns instead of what on the other side was euphemistically described as "desert landscaping." Every second or third house on Griffin's block had a pool. And the neighborhood was white, of course. How much of this had Sunny's mother prepared him for before allowing him to attend Laura's party? How, he now wondered, had he been invited in the first place? Had Joy insisted, or had Laura done it on her own? He was the smartest kid in her class, and had been since grade school. His name was always coming up in conversation, though usually the subject was honors and awards, not romance. "Did somebody dance with him at least?"

"Yes," his wife told him, clearly annoyed now. "Laura did. And Kelsey."

What was vague in Griffin's recollection was the exact chronology of all this. By that birthday party he and Joy must have already been making plans to leave L.A., hadn't they? Was it that very night that had firmed his resolve to look seriously for a teaching position back East? No, that was a trick of memory, surely. Yet he did seem to remember not liking Laura's friends, especially that cluster of boys, and one in particular who, smirking, had elbowed another and pointed to Sunny Kim standing alone on the patio. But there'd been other factors. The old days, wild and free, finally seemed to be over. Even Griffin had to admit it. Laura's birth was part of that, but by then he'd begun to suspect there was something wrong with Tommy, whose second, short-lived marriage had quickly ended up on the rocks and who now was drinking more heavily. Griffin was pretty sure the drinking was more effect than cause, and Tommy admitted as much but claimed it wasn't something he wanted to talk about. All of which put a strain on their writing partnership. They'd always been good at different things. Tommy, smooth and personable and quick-witted, loved to pitch ideas. He always saw a story in terms of its overall structure, leaving Griffin to write the dialogue, make sure the scenes were alive and the narrative tracked. But now, with Tommy viewing things through a prism of empty vodka bottles, Griffin found himself doing more and more of the work, not really even trusting Tommy to do the pitch without him.

Just as troubling, Joy seemed actually to be settling into their "lovely home." Now *he* was the one reminding *her* of the Great Truro Accord, that the idea had always been to sell the Valley house and use the equity for a down payment back East. Finally, in the second decade of their marriage, he was beginning to understand that his wife's natural inclination was toward contentment. Their present house and their life in L.A. had grown on her. She adored Laura so completely that their daughter seemed like the only thing that had ever been missing from their lives. And though she never said so, he also suspected she wasn't sure she wanted to be so far away from her family, on the other side of the country. It was this, of course, that he truly resented. There'd been a time when Harve and Jill had themselves talked of returning to the East, but Harve was now talking about investing in a planned community called Windward Estates (Breakwind Estates, Griffin had immediately dubbed it), where they could map out their entire future in advance. On special occasions they could still entertain the family in the big common areas that centered around a mammoth pool and clubhouse, while they downsized into a smaller house that Jill wouldn't have to work so hard to maintain. Later, they could downsize further into a condo, then into the attached assisted-living facility, then into the best nursing home money could buy, all right there in Breakwind.

He'd described all this to his son-in-law on the phone with great enthusiasm. "What if you buy in and then change your mind?" Griffin asked.

"We won't," Harve said. "Not once it's made up. Haven't you figured this out about us yet?"

Actually, he had.

It was possible Griffin was misremembering, but it seemed to him now that the need to break free of Joy's family, to make the Great Truro Accord work for him instead of against him, began to crystallize in his mind the night of Laura's birthday party, when Sunny Kim told him they had a lovely home. He knew that if he wasn't careful he was going to be trapped in that lovely home for the duration. Had he and Joy argued later that night? He couldn't recall. He'd recently received an offer to teach screenwriting in a fledgling film program in the Cal State system. Had Joy encouraged him to consider it, in order to give up screenwriting (as they'd always planned) but stay in California (as they hadn't)?

What did it matter? They'd done what they'd done, and it was all a long time ago. Little Sunny Kim now stood before them, a grown man. Laura had become a radiant young woman. His long-time agent and friend, who'd once terrorized their daughter with his canine antics, had woken up dead. Jesus.

A few yards from the ceremonial arch, a perspiring string quartet stopped abruptly, mid-Pachelbel, on some invisible signal, and began a somnambulant rendition of the "Wedding March." Everyone turned to watch the wedding party descend the porch, two by two, and wind down the sloping lawn. Andy, Laura's boyfriend, had been commissioned to handle the photography, and he trotted halfway up to catch each bridesmaid and groomsman as they passed.

"Laura's friend is nice," Griffin overheard Sunny tell Joy. "I think she's in love."

"There she is," she whispered to Griffin when Laura appeared on the porch, radiant and squinting into the sun, on the arm of a burly groomsman half a head shorter than she. Partway down the lawn she snagged a stiletto heel on the uneven ground, nearly rolling an ankle, and Griffin saw Sunny flinch, but she quickly righted herself and told her escort (unless Griffin's long-distance lip-reading was mistaken) that she was a klutz and always had been.

When Kelsey emerged on her father's arm, Joy took Griffin's hand and said, "Oh, my. Look how beautiful she is."

"Yes," Sunny Kim agreed, but he wasn't looking at the bride.

7

Halfway There

Each of the large round tables in the reception tent was set up for twelve, but table seventeen had only eight actual "leftovers." The resulting gaps in the seating were an additional impediment to conversation among these strangers. Well, not complete strangers. Griffin was surprised to recognize the unhappy couple from the Olde Cape Lounge. The woman was dressed more modestly today, and her face immediately lit up when she saw him, as if his unexpected presence was further evidence that the world was a marvelous place, that it offered genuine miracles on a daily basis. Her companion seemed to have forgotten him completely. ("We met where? . . . Oh, right, *that* fuckin' place.") He'd worn a tie for the ceremony but took it off now in the tent, unbuttoning the top two buttons on his shirt as if to allow his chest hair to breathe. The table's extreme distance from the bridal party wasn't lost on him, though he seemed cheered by its proximity to the tent's back flap, on the other side of which the caterers were scurrying. "Maybe we'll get fed first, at least," he grunted in Griffin's direction, mistakenly concluding, just as he had the night before, that they were natural allies in an otherwise hostile world.

"We're Marguerite and Harold," the woman announced when

everyone was seated and Sunny Kim suggested they all say something about themselves, where they lived and their relationship to the bride or groom. Marguerite owned a shop called Rita's Flower Cart in the San Fernando Valley, not far from where Griffin and Joy had lived. She'd moved to California, she said, after she and her husband decided to call it quits. Only when Harold interrupted to say, again mostly to Griffin, "Don't ever think a woman will go away just because you divorce her," did he realize this was the ex-husband she'd alluded to. And only when she said she'd bought a house right around the corner from the bride's parents and described it a little did he and Joy realize that it was their old house. They'd moved to Connecticut before the closing, so they'd never met the buyer.

At any rate Marguerite and the Apples had become such good friends that Kelsey now referred to her as Aunt Rita. Harold, she told the table, hooking her arm through his, lived in Boston ("Quincy," he corrected) and worked in law enforcement ("Private security"), so when she heard the wedding was going to be on Cape Cod, where the groom's parents had a house, she called Harold "out of the blue"—without even thinking about it, really, the phone just suddenly in her hand—and asked if he wanted to go to a wedding in June, to which he'd replied, "As long as it's not ours." That sporty riposte had reminded Marguerite that one of the things she'd always liked about Harold was his "dry sense of humor." So she'd flown out a few days early, and they'd spent the time getting reacquainted, and it had been, she said, scrunching up her shoulders as she'd done the evening before when she decided on a cosmo, really kind of romantic. She turned to Harold, clearly hoping he wouldn't correct her here as well. "Yeah, well, sex was never the problem," he conceded.

"I bet I know what was," Joy murmured, loud enough for Griffin, on her left, to hear and possibly Sunny, on her right, too, though he gave no sign of it. As Marguerite was talking, a bottle of champagne was brought for toasts, and Sunny uncorked it and poured full flutes (ladies first, to Harold's clear chagrin), shorting Harold just a bit with the last of the bottle. Intentionally, Griffin hoped, but thought probably not.

A precedent had apparently been set for the women at the table to speak for the men, and Joy went next. As she talked, Griffin found himself thinking how different it would've been if he was the one giving the synopsis. He had no intention of correcting her, à la Harold, but he did feel a stirring of guilty sympathy for him. Joy explained that their daughter, Laura, was the maid of honor and had been best friends with Kelsey, the bride, since they were girls, and of course she and Griffin had been friends with the Apples when they lived in L.A. This last bit struck him as more convenient than true. Sure, they'd all been friendly enough but never actually socialized, he and Joy having had little in common with Kelsey's accountant father and evangelical mother, though Joy had been willing to suffer her religiosity given that the girls were best friends.

But never mind L.A. It was how Joy characterized their present lives, though factually accurate, that really rankled him. Griffin, she told the group, was a college English professor ("We'll have to watch our grammar, then, won't we?" said Marguerite, again scrunching up her shoulders), making no mention of his screen-writing career. Okay, granted, he was partly to blame, since normally he preferred not to bring that up. People immediately wanted to know what movie stars you knew and whom you had to know to gain entry into such a glitzy profession. They also were curious about what movies Griffin had written, and then he'd have to admit that only one or two of his and Tommy's really stood up. Toward the end they'd been reduced to writing low-budget, made-for-TV movies, so better, really, not even to open the door.

Yet in this instance it seemed that Joy wasn't so much acting in deference to his wishes as simply stating what she considered to be the facts. As part of a past they'd by mutual consent put behind them, screenwriting was no longer germane. Which was now also why Sid's call had initially slipped her mind. It was even possible she thought Sid's death meant not just the end of Sid but of Griffin's screenwriting career, the last dangling thread neatly snipped. He was now only one thing, a professor of English at a very good liberal arts college, whereas before he'd been two. She herself was the assistant dean of admissions, she informed them, and this, though it was the precise, unembellished truth, annoyed him as well. After all, he was tenured and she wasn't, but to hear her tell it, anybody would have thought she outranked him. That sort of petty caviling was worthy of his mother, of course, and all the more *un*worthy of him, because Joy hadn't meant it that way at all. Still, he was relieved when his wife let her voice fall, and the attention shifted to the two hefty lasses across the table.

They were from Liverpool, and their accents nearly impenetrable. Their spirits were extraordinarily high, even for the present occasion, and so far they'd giggled enthusiastically at everything anybody said, as if prior to taking their seats they'd been informed that the other guests at this table were all professional comedians. Griffin's experience of lesbians was largely limited to the academic variety—a grim, angry, humorless lot—so he was unprepared for these girls' good cheer. They demonstrated that British habit of turning simple, declarative statements into questions and then waiting a beat, as if for a response. They'd known the bride for years and years, hadn't they? Ever since she'd come to Norwich, to the University of East Anglia, that is, where she hadn't known a soul, had she? But they'd gotten her sorted quick enough. That first Friday afternoon after class they'd pulled her out of the residence hall by force and hauled her down to their favorite pub for a pint, and then introduced her to all the other good pubs and also their *chooms* (*Their* what? Griffin thought. *Oh, right, their* chums), and when the holidays came round they'd dragged her home to meet their mums and dads, and it had all been ever so much *foon*, hadn't it? Still, you could've knocked them down with a feather when they got invitations to the wedding, because they hadn't neither of them ever come over to the States before, had they?

By the time the girls finished, they were holding hands, which Marguerite apparently took for a show of moral support between foreigners, because she asked if either of them was married or engaged. "*Booth* of us," one of them replied, giving her partner's hand a squeeze, "to each *oother*," as if to admit that their sexual preference might be a local custom that hadn't yet made its way across the pond. Apropos of nothing but her own embarrassment at not recognizing them as a couple, Marguerite then remarked she'd always wanted to go to England but never had, the reason being—and here she elbowed Harold—that nobody'd ever been nice enough to take her. "Women," Harold said, turning again to Griffin. "They just never can give it a rest."

Marguerite nudged him, noticing he'd already drained most of his champagne. "That's for the toasts."

"Complete this sentence and win a prize," Harold told her. "Give . . . it . . . a . . ."

Having no women to speak for them, the final two—Sunny and a man in a wheelchair—had no alternative but to plead their own cases. The latter had a lopsided smile, if that's what it was and not a grimace, that bespoke a recent stroke. During the previous introductions he'd stared steadfastly at his cutlery as if he expected the utensils to become dangerously animated. There was a vacant chair, complete with place setting, on either side of him, suggesting that everyone had concluded his condition might be contagious. In a loud, braying voice he announced that he was the groom's sixth-grade math teacher, which cracked the lesbians up more than anything anybody'd said so far. "*Animal House,*" Griffin whispered to Joy, who, no surprise, didn't get the reference. Though she enjoyed movies, even their most iconic moments left no lasting impression on her, and she'd always considered his own ability to quote such scenes verbatim as rather perverse.

Which left Sunny, who managed to say only his name and that he lived in Washington, D.C., before the DJ chose that moment to conduct a sound check of his nearby equipment. Harold swiveled in his chair to watch, a clear indication that he couldn't care less who Sunny was or what he'd done to be stranded at the misfit table. A loud peal of laughter from the front of the tent attracted the attention of the lesbians, who stood to applaud something, Griffin couldn't tell what, and the man in the wheelchair resumed staring at his knife and fork. The Griffins, of course, didn't need to be introduced to Sunny, which left only Marguerite to give him her undivided attention. "Go on," she said. "I want to hear *all* about you," and if Griffin hadn't already decided to like her, he would have then. But the best man had risen to give the first of the afternoon's strained comic toasts, and Sunny, ever good-natured, turned his chair around to watch and listen.

By the time they were invited to raise their glasses in a toast to the bride and groom, Harold's glass was empty. Perhaps to emphasize this fact, after everyone else had drunk to the toast, Sunny rose to his feet, his glass held high, and proposed a toast of his own for table seventeen. "Here stop and spend a social hour in harmless mirth and fun," he intoned, grinning, for some reason, at Griffin and then Marguerite. "Let friendship reign. Be just and kind and evil speak of none." After which they all leaned forward to clink glasses, and Griffin found the *ting* of Harold's empty flute against all the other full ones particularly rewarding.

"What an odd toast," Joy whispered. "Do you suppose it's Korean?"

"I don't think so," Griffin said. It felt not only familiar but recently so. He could feel the dim memory spooling toward the front of his brain, but then his cell phone vibrated and it was gone. "Again?" Joy said in disbelief when he showed her who it was.

"I'll take it outside," he said, getting to his feet. "Mom, hold on, okay?"

It took him a minute to get out of the tent, and when he put the phone to his ear, he realized that his mother, unaccustomed to being told to wait, had been talking the whole time. "Mom, I haven't heard a word of this. Is everything all right?"

"Of course everything's all right."

"Then—"

"Have you done it yet?"

"Done what?"

"Put your father in the drink."

"I'm sorry?"

"Scattered his ashes. Laid him to rest."

"Not yet, no."

"I think you should put him on the bay side. He was that kind of man, don't you think? Wordsworth was his favorite poet. 'Emotion recollected in tranquility' and all that nonsense, which all boiled down to being afraid of the surf. He hated being tossed about, feeling the power of something greater than himself."

The music from inside the tent ratcheted up now, and Griffin turned his back (as if that would help) and covered his other ear with his hand (which did help, but not much).

"What is that awful racket?" his mother wanted to know.

"Music. I'm at the wedding, Mom."

"What wedding? You told me you were there to scatter your father's ashes."

"I told you several things. You remembered one of them."

"Somewhere on the North Shore, I think. Maybe Sandwich."

"That's barely on the Cape," Griffin said. "You hated Sandwich. We might as well put him in the Canal."

"I don't know who you mean by *we*. I'm simply making a suggestion. The decision is yours."

"I'll think about it," he said, and should have hung up right then. Instead he asked, "Do you remember the Browning family? From the Cape?"

"Don't tell me you ran into them."

Which was surprising. He hadn't expected the name to register, and that it did immediately made him curious. "Are we talking about the same people? I must've been eleven or twelve and—"

"Twelve. They were in the cottage across the way. There was a horrible muddy playground in the center of things, and they were diagonal. Near Orleans, wasn't it? Anyway, I wouldn't put your father there. Think North Shore. Find some calm, brackish water and pour him in. He'd prefer it. Actually, the Canal isn't such a bad idea—"

"Mom, about the Brownings—"

"You abandoned your father and me the entire two weeks. All we heard about was Steven Browning. Your father thought it meant you were gay."

"Peter," he corrected her, annoyed that both Tommy and his father had leapt to the same erroneous conclusion. Was loneliness in a twelve-year-old so difficult to diagnose?

"Don't you remember how you melted down that last night when we insisted you spend it with us?"

"*You* insisted?"

"And the tantrum you threw at the restaurant? The Dry Martini? No, that's not right. The *Something* Martini, it was called. Anyway, don't tell me you've forgotten how I sat up with you all night, trying to console you?"

"You're making this up, right?"

"And the next morning you refused to get in the car. God, what a little pill you were."

"There was something wrong with the little Browning girl, wasn't there? Peter's sister."

"Asthma, I believe. Something respiratory. The sea air was supposed to be good for her, but she ended up dying. And then of course Steven in Vietnam."

"Mom, what are you talking about?"

"I'm talking about your friend Steven Browning dying in Vietnam."

"Mom, he's Peter. And anyway, how in the world would you know what happened to him or his sister? We never went back there. We never saw any of them again."

"We exchanged addresses before we left, don't you remember? Steven wanted to keep in touch. He wrote you several letters, but you refused to write back. We got Christmas cards for a couple of years. The mother wrote when the little girl died, and then later about Steven. You were gone by then."

"Why would you remember all this, Mom?"

"Why shouldn't I remember things?"

"It's unlike you. Especially people like the Brownings. You and Dad looked down your noses at them."

He expected her to deny this accusation, but she didn't, which meant she either hadn't really heard it or preferred not to. Maddening, the way she blithely shopped among his conversational offerings, as if she were at a fruit bin looking for an unbruised pear. "Wait till you're my age and memory is all you have."

It was on the tip of Griffin's tongue to say that, based on this conversation, he wasn't sure she had even that.

"Happy memories in particular you hold on to."

"That was a happy memory? That vacation?"

"Well, it wasn't *un*happy. The wheels hadn't come off yet for your father and me. He hadn't started the cheating yet."

"Of course he had. You both had."

"Not the really nasty, vindictive stuff. We were still in love, despite everything."

"That's how you remember it?"

"That's how it *was*."

"I need to get back to the wedding, Mom."

"You haven't told me what you think."

"About what?"

"About the North Shore, though I have to admit your Canal idea is growing on me."

"Why would you care, Mom? Could you answer me that?"

"Because if you put him on the North Shore, you can scatter me on the South."

"Mom, we've had a lot of ridiculous conversations over the years, but this is one for the record books."

"Remember how I taught you to bodysurf?"

"Peter Browning taught me to bodysurf. Him and his dad."

"No. They all knew how, and you were embarrassed because you didn't. You were scared to try. Your father was frightened of the undertow, so it was up to me."

"Gotta go, Mom."

"I'd just feel better if the Cape was between us, me on one side and him on the other."

By the time Griffin returned to the tent he'd missed the bride and groom's first dance. Kelsey was now dancing with her father, clearly for the first time ever, and her new husband with his mother.

"What now?" Joy said.

He told her about his mother's insistence about where all the ashes should go. "I think she's losing her mind. She's rewriting history. Inventing memories."

Under the table he felt Joy take his hand, perhaps in sympathy for having to deal with his mother, but more likely because Laura and Andy had joined the others on the makeshift dance floor, where they looked like what they were, two young people who'd waited what had seemed like forever to find each other. Now they clung tightly together in the understanding of how lucky they were, that in another equally plausible scenario they wouldn't have met, still be alone, still looking. It was hard to take your eyes off them, and for Griffin the pleasure of watching them would have been pure and fully sufficient if Sunny hadn't also been in his line of sight. He tried not to look at him, at least not directly, tried not to think of him as the boy standing by himself at that long-ago birthday party, pretending not to be alone. But somehow that opened the door to another unpleasant, totally unrelated thought. Was it possible his mother was right, that Peter Browning had been killed in Vietnam? Griffin felt something like panic rise at the possibility, a physical sensation at the back of his throat. But really, it was highly unlikely, he told himself. The son of two teachers, he'd have gone to college and gotten a deferment, as Griffin himself had done. By the time his own deferment ran out, the war was over, and it would have worked out the same way for Peter. His mother had sounded certain on the phone, but then she always did, never more so than when she was dead wrong. If somebody asked her tomorrow what the Browning boy's name was, she'd answer *Steven,* and she'd be sure about that, too. Was it really possible that she remembered sitting up all night in that cottage trying to comfort him? When had she ever done anything like that? And they definitely hadn't gone to the Blue Martini that night. What she was remembering was that that's where she and his father had planned to go before he screwed things up. But asthma for Peter's sister sounded right, and he supposed she might have died. But had Peter actually written to him, as his mother claimed? That was how it went with all her recollections. She'd get just enough details right to make you doubt your own memory, but in the end her stories never tracked. They played out like his still-unread student story, the one now with missing pages.

When the DJ segued from the first slow dance into an earsplitting Bon Jovi tune, the lesbians, howling with laughter, as if this were the best joke yet, leapt from their chairs and skipped, their arms windmilling, onto the dance floor. "I hope you don't imagine you're going to be allowed to sit here on your hands, mister," Joy shouted, rising from her chair. Across the table, Marguerite was prodding stolid Harold to his feet as well.

"Okay, but hold on a minute," Griffin said. Because if Marguerite succeeded in dragging Harold out for a dance, and he and Joy went, too, that would leave Sunny sitting there with the stroke victim, and he couldn't bear for that to happen.

But then their beautiful daughter appeared and took Sunny by both hands and was pulling him to his feet. He was shaking his head no, saying no, he was fine, but Laura wasn't about to let go, so he had no choice but to be led onto the dance floor, where they joined Andy and the lesbians and the bride and groom and all the other fits and misfits.

"I know. She's wonderful," Joy said, reading his mind, as they, along with Marguerite and Harold, joined everyone in the crowded center of the throbbing tent. "You worry too much, you know that?" she said, nodding at Sunny, who was holding his own with the other young people. A little stiff, maybe, but better than Griffin would have predicted. He'd unbuttoned his suit jacket and lowered his tie enough to unbutton the top button of his shirt. He probably would never do anything with abandon. Dancing was too much like instant messaging, and Sunny would always fear spontaneity. But he felt the music, you could tell, and he even had some moves. Had he anticipated this moment and taken lessons, studying fun much as he'd studied political science and molecular biology at Stanford, practicing, as he'd done as a boy at home, how to tell Griffin they had a lovely home?

Griffin suspected that what Joy really meant when she said he worried too much was that he had too little faith—in the world, in her, in himself, in their good lives—and sometimes got important things wrong as a result. Searching for evidence of a fundamentally crappy world, he glanced back at table seventeen, expecting to see the stroke victim sitting there forlorn and abandoned. But the groom's parents had come over and were wheeling their son's old math teacher to their side of the tent. Griffin couldn't tell whether the frozen grimace on the man's face represented joy or pain, but decided, arbitrarily, on the former.

The dance floor was now an official frenzy. Everyone under the age of thirty was shouting the song's refrain: "Oh-oh! We're halfway there!"—pumping the air in unison with defiant fists—"Oh-oh! Livin' on a prayer!"

Halfway there. Was this what it came down to, Griffin wondered, his own fist now pumping in solidarity with those younger than he. Was this the pebble in his shoe these last long months, the desire to be, once again, just halfway there?

Later, back at the B and B, he and Joy made love. It had been a while, and by the time they finished, the panic Griffin had felt after his mother's phone call had dissipated. Sex always had that effect on him—the release it offered—and he was grateful for it and also that his mother hadn't called just then. He made a mental note to call her tomorrow and firm up his plans to pay her a visit, maybe even see if she wanted to come to the Cape for a few days later in the summer. How long had it been since she visited? More than a decade, surely. That would give her something to look forward to. Unless he was mistaken, there'd been something panicky in her own voice tonight, though she'd tried to disguise it. Why should she care, really, where he scattered his father's ashes? He'd asked her and, naturally, received no answer. Of course, assisted-living facilities were table seventeens for the elderly, where virtual strangers were thrust into proximity by neither affection nor blood nor common interest, only by circumstance: age and declining health. No wonder she was going batty. With no one to say otherwise, she seemed to be revising her life so as to please herself. If so, fine. He didn't object. Except that she seemed to be revising his as well and expecting him to sign off on it.

Looking over at his sleeping wife, he felt another surge of almost painful affection, like the one he'd felt in the tent when Laura had validated their marriage, their love, with her great generosity and kindness. Joy was by nature a modest woman, quick to cover up, but sex always loosened her a little in this respect. She lay naked next to him now, lovely. Her body had thickened over the years, but it was still fine, and he desired her even more now than he had when they were younger and the sexual experience more intense. He watched her breathe for a minute, studied the trace of a smile on her lips, its source only in part their lovemaking. Back at the reception tent, when they finally decided to call it a night, Laura had detached herself from her friends, all of whom still crowded the dance floor, and come over to whisper in her mother's ear that Andy had proposed during that first dance while they'd been watching. It took Griffin's breath away to think that in the very moment of her great happiness, his daughter had remembered Sunny Kim and come to fetch him into the festivities. And he felt certain that he'd never in his entire life done anything so fine.

As he lay there, growing drowsy, he became aware of sounds on the other side of the wall, as of a headboard, first gently nudging, then bumping, then roundly thumping the wall. Harold and Marguerite? Listening, he thought he could hear a woman's voice, muffled but enthusiastic to the point of ecstasy. Was it even remotely possible that Harold could bring a woman—any woman—to such a climax? He doubted it. Halfway through the reception, he'd gone up to the hotel in search of the gents and had seen Harold sitting alone in the four-seater bar, watching a ball game. Feeling sorry for Marguerite, as he had the night before, he'd danced with her a couple times, and she'd given him her business card, making him promise that if he came to L.A. to write a movie and needed to buy flowers for some gorgeous actress, he'd come to *her* shop. And she'd know if he didn't, she warned, don't think she wouldn't. It had been a great wedding, hadn't it? Marguerite hated to think what it was costing Kelsey's parents. Her one regret about the trip was that she and Griffin had never figured out what that sign in the restaurant meant, which they definitely would've if he hadn't been such a party pooper and left early.

Suddenly Griffin was laughing so hard the bed shook, waking Joy in the process. "What?" she said, pulling the sheet up over her bare breasts, ten minutes of sleep sufficient to restore her customary modesty.

"I'll tell you in the morning," he said. "I just thought of something. Go back to sleep."

What he'd remembered was Sunny's strange toast: *Here stop and spend a social hour in harmless mirth and fun. Let friendship reign. Be just and kind and evil speak of none.* He'd thought at the time that the words were familiar, and now he knew why, picturing the sign on the back bar at the Olde Cape Lounge, plain as day but for the spacing.

Griffin lay there in the dark, grinning. The sounds of lovemaking continued on the other side of the wall, and at some point it dawned on him that it had to be the lesbians, and shortly after that he was asleep.

PART TWO

Coastal Maine

(Second Wedding)

8

Bliss

How quickly it had all fallen apart. Even a year later, most of it spent in L.A., the speed of what happened after Kelsey's wedding took Griffin's breath away.

For the first time in what seemed like forever he'd slept through the night and awakened to a sense of profound well-being, his funk, or whatever the hell it was, having finally fled. The morning breeze billowing the chintz curtains smelled of the sea, reminding Griffin of their honeymoon in Truro. Later in the morning they'd drive there, and this, too, made him happy. Joy was usually an early riser, but last night's sex, together with too much to drink, had made her lazy and content as well. When he touched her bare shoulder she purred like a cat, which might mean she was amenable to a reprise of last night's intimacy, though it was also possible she was just enjoying the special indulgence of sleeping in after the long, grueling semester. Or remembering that Laura was now engaged. Before Griffin could make up his mind which it was he'd drifted off again.

It was almost ten-thirty when he felt Joy get out of bed and heard the shower thunk on in the bathroom. The long, languid summer, two and a half glorious months without classroom responsibilities, stretched out before him, all the more real, he supposed, for beginning here on the Cape. Two days ago he'd been hoping he might spend them writing whatever Sid—the poor bastard—had to offer, but that wasn't going to happen. So be it. After last night's conversation with his mother, he was thinking again about taking another run at "The Summer of the Brownings." The little girl's death, whether or not she was right about that, would give the story some added weight. He'd cut back big-time on the characters based on his parents, unwelcome intruders that they were. Asserting his authorial prerogative, he'd reduce the story to its essence: an innocent summer friendship set against the backdrop of a terrible reality both boys are aware of but can't quite acknowledge directly. This new strategy would force Peter into the narrative foreground, not a bad idea, either. He might even weave in some harbingers of Vietnam.

He was busy revising the story in his head when his cell phone commenced buzzing on the nightstand like a fly on its back. He usually turned the damn thing off before going to bed, but last night he'd apparently forgotten.

"Griff," said Tommy. "What's happening today, locusts?"

"No clue," Griffin said, though sun was leaking through the chintz curtains. "What're you doing up so early?"

"I've *been* up," he said. "Anymore, I pee three times a night, at least. Don't tell me you're spared this, because I hate you already."

"Why?"

"Same old reason. The woman you're married to. All my life I've been a good woman shy of true happiness. It's tragic, really."

Neither man said anything for an awkward beat. In the next room the shower thunked off.

"Anyway, Sid gets planted later this morning."

"That's not wasting any time."

"As per Jewish custom. We have Jews out here, remember? Also Negroes and Hispanics. You forget, living there in pale New England."

The bathroom door opened, and Joy came out, toweling her hair dry. *Who?* she mouthed. Griffin could tell from her smile that she expected it to be Laura.

Tommy, he mouthed back, and she quickly covered up, as if his cell were equipped with a streaming-video camera.

"There's going to be a big memorial do in a couple of weeks, though," Tommy was saying, and he rattled off the names of half a dozen stars and directors, all former Sid clients, who'd already committed to attend. "You think you'll come?"

"I don't see why not. Once I get my grades turned in, I'm a free man."

"Why don't you and Joy come out for a week. Hell, two weeks. We'll have some laughs."

Joy was now bent over the small pad of B and B stationery, scribbling something.

"I'm working on this thing right now that's going nowhere," Tommy continued. "You can read it and tell me what's wrong. If you're nice I might even let you fix it. And Joy will hit it off with this woman I'm seeing. It'll be like old times."

Joy tore the page off the tablet and showed it to him: *Don't commit me.*

"Sounds like fun," he said. "Joy's shaking her head no, but I'll work on her."

At which her face clouded over and she returned to the bathroom, closing the door behind her. Just this quickly last night's magic, the sense of well-being it had engendered, evaporated.

Half an hour later they were in the car, having checked out of the B and B. They'd lolled in bed too long to take advantage of the second *B*. Even the giant coffee urn had been cruelly removed from the dining room by the time they'd both showered and dressed. The apologetic owner said they could leave one car there, drive the other to Truro, then pick it up on the way back. Joy disliked Griffin's roadster, which felt unsafe compared with her SUV, and her hair would be a lost cause by the time they arrived, but she gave in grudgingly when he observed there wasn't much point in having a convertible if you weren't going to put the top down on a bright summer day on the Cape.

"That was Route 6," she remarked when he drove beneath it. The divided highway was the most direct route to the Outer Cape.

"Are we in some kind of hurry?" His plan had been to take two-lane 6A, a much more scenic drive that hugged the shoreline. If they happened on a likely spot, they'd stop and scatter his father's ashes.

"No," Joy said, "we're certainly not."

The day was warm, but the emotional temperature had plummeted.

"Can I use your phone? I forgot to put mine on the charger last night. It's running on juice."

Running on fumes? Because she forgot to juice the phone? Griffin opened his mouth, then closed it again, handing her his phone without comment. After last night's festivities, it was far too early to call Laura, but he held his tongue about that, too.

"Hi, sweetie," Joy said, after several rings, "did I wake you? Oh, I'm sorry. I just wanted to tell you again how thrilled we are."

With the top down, Griffin could hear his daughter's voice but not what she was saying. Probably going over again what Andy had said last night, how he'd asked, the whole play-by-play. It was the kind of conversation she and her mother delighted in, and Joy, glum a moment before, was smiling now, the world made right again. Griffin told himself not to be bitter.

"We're on our way to Truro," she was saying. "No, just for tonight. I need to get back, and now it's looking like your dad may be going to L.A., so . . ." A beat, then: "No, he's fine." Another pause. "Please be careful driving home." She hung up and returned his phone to the cup holder.

"If you really need to get back, we don't have to go to Truro," Griffin ventured. "It was your idea."

"I know whose idea it was."

Griffin couldn't understand how they'd gotten there so quickly, but they were clearly on the cusp of a serious falling-out, like the one that had sent him off to Boston and the Cape by himself. The thing to do, obviously, was to avoid hostilities. The day was drop-dead gorgeous, and with a little patience and forbearance there was no reason they couldn't reclaim the better emotional place they'd found the night before. In a couple hours they'd be at the inn where they'd honeymooned, and all would be well. That was what he wanted, wasn't it?

"It's just that your story has some continuity problems," he said, deciding that he'd push this far and no further. Because if Joy really wanted to have this out, better to do it now.

"It's not a story. Or a screenplay. It's my job. My life."

"Our lives."

When she didn't say anything to this, he continued. Impossible, really, to stop, once you'd started. Still, best to be conciliatory. "All I meant was, if you're too busy at work to go to L.A., fine. But if you're really that busy, why are we going to Truro? *That's* what I'd like to understand." Okay, the emphasis maybe wasn't entirely conciliatory.

"No, that's what you *don't* want to understand."

"Meaning?"

"Meaning what you're determined *not* to understand couldn't be simpler. It makes no sense to go all the way to L.A. unless we stay a week. I can't afford that much time away right now. *Your* semester's over. I'm happy for you. But I'm still flat out. I have two new staff to hire and a new boss to train. The day will come when he can spare me for a week, but not now. Truro is one day. I wouldn't be working on the weekend anyway. So tomorrow I'll miss *half* of one day. Not a whole week. You can pretend that doesn't make sense, but it does."

Which it did, as far as it went. "Fine," he said. "Now I understand."

"And I really hate it when you do that."

"When I ask you to explain something? I'm not entitled to understand your thinking?"

"No, I hate it when you talk to me in script metaphors. My 'story isn't tracking.' It has 'continuity problems.' Like I'm making things up. Like we're still in L.A. Like you wish we'd never left. Like you regret the life we have."

Of course he knew better than to say what came next, though it wasn't the words themselves. If he'd delivered the line with a good-natured, self-deprecating grin, all would have been well. That's probably what he was trying for, but he could feel the tight grimace on his features when he said, "Aren't you going a little 'over the top'?"

Before Joy could respond, his cell vibrated in the cup holder, and irritation morphed instantly into full-blown rage. "*What*, Mom?" he said through tightly clenched teeth. "What? What? What?"

It took a while, but they finally found where they'd honeymooned. It was smaller than Griffin remembered but otherwise unchanged, except that it was no longer an inn. An elderly woman in a straw hat was weeding the mulch around some new plantings on the front lawn. She looked up when she heard the car door shut and struggled to her feet as he approached. "It's hell getting old," she said, shading her eyes with one hand, scout fashion. "I'd like to ride in a car like that once more before I die."

"You just might be the woman of my dreams," Griffin said.

"Who's that, then?" she wondered, indicating Joy.

"My wife. She hates it."

"Her hair, right?"

He nodded.

"Attractive woman. What can an old lady do for you?"

"This used to be an inn," he told her, aware that this might not be news to her. "My wife and I stayed here on our honeymoon. Thirty-four years ago."

"I've owned it almost that long," she said, turning to regard it. "Bought it with my husband. Then the rat-bastard up and died."

"I'm sorry."

"*You're* sorry?"

She turned back to look him over. She had the palest, most piercing blue eyes he'd ever seen, full of kindness but even more full of intelligence. He'd hate to have to lie to her for a living. She looked in Joy's direction. "So what's wrong?"

"We've been arguing."

"I'm sorry."

"*You're* sorry?" he said. "Can you recommend an inn here in Truro?"

She shook her head. "Between here and Provincetown there isn't much but motels. Borderline sleazy, most of them. You want something nice, you'd best head back toward Wellfleet. Couple of good inns there."

"Thanks. We'll take your advice."

"Do that."

"If you don't mind my saying, I don't think I've ever heard a woman of your generation use the term *rat-bastard* before."

"I used to be a writer. Still love words, the sound of them. *Fart-hammer* is my new favorite, though I can't seem to find a sentence to put it in."

"What did you write?"

"Biography, mostly. A poem or two, when the fit was on me. 'Strange fits of passion I have known . . .' "

" 'And I will dare to tell, / But in the Lover's ear alone, / What once to me befell,' " he continued. But if his ability to finish the stanza impressed the old woman, she gave no sign. "My parents were both English professors," he explained, stifling the urge to tell her that one of them happened to be in the trunk of the car. "I'm another, actually. And a writer, too."

"Hah!" she said. "No wonder your wife's in tears."

It was true. Joy was crying. She hadn't been when he got out of the car, but now she was. Silently, but not trying to hide the fact, either.

"Go to her," the woman suggested.

"I can't stay here?"

"I'm sorry, no."

Back in the car he took a deep breath. "Are you going to tell me about it, Joy? I know you called him back when I was in the shower." He'd seen it listed on the phone's recent calls list.

She didn't pretend not to know what he was talking about, and he was grateful for that. She wiped her tears on the back of her wrist, and for a moment they just sat there. The old woman had gone back to her weeding, though Griffin had the distinct impression she hadn't forgotten about them.

Finally, Joy said, "We can talk about it if you want. But first call your mother back."

"Why?"

"Because she's your mother. Because you yelled at her. Because she's old. Because you've only got one."

That night Griffin's insomnia returned with a vengeance, payback, apparently, for the previous night's blissful sleep. Joy, to her credit, had tried to head the argument off. "We don't have to do this," she said after he called his mother back, leaving a brief apology on her machine for barking at her and promising to call again later in the week to discuss a visit. "There's no need. Nothing happened."

But she seemed to know they'd quarrel, and that the argument would be the most intense and bitter and wounding of their marriage. They'd finally quit out of exhaustion sometime after midnight, and since then he'd lain awake listening for the clock on the nightstand, which buzzed faintly every time the minute hand changed over. Amazing, really, how many bad thoughts you could cram into the sixty seconds between buzzes.

The day he found Joy sobbing in the shower, some part of him had known Tommy had to be involved. Even back when he and Elaine were still married and they were a foursome traipsing off to Mexico, Griffin knew about his friend's crush on Joy. Out on the balcony of their resort hotel, working through some crucial scene, he would look up from the typewriter and see Tommy staring down at the pool below, and he could tell it was Joy he was looking at, not his own wife. Nor was his partner much interested in disguising the fact. "Lucky fellow," he'd say before they went back to work. It had been part of the narrative of their long friendship that Griffin was born fortunate. Raised by two college professors, he'd gone to good schools that without exception identified him as gifted. Tommy, who was several years older, had grown up in a series of foster homes, knocked around rough urban public schools, his dyslexia undiagnosed, and was thought by everybody, including himself, to be dumb and lazy. First the army, then the community college where he'd met Elaine, after that some studio gofer work. "We're both lucky," Griffin would respond with a sweeping gesture that included their lovely young wives, the pool deck below with its palm trees and swim-up bar, the ocean just beyond the pink patio walls, the portable typewriter that provided them with all of this. "Yeah, sure," Tommy always replied, "but there's luck and then there's luck."

At what point had his feelings for her been reciprocated? This Joy had refused to tell him, asking what difference could it possibly make, so he'd spent the long night scrolling back through their marriage, especially the times he'd behaved badly. There'd been a fair number, he had to admit. Had his wife already fallen for Tommy the day she told Griffin she hated jazz? Probably not, but the seed might well have been sown that early. It was also around this time, he recalled, that Tommy had been desperately trying to locate his birth mother. "Why, for Christ sake?" he'd asked him one drunken night, hoping to diminish his friend's need for something that was bound to disappoint him. "Don't you realize how fortunate you are?"

"Jack," Joy said, cautioning him.

"No, look at the man." Griffin appealed directly to her here. "He has no baggage. He moves about the world a free man. He possesses large, untapped reserves of the very ignorance that bliss was invented to reward."

"Yeah," Tommy said, "but the thing is, she's out there somewhere. And she's older now. Things change. What if she's wishing she never gave me up? What if she wants to tell me how sorry she is?"

"That's what you don't understand about parents," Griffin explained. "They don't apologize. *We* apologize. Take this last weekend." Again he turned to Joy, who, knowing what was coming, looked away. "We're summoned to Sacramento, right? It's the twins' birthday. The rest of the family's going to be there so of course we have to be there, too. It's Momma Jill making the pitch. On and on. When she finally lets her voice fall, we explain that we can't—"

"*Who* explained?" Joy interrupted.

"They're *your* parents," Griffin pointed out.

Tommy and Joy exchanged a suffering look.

"Explain," Griffin continued, "that we're under deadline on this script—"

"Yet again," Joy added.

"So," Griffin said. "End of discussion? Hardly. Now it's Poppa Jarve's turn—"

"You *promised* you weren't going to do that anymore," Joy said, still gazing off into the distance. Griffin had recently taken to calling him (never to his face) not Harve but Jarve, so he wouldn't be the only one in the family whose name didn't begin with a *J*. Joy had found that funny at first but quickly changed her mind, claiming it was mean-spirited.

"And we have to go through the whole thing all over again."

"Who has to?"

"Because to *Harve*, what you and I do for a living isn't real work."

"He does have a point," Tommy said, raising his margarita so they could clink glasses.

"But we stand firm and—"

Tommy and Joy, together, this time. "*Who* stands firm?"

"So now, because we can't go to Sacramento, everybody's feelings are hurt."

"We could've gone," Joy corrected. "We chose not to."

"But that's my point," Griffin said. "We're adults. Shouldn't we be *able* to choose? Every night this week you've been on the phone apologizing. First to your father, then your mother, then your sisters, then your father again." He turned his attention back to Tommy now. "This is why our ancestors came to America. To ditch their symbolic parents. To become grown-ups in their own right."

"I'm not saying we'd start some heavy relationship, my mother and I," Tommy tried to explain. "I'd just like to know if she's alive or dead . . . if she's, you know, okay."

"Isn't that *her* job?" Griffin said, getting worked up on his friend's behalf. "To wonder if *you're* okay?"

Now Tommy appealed to Joy. "Do you ever win an argument with this guy?"

"Let . . . me . . . think," Joy said, leaning toward Tommy so he could rub her neck, pausing just a comic half beat before saying, as if it had never occurred to her before, "Why, no."

Later that same night, though, when he and Joy were in bed, the discussion had turned more serious. "Why shouldn't he yearn for his biological mother?"

Okay, Griffin conceded, it made perfect sense that he should. But what made such yearning possible was that he didn't know the woman. He expected Joy to object to his cynicism, but instead she snuggled up against him and said, "We hurt their feelings, my parents'. That's why I apologized."

Who said she never won any arguments?

Another buzz, another minute.

Joy had known about Tommy's crush on her, of course. How could she not? She just hadn't expected ever to feel the same way about him, she told Griffin. One day she just woke up and realized she did. But *what* day? When?

After Laura, was Griffin's best guess. It was the birth of their daughter, together with Tommy's divorce, that really changed the dynamic of their lives. It was then that he'd finally given in and accepted Harve and Jill's offer of a loan. Which guaranteed, Griffin complained to Tommy, that he and Joy were now officially hitched to the parental sled. They'd have little choice but to obey every summons to Sacramento. Tommy took Joy's side, of course. What could be more natural than for her to want their daughter to know her grandparents, her aunts and uncles and cousins? She simply wanted Laura to grow up with the kind of family memories she herself cherished. Who wouldn't? (Griffin, for one, but he understood his orphan friend's question to be rhetorical.) Tommy, who desperately wanted a family, and Joy, who had one—they'd made an effective tag team. "Look," she said, "we're talking about a week-end every other month. I'm no fonder of their gated community than you are, but taking their money doesn't mean we have to start voting Republican or something. Sacramento's purely logistical. Where else is the family supposed to gather if not at my parents'? Our apartment?" Plus, she went on, the timing was right. Vietnam had been over for years. They were in their late twenties now, and it was time to start applying a salve to all those never-trust-anyone-over-thirty generational wounds.

"Hey, talk to your old man," Griffin said, because it was Harve who always brought up the war, Harve who stubbornly refused to admit it had been a mistake, Harve who loved to pronounce that the domino theory "had never been disproved," as if the war's detractors had failed at this, too. Besides, he thought but didn't say, no such reconciliation was needed where *his* parents were concerned. As old-school lefty intellectuals, it never would've occurred to either of them that Asian adventurism could be anything *but* monumental folly. Better yet, they lived on the other side of the country, still completely involved with the continuing psychodrama of their own screwed-up lives. They neither demanded nor particularly encouraged visits. They'd never feigned any interest in children, and a grandchild was unlikely to alter that. When Griffin called to tell her Joy was pregnant, all his mother said was "So she finally got her way, then." *She.* Unbelievable. By that point they'd been married for—what, seven years? And his mother still didn't call his wife by name, just the feminine pronoun. Who could be expected to remember and use the names of people who hadn't done graduate work? On the rare occasions when either of his parents phoned, Griffin always took the call in the den behind a closed door. "You don't have to do that," Joy would remind him when he emerged again, ten or fifteen minutes later, usually in a foul mood.

"No reason to inflict them on you," he'd reply, and she'd let it go because, of course, the intended implication was all too clear. A plague on both their houses was the bargain he'd tried to drive back in Truro, and he meant to keep up his end, even if she didn't.

The entire time Joy was pregnant, nobody had been more solicitous of her than Tommy. In honor of little Enrique (he was convinced it would be a boy) he'd quit drinking—to clean up his act, he claimed, to be worthy of his godson. Griffin remembered vividly the first time he held the baby, how reluctantly he'd handed Laura back, then turned to him and said, "Mr. Lucky." And how right he was. Griffin had known it the moment he took his daughter from the nurse at the hospital, sensing in her ferocious, squirming little body reason enough for his own existence.

But here was the thing. Tommy had known it all along, as Joy swelled and waddled, whereas Griffin, God help him, when he looked at his pregnant wife, kept hearing his mother's disembodied voice: *So she finally got her way, then.*

Yeah, it must have been around then, he decided, and who could blame her? How could Joy not feel affection for a man who'd happily drunk mineral water during her pregnancy so she wouldn't be the only one abstaining from alcohol? Tommy'd called the house right after Griffin left for work that morning, Joy explained, and not even to speak to her, that was the ironic part. He'd heard about some writing gig he thought Griffin might be interested in. But then he'd asked her how things were going, and she'd just broken down. Her mother had recently been diagnosed with breast cancer and was beginning treatments that week, and now here she was on the other side of the country, with Laura growing up fast, becoming a young woman before she'd gotten her fill of her as a child, and, well, hearing Tommy's voice on the line had made her realize that he, not Griffin, was the one she'd really wanted to talk to about everything, Tommy who would understand the sense of loss coming at her from all directions. He'd been, it came home to her as she sobbed there in the shower, her best friend. He might have been more if she'd allowed it. Maybe she should have.

Buzz. Griffin watched the alarm clock's minute hand turn over.

At six, he rose and slipped quietly into a pair of shorts, an old polo shirt and sandals. He was pretty sure Joy was awake, too, that she'd slept no more and no better than he had, so he wasn't surprised when she spoke.

"Do you really have to do this now? Have you looked outside?"

"I won't be long. Go back to sleep."

Outside, Wellfleet was lost in dense, liquid fog. She was right, of course. The sensible thing would be to wait for it to burn off, but he was determined to disprove without further delay the most ludicrous of the charges his wife had leveled against him. By midmorning they'd be back in Falmouth to pick up Joy's car and head back to Connecticut, to the life they'd managed to undermine so thoroughly.

It was far too wet to put the top down, but he did it anyway, hoping he'd be less blind. By the time he inched down the mussel-shell drive into the street, the inn was completely swallowed by the fog, and his shirt collar was cold and soaked through. Somewhere in the distance he heard the lonely tolling of a buoy, but he had no idea which direction the sound was coming from.

The town dock was probably his best bet. There might be people around even this early, but anyone standing more than a few feet away wouldn't even know he was there, much less what he was up to. This assumed, of course, that he could find the dock. But if he couldn't, no big deal. Except for its outer tip at Provincetown, the Cape was narrowest here at Wellfleet, just a couple miles wide. You couldn't drive very far in any direction without coming to water of some sort, an inlet or a freshwater pond. Creeping forward at a pace that barely registered on the speedometer, he squinted into the gray soup, trusting that he'd see what he was about to hit before impact. Because it would be ironic if he got in an accident while driving to scatter the ashes of a man so prone to them.

Had he ever in his life been so exhausted? Not having slept was part of it, but the quarrel itself, he knew, was what had drained him. He and Joy were no strangers to argument, of course. What couple married thirty-four years was? But usually their disputes were contained. They were about something, not everything. Yesterday's had started out like that, focused on his wife's admission that yes, for a time she'd been in love, or something like love, with his old friend. But that perimeter had quickly been breached by Joy's claim that the issue between them now was about him, not Tommy. Since his father's death nine months ago, she said, his dissatisfaction had become palpable, as was evidenced by how excited he'd become at the prospect of a screenwriting gig. What he wanted, she told him, was his old life back, to be young and free again. She understood how losing a parent could cut you loose from your moorings. She'd lost her own mother, hadn't she? But moving back to L.A. (and *that* was his real intention, she insisted, next week's visit being just the opening gambit) wouldn't make either of them young again, nor, she was dead certain, would it make him happy.

Griffin had laughed at the notion that he was "unmoored" (or even fazed, for that matter) by his father's passing, and though he grudgingly conceded that the notion of moving back to L.A.— getting back in the *game,* for Christ sake—had its attractions, he denied categorically that he harbored any illusions about the place restoring his youth. If anything, the culture out there would have the opposite effect by making him feel his age even more acutely. But did the fact they weren't young anymore mean they had to be prematurely old? Why spend the rest of their lives in curriculum meetings and eating in the same three or four local restaurants with the same bunch of dull academics? Did they have to be so *settled*?

Wasn't that the same as "settling"? They'd left L.A. because of Laura, but she was an adult now. By this time next year, she'd be married. Obviously, their circumstances had changed. Couldn't their thinking and future plans reflect this?

What would be so wrong with, say, dividing their time? This past winter had been brutal. Even Joy had to admit that. Why not keep an eye out for an apartment in L.A. where they could spend each spring semester? Okay, the college wouldn't be thrilled by him going down to half-time, but before leaving on this trip, he'd floated the idea past the dean of faculty, who'd said that the school, rather than risk losing him entirely, would likely be flexible. Once they were back in L.A., Griffin could reestablish his contacts in the film world, and the money he'd make there would more than offset the loss of academic income. But for Joy *settled* wasn't the same as *settling*. To her, settled just meant that they'd chosen wisely all those years ago. She happened to love the life they were living now; moreover, it was one they'd agreed on. And what would become of her full-time job when Griffin went to part-time? Was she expected to sit and watch while he had his middle-age meltdown?

Thus far, Griffin had held his own. He'd always wielded superior rhetorical skills (*Do you ever win an argument with this guy?*) and over the last decade he'd honed them further in the classroom. But admit it, he wasn't on his game. He never should've allowed their dispute to expand beyond her and Tommy, and even to his own ears, his voice, though he was careful not to raise it, sounded shrill, almost desperate. Usually, by this point Joy would have become frustrated and given in, yet the quarrel ground on. It was like a poker game where the wagering suddenly accelerated, each player raising instead of calling, then raising again, until all the blue chips were in the center of the table, more than either could afford to lose, or, maybe, in this case, to win. His father's death, she kept insisting, was the true source of his current malaise, and her steadfast refusal to surrender this causal linkage had thrown him off his stride. Truth be told, the chronology did give him pause, because the idea of returning to L.A. *had* taken root not long after his father's car was found at the turnpike rest stop. Since then he'd become more aggressive about looking for film work, checking with Sid every couple of weeks to see if he'd heard of any assignments he might be right for. He never made those calls when Joy was around, but of course they'd showed up on their long-distance bill, and she'd put two and two together. And he couldn't really blame her for being angry that he'd sent up a trial balloon with the dean of faculty before broaching the subject with her. Why had he done that? Because he'd been pretty sure she'd hate the idea, maybe even veto it preemptively. So he'd gone ahead without her.

Reluctantly, Griffin was forced to entertain the possibility that he was in the wrong. Maybe her case against him wasn't airtight, but it was fundamentally sturdy, whereas his defense against her accusations was merely skillful, artifice teetering on the head of a pin. Panicking, he'd tried to retreat to more solid ground. If he had a few secrets about phone calls to his agent and conversations with his dean, what about the whopper she'd been keeping all these years? *He* wasn't the one who'd fallen in love with somebody else; *she* had. And indeed it was this knowledge, the details of it, that kept playing on a loop through his brain, like a pivotal scene in a script (yes, Joy would hate the metaphor, but there you were) that was out of kilter, jeopardizing the whole.

INT. TASTEFUL B&B ROOM: NIGHT.

A man (mid-fifties, slender and moderately good-looking despite his receding hairline) is peering out the window, but his haggard face is reflected back at him in the glass. A woman his age, beautiful but despondent, is seated on the four-poster bed, her head in her hands. Clearly, they're arguing and have been for some time.

HUSBAND

Is it over? Can you at least tell me that much?

WIFE

(looking up in disbelief)

Over? Can't you see it never even started?

HUSBAND

Okay, say I believe you and you never—

WIFE

Say you believe me?

HUSBAND

(ashamed of himself)

Even if it never . . . My question is, are you afraid
to see him again? Is that why you won't go to L.A.?

WIFE

I don't know . . . Maybe.

He turns to face her now. Neither speaks for a long beat.

HUSBAND

Explain something to me. How come you get to
be disappointed with our life and I don't?

WIFE

(shaking her head)

Don't you see? I'm *not* disappointed. That's why
I'm not willing to risk what we have. We're
talking about something that happened a long

time ago. It shouldn't have, but it did. I let my
feelings get the better of me, and I'm sorry for
that. I'm sorry yours got hurt. But *I chose you.*
Aren't the last two decades proof?

But he still can't believe she was in love with someone else,
ever.

> HUSBAND
> *(petulant)*
> Proof you love your daughter.

> WIFE
> I do love our daughter.

> HUSBAND
> *(bitter)*
> Plus, how would you explain to Harve and Jill
> and Princess Grace of Morocco that you loved
> somebody new? That would mean you changed
> your mind about something, and nobody in your
> family ever does that.

CLOSE ON THE HUSBAND. He knows better than to
continue in this vein, but he can't help himself.

> HUSBAND (CONT'D)
> What is it your father always says? Nobody's ever
> disproved the domino theory?

> WIFE
> At least we're finally addressing the real subject.

HUSBAND
(*incredulous*)

Which is?

WIFE

Our parents.

HUSBAND

Hey, *my* parents couldn't be more out of the
picture. They have been right from the start.

WIFE
(so *sad)*

Can't you see, you've got it all wrong. You always
blame *my* parents for intruding into our lives.
You think I'm spared when you take your
parents' phone calls in the den with the door
closed.

HUSBAND

Let me see if I understand this. Are you really
saying my parents are the reason you fell in
love with Tommy?

ON THE WOMAN NOW. She's on her feet, facing him,
gaining confidence. In all their married lives, she's never
so openly confronted him before.

WIFE

I'm saying that out of sight isn't out of mind. You
think you don't let your mother into your life—
into *our* lives—but you blame *her* when a bird

craps on you. Think about that. You believe your
father's gone because he died, but he *isn't* gone.
He's haunted you this whole year. Right now he's
in the trunk of your car, and you can't bring
yourself to scatter his ashes. Do you think maybe
that *means* something?

Griffin came to a stop sign, or what he assumed was a stop
sign—something octagonal, possibly red. He listened for the
approach of an oncoming vehicle, but there was no sound, nothing
except the tolling of that far-off buoy. He took a left, recalling, or
seeming to, that this would take him through the village and down
to the harbor. But that was somehow wrong, because almost immediately the road was lined on both sides by dark, ghostly trees
instead of houses, which meant he was heading away from the harbor. Never mind. It didn't have to be the harbor, or even saltwater.
All that had seemed to matter yesterday, but not today. The important—no, critical—thing was to dispose of the man and, in doing
so, win the only winnable part of yesterday's argument. That was
the crux of Joy's case. That *his* parents, despite their physical
absence, had intruded on their marriage as much as hers had, that
he perversely wanted them to. If he could prove her wrong about
this, then maybe her whole argument would collapse.

Outside of town the fog was, if possible, even thicker, and Griffin's hair was now as wet as if he'd just stepped out of the shower.
Turning on the wipers helped a little, but his headlights, even on
low beams, just made matters worse. Every quarter mile or so he'd
pass a mailbox that marked a narrow dirt road where he could turn
around and head back into town, but for now, not wanting to
appear indecisive even to himself, he was content to keep moving
forward. A minute later he passed beneath a highway—Route 6, he
guessed—which explained why he hadn't come to the shore yet. In

another mile or two, if this road was reasonably straight, he'd reach the National Seashore on the Atlantic side. Hard to imagine a more remote stretch, especially at this hour of the morning and in this weather. No chance he'd be interrupted there.

WIFE

You want this to be about one day—the day you found me so brokenhearted—but it isn't. You're unhappy every day, and it's getting worse. You're a congenitally unhappy man.

HUSBAND
(choking back his emotions)
I'm never happy? I wasn't happy last night?

WIFE

Okay, last night, for a few short hours, you were. But you always retreat, Jack. It's like you're afraid it won't last. Like if you admit to being happy, someone will steal it from you.
(A BEAT, while he considers this)
Yes, there was a time when my heart went out to Tommy, and yes it got broken. But I mended it. I mended my heart.

ON THEIR REFLECTION IN THE GLASS. His, in the F.G., goes OUT OF FOCUS as hers comes in.

WIFE

I'm sorry I haven't been able to mend yours, because God knows I've tried. I'm exhausted from trying.

HUSBAND
(looking gut-shot)
Maybe you should stop.

WIFE
(heartsick, looking away)
I have. That's what you've noticed these last few
weeks. Me stopping.

FADE OUT.

Congenitally unhappy. The word was not hers, of course. In
thirty-four years he'd never known her to use it until yesterday. But
Tommy loved it, even though Griffin always had to correct his
spelling—*congental* or *congentle*—on the page. ("Think of genitals," he'd advised, to which Tommy had responded, "I don't like to
think of genitals. I'd rather spell it wrong.") No doubt he'd used the
word yesterday when Griffin was in the shower and she called him
back to explain why she wouldn't be coming along to L.A. Griffin
could imagine how the conversation had gone, Joy confiding how
their marriage was deteriorating, how they seldom made love anymore, how his ambient discontent had deepened to the point of
pathology, how he'd been driving around for the better part of a
year with his dad's ashes in the trunk of his car. And Tommy—
because in the end he was Griffin's friend—advising her not to be
hasty. "This shit ain't new, kiddo. The guy's always been a congeni-
tal malcontent. He doesn't even realize he's doing it. Remember the
famous house categories, back when you guys were looking? Can't
Afford It and Wouldn't Have It As a Gift? Tell me that isn't Griff all
over. This is the man you married when you could've married me,
Mr. Happy-Go-Lucky."

Griffin couldn't help but smile at this imagined conversation, how he didn't come off very well even when he himself held the reins of invention. But it was true that back then he'd adopted his parents' mantra. Tommy and Joy had made relentless fun of him, even after he explained that he'd just been riffing on how his parents had classified at a glance every single property in the fat Cape real-estate guide, that *his* use of these same categories was meant to be ironic. But Tommy hadn't bought any of that. "Explain irony to me," he said. "I went to school, but that's a concept I never really understood. Ironic guys like you confuse me especially."

When the trees fell away on both sides of the road, Griffin heard surf pounding nearby, though he knew how deceptive the sound could be. One summer (before the Brownings or after?) his parents had rented a place with a second-story deck, from which you could see the ocean beyond the dunes, a good quarter-mile away. Each night he fell asleep in profound stillness, only to awaken to crashing waves right outside his window, as if during the night the turning tide had breached the dunes. But when he rose and joined his father on the deck, the ocean was right where it had been the day before. His father had explained it, how the wind had changed during the night, now pulling the sound toward them instead of pushing it away, and this made sense, the way science always does, because you know it's supposed to. But the next morning, when Griffin again awoke to the same thunder, the explanation felt inadequate to the experience. The sound was just too close, too loud, and again he expected to find the lower rooms of their rental cottage flooded. Only repetition—the same thing happening night after night—had diminished and finally banished the magic.

But the beach *was* near. He could smell the salt, and this close to the shore, the fog had begun to dissipate. Squinting, he was able to make out a line of rolling dunes and beyond it a pale yellow orb, like a lamp with a forty-watt bulb covered by a sheet, near where he imagined the horizon to be. For a while the road he was on paralleled the shore, then abruptly ended in a large dirt parking lot. A lone pickup truck was parked there, probably some intrepid fisherman trying to get a jump on the blues.

A weathered boardwalk ran between the dunes, at the end of which Griffin slipped off his sandals. Looming ahead was some sort of structure—a building on the beach, maybe, or a ship at anchor?—but he couldn't tell which until he got closer and the ghostly shape resolved itself into a restaurant with a large wraparound deck and a ship's mast growing up through the roof. A rear door stood wide open, and he could hear someone moving around inside. The owner, probably, someone swamping the place out before the other employees arrived. Possibly even a thief. If whoever it was saw him and demanded to know what he was up to, what would he do? Raise his father's urn by way of explanation? He hurried along before any such embarrassment could come to pass.

Almost immediately he could tell his plan was deeply flawed. From the boardwalk the waves looked to be breaking about knee-high, but now he saw it was more like waist-high. The restaurant had become just a gray silhouette in the mist behind him, and he was reluctant to go much farther up the beach. After all, the building marked the entrance to the parking lot, and if he allowed it to disappear completely, how would he find his car again? What he'd been hoping for, he realized, was a stone jetty or a pier, something that jutted into the water, something he could walk out on and, at the far end of, release the ashes into the churning sea. But there was nothing of the sort, which meant he'd have to wade out into the surf, submerge the urn and open it into the undertow. That would require dexterity, timing and, he feared, a good measure of luck. The lid was secured by two flimsy-looking metal clasps that would probably fly open if he got hit by a big wave before he was ready. It'd be more sensible to dig a hole at the water's edge, pour the ashes in and cover them over. Later, when the tide came in, the push and pull of the waves would mingle the ash with sand and water, and his father would at last become part of the grit of the world. How different was that, really, from pouring the contents of the urn off the end of a dock or over the side of a boat?

Well, it *was* different. Plus, now that he looked more carefully, he saw the tide was already in. The water might not come any farther up the beach.

> WIFE
> Is it possible you haven't scattered your father's
> ashes because you need him in some way?

> HUSBAND
> *(stern, cold)*
> Need him? My *father?* I didn't need him alive.
> Why would I need him dead?

He took a deep breath, kicked his sandals aside and, gripping his father with both hands, entered the surf.

Driving back to Wellfleet, completely soaked, Griffin noticed what had been shrouded in fog when he was coming from the other direction. There, arranged in a horseshoe just as he remembered them, were the cottages where he and his parents and the Brownings had stayed that summer. At first, he wasn't sure he trusted his eyes. That he should stumble on the place now seemed beyond improbable, as if the physical world were suddenly and mysteriously linked to his own psychic necessity. Having passed the entrance, he pulled onto the shoulder and backed up, his tires grinding on the gravel in the stillness.

On second thought, maybe it wasn't the same place. The sign, OFFSHORE COTTAGES, WEEKLY/MONTHLY RENTALS, didn't ring any bells, and in the center of the horseshoe, where the playground had been, there was now an in-ground pool enclosed by a chain-link fence. Beyond this were a shuffleboard court and several stone barbecue pits topped with heavy metal grates. But after more than four decades wouldn't it have been even stranger if there *weren't* significant changes? More difficult to reconcile was his memory of being able to walk to the beach that summer, which had to be a good half mile away. Had he conflated elements of the Browning summer with other vacations? Perhaps he'd added the detail of walking to the beach when he wrote about it as an adult, and it had been assimilated as memory.

About half the cottages looked occupied. Otherwise identical, each was painted a different pastel color and named—Sea Breeze, High Tide, Quarter Deck, Scallop Shell. Did he actually remember his parents making fun of the kitschy names, or was this just something they would've done? It was still only seven-thirty, too early to call his mother and ask. Besides, even after talking to her, he still wouldn't know.

If these were the same cottages, then Dunwanderin would have been theirs—two-thirds of the way up the right-hand side of the horseshoe. It faced diagonally across the pool patio toward what would have been the Browning cottage. Feeling his sleepless exhaustion drag him down, Griffin put the car in park and closed his eyes, allowing himself to become again a twelve-year-old boy in the backseat of his parents' car. The memory of their arrival here that first day was suddenly there, more vivid and detailed than ever before—his mother and father just staring at the cottage, neither making any move to get out. What they were doing, he knew from experience, was comparing the actual cottage with the description of it they'd been sent last January by the Cape Cod Chamber of Commerce, the brochure's *charming* becoming *tiny*; *rustic* becoming *dingy*; *fully equipped* becoming *attic furnished*. In other words, crappy.

"Good," said his father finally, his voice full of false cheer, "there's a deck."

"That?" said his mother, pointing. The warped, splintered boards weren't even bordered by railings, and tall, spiky black weeds were sticking up between the planks. "You call that a deck?"

"Hey, there's a table and four chairs, right? Perfect for us. You, me, Jackeroo and Al." Clearly, he'd come to a decision, and he meant to make the best of the situation. It had been a long drive from the Mid-fucking-west, and Griffin's mother had been angry the whole way, failing to cheer up even when they crossed the Sagamore and his father had bravely broken into "That Old Cape Magic." The New York State Thruway motel where they'd stayed the night before had been crappy, and this was going to be crappier still.

A screen door banged on the other side of the compound, and a little girl, shrieking with delight, came running toward them, her brother at her heels. They both stopped near the swing set, heads cocked, taking the measure of the newcomers. (At the wheel of his convertible, some forty-five years in the future, Griffin could feel himself smile at the sight of them.)

"Wonderful," his mother said, no doubt envisioning an army of bratty kids, every cottage swarming with them. "Just great."

"Mary, it'll be fine," Griffin's father said. "Next year we'll do better. They never freeze salaries two years in a row."

"I like it," Griffin piped up from the backseat, sensing his father needed an ally. There was a tiny window under the eaves on the cottage's second floor, and he'd intuited correctly that this room would be his.

His mother stared straight ahead, incredulous. "We're paying *how* much?"

"It'll be fine," his father repeated, "unless you *prefer* to be miserable."

"It's like an oven up here," she remarked when they shouldered open the door to the tiny room under the eaves. Not much bigger than a closet, it was only about five feet in height from floor to peak. His father, no giant, had to duck when he entered. "This is the kids' room, all right," he said when Griffin's mother, shaking her head in disgust, went back downstairs. Three cots with thin, stained mattresses crowded the room, two along opposite walls, the third folded up behind the door. His father threw open the tiny window, and together he and Griffin repositioned one of the cots directly beneath it to catch any stray breezes. At the base of one wall, where the A formed by the roof was at its widest point, were built-in storage compartments.

"Wanna bet that's where they keep the games?" his father said, pulling on the stuck door. His parents never brought games of their own on vacation, preferring to see what each new rental provided, though they were usually very old board games with pieces missing, unplayable. When the door didn't budge, he yanked it harder. This time it opened and his father yelped, pulling his hand back fast, as if from a fire, and then made the mistake of straightening up, the crown of his head smacking the low roof beam. "Ow!" he said, rubbing it with both hands. Whenever he injured himself, he looked betrayed, as if somebody else, maybe Griffin, was responsible. He complained of having what he termed a "low threshold of physical discomfort," what Griffin's mother termed "being a big baby." He came over now, bending low so Griffin could examine his scalp. "Is the skin broken?"

"Sort of," Griffin said. An impressive knot was rising where his father's hair was thinnest. The skin was abraded, a dozen tiny spots of blood just starting to form.

"Bleeding?"

"Just a little."

Now his father was examining his injured thumb, where a dark splinter had been driven under the skin. "This vacation isn't starting very well, is it?"

Griffin admitted it wasn't.

"Your mother . . . ," he began, but broke off in order to chew at the splinter.

Griffin waited.

"Damn," he said, showing Griffin this wound, too. "It's *in* there." The thick end of the splinter was close to the surface, the slender end, a mere shadow, much deeper.

"What about Mom?"

"Right now she's on the warpath, but she'll calm down." He seemed to be talking to himself more than to Griffin. "She just needs . . ." He let his voice trail off again, as if to admit that he had no idea, really, what his wife needed, then went back to gnawing on his thumb.

They could hear her opening and closing kitchen cabinets downstairs. "No wineglasses," she muttered. "Not a single goddamn wineglass." Then, calling up: "Bill! You're *not* going to believe this."

"Gotta go," his father said, grinning sheepishly, and headed downstairs.

There was no chest of drawers in the room, so Griffin laid out his week's worth of vacation clothes on the extra cot and shoved his suitcase under it. When he thought he heard scurrying in the shadows of the storage cabinet, he quickly shut the door with his foot. Kneeling on the bed, he peered outside. Even with the window open, the room was still stifling hot, with barely enough breeze to flutter the curtain. On the sill a big green fly, dazed, was buzzing around on its back. It had been trapped between the window and the screen, but now, with the window up, its freedom was at hand. Its mind, though, if it had one, hadn't adjusted, the old hopeless reality holding sway. Griffin watched the stupid thing spin and buzz until he heard a door open below and his mother emerged onto the deck, where she just stood with her arms crossed. When his father appeared a moment later, Griffin had a good view of the top of his head, where the tiny spots of blood had connected in a purple blob.

"Look," he said, bending down to show her.

"Good," she said.

"This, too." He was showing her the splinter now, and she winced—something about this smaller thumb injury apparently touched her in a way the larger one hadn't.

"You're a mess," she said, not unkindly.

His father lowered his voice then, but Griffin could hear him anyway. "She doesn't mean a goddamn thing to me. You know that."

His mother shook her head in despair. "I thought we agreed we weren't going to do this anymore. Either one of us."

"We did. I don't know what comes over me. I hate myself. Really, you've no idea how much. I don't know why you have anything to do with me."

His mother allowed herself to be gathered into his arms then, and they stood there for a long time without speaking. "Okay," she finally said, as if surrendering something large, something she'd meant to cling to. "We're on the Cape."

"And it's great."

She nodded, surveying the cottage and the entire compound once again. Griffin could tell that while nothing had changed, things looked better to her now than they had ten minutes ago. She took his father's hand and examined the splinter more closely. "Come on," she said. "Let's go find some tweezers."

"Hello, Indiana!" came a hearty male voice, and when Griffin looked up, the two kids and their parents were coming toward them, waving enthusiastically. Apparently they'd noticed the out-of-state license. Griffin saw both his parents stiffen at being personally linked with the Mid-fucking-west. When they turned to greet the other family, he couldn't see their faces anymore but knew they were offering the newcomers their most forced, rigid, unnatural smiles, the ones that convinced exactly no one, but, because they were identical, carried a certain authority. He noticed his mother had put her arm around his father's waist, which meant that at least as far as these people were concerned, they were a single entity again, with the same contemptuous mind.

Strange, Griffin thought, opening his eyes on the present. He'd used none of this in "The Summer of the Brownings." He'd meant for the story to be about the Brownings and felt that his parents, or rather the parents of the boy in the story, had already taken up too much narrative space. He'd wanted to focus on his friendship with Peter, with a subplot on the crush he'd had on the boy's mother, the dawn of something like sexual awareness in a twelve-year-old. Except this wasn't what the *experience* had been about. The idea that there might be something seriously wrong between his parents had not been new that summer. Their unhappiness, together and separately, had been a given throughout his childhood. That was why they needed the Cape, even more each passing year, to make things right between them, at least for a while. The Browning summer was just the first when he'd begun to understand what ailed them. If he'd had a true sexual awakening that summer it was this: what was wrong between his parents was about sex. At the time, that was as precise as he could make it, and he yearned neither for additional information nor further illumination. Indeed, to keep these at bay he'd escaped into that other, happier family. The Brownings had offered the refuge he needed, though any happy family would have probably served the same purpose, which meant he hadn't so much told the story of that summer as avoided telling it. That was why a puzzled Tommy had concluded it must be about a kid discovering he was gay. *Poor fucking kid,* he'd said, perhaps sensing the presence of the real story that never got written. Griffin looked up at the dark window under the eaves now, half expecting to see his own worried twelve-year-old face still framed there.

The irony of all this, Griffin realized, was one even Tommy, who'd once jokingly asked him to explain irony, would appreciate. Because Griffin had attempted to do in the Browning summer story precisely what his wife was now accusing him of having done in their marriage: he'd tried but failed to keep his parents out. Right from the start (of the story, of his marriage), despite his best efforts, they'd managed to insinuate themselves. When Joy suggested they honeymoon on the Maine coast, Griffin convinced her that what they needed was a dose of the old Cape magic, that weakest of marital spells. In Truro they'd made plans for a life based on what they foolishly thought were their own terms, Joy articulating what she wanted, Griffin, tellingly, what he didn't want (a marriage that even remotely resembled his parents', as if this negative were a nifty substitute for an unimagined positive). Even as he rejected their values, he'd allowed many of their bedrock assumptions—that happiness was a place you could visit but never own, for instance—to burrow deep. He'd dismissed their snobbery and unearned sense of entitlement, but swallowed whole the rationale on which it had been based (Can't Afford It; Wouldn't Have It As a Gift). Joy's contention that his parents, not hers, were the true intruders in their marriage had seemed ludicrous on the face of it, but he saw now that it was true. They were mucking about still, his living mother, exiled in the Mid-fucking-west (justice, that) but using seagulls as surrogates, his deceased father, reduced to ash and bits of bone, still refusing to take his leave.

He'd tried. Joy probably wouldn't believe him, but he *had* tried. Failed, sure, awkwardly and foolishly, but was he not his father's son? He'd gone out a good twenty yards into the cold surf, turning his back to the waves as they broke, holding his father out in front of him with both hands like a priest with a chalice, as if keeping the urn dry until the precise moment of submergence were a necessary part of the idiotic liturgy. *He's haunted you this whole year,* Joy had accused. *Right now he's in the trunk of your car, and you can't bring yourself to scatter his ashes. Do you think maybe that* means *something?* And so, by God, as soon as he was waist-deep, he'd put an end to the folly.

Except that when he plunged the urn into the turbulence and positioned his thumbs under the latch that secured the lid, the sand beneath his feet gave way to the very undertow his father had always feared, and Griffin lost his balance. To regain it, he held his arms out to his sides like a surfer. Had he dropped the urn then, or had the next wave knocked it out of his hands? He couldn't remember. One second he had it; the next it had disappeared into the churning froth. *Lost*, he remembered thinking as he lunged after it, feeling around in the surf with both hands like a blind man until the next wave, larger, knocked him flat. Regaining his feet, he thought, *My father is lost.* Hilarious, really. After all, he'd been dead for nine months. But he was *lost* only now, this instant, and somehow this was worse than *dead*, because *dead* wasn't something Griffin could be blamed for.

How long had he stood there, paralyzed, mortified by his clumsy incompetence, wave after wave leaping past him onto the shore? *Do something*, he thought, panicked, but what? How many times as a boy had he watched his father seize up in the middle of a room, a portrait of indecision, with no idea of where to turn, an angry wife tugging him in one direction, a pretty grad student who'd confused him with the romantic hero of some novel they'd been studying pulling him in the opposite? It was as if he'd concluded that if he remained where he was long enough, whatever he wanted most would come to him of its own volition. Griffin remembered willing him to act, to *do something*, because it frightened him to see anybody stand frozen in one place for so long, unable to take that first step, the one that implied a destination. Now, waist-deep in the roiling surf, the sands shifting dangerously beneath his feet, he finally understood. Because of course it was the *doing* that had brought him to this pass, and now, having *done* the wrong thing, the thing he never would've done if he'd been thinking clearly, there was nothing further *to* do but hope that chance, not known for compassion, would intervene in his undeserving favor.

Which in defiance of both logic and expectation it finally did, the dreaded undertow returning his father's urn in a rush of sand and water, banging it hard against Griffin's anklebone, and this time his blind hands located it in the froth. He yanked the urn from the surf intact, its latches, somehow, unsprung.

Found. That was the word that leapt into his consciousness, like a synonym for *triumph.*

Back at the B and B Joy was packed and waiting. If she noticed the condition of his clothes, she didn't say anything, nor did she remark on the fact that, when he popped the trunk and tossed in their bags, his father was still in the wheel well. Her silence alone was an eloquent indictment. He considered telling her that he'd stumbled on the very place where his family had vacationed when he was twelve and as a result he at last knew how to go about revising "The Summer of the Brownings." But why should she care?

They took Route 6 as far as Hyannis, then Route 28 to Falmouth, all of it in silence. His cell phone vibrated once, but he saw it was his mother and let it go to voice mail. He was simply too dispirited to talk to her, especially with Joy in the car. Old habits like taking her calls in private were the hardest to break. In Falmouth they transferred Joy's bag into her SUV, an act disturbing in its symbolism, since both vehicles were bound for the same destination, their home.

They headed in tandem for the Bourne Bridge, Joy in the lead.

What he needed to do was think about the future, to figure out how to get back to the place they'd been the night of Kelsey's wedding. Hard to believe, but that was just twenty-four hours ago. It felt like a lifetime, as if he and Joy had been traveling, lost, up and down the Cape forever. Odd that the future should be so difficult to bring into focus when the past, uninvited, offered itself up so easily for inspection. According to his mother, he'd pitched a fit, refusing to get into the car when it was time for them to leave the Cape that Browning summer, but that wasn't how he remembered it at all. As his parents were loading the car, the man they'd rented the cottage from had come by to pick up the keys.

"What's this?" his father asked when he was offered a bright red folder.

"Next year's rates and availability," the man told him. "You get first crack and a hundred dollars off because you stayed with us this year."

"I don't think we're interested."

The man glanced at Griffin's mother, then, to see if husband and wife were on the same page about this, and finally at Griffin himself. "How about you hang on to it, young fella," he said, perhaps sensing that returning to these same cottages next summer was what Griffin wanted more than anything in the world. "In case they change their mind."

No one had spoken a word by the time they got to the Sagamore. Griffin's mother looked like she meant to say nothing all the way back to the Mid-fucking-west. His father's thumb had seemed to heal, but the splinter had resurfaced, and he'd chewed on it until the thumb became infected. It was now swollen to twice its normal size, and when the car rumbled onto the bridge, perhaps remembering that this same splinter had elicited sympathy a fortnight earlier, he tried to show it to Griffin's mother, but she just looked away. He should've quit right then, but knowing when to give up wasn't one of his father's strong suits. "Am I running a fever?" he said, leaning across the seat so Griffin's mother could feel his forehead. "I'm burning up, aren't I?"

But she just continued to stare out the window.

"Fine," his father said, leaning back, his brow untouched. "Just great."

"Just great," Griffin now echoed as the Bourne Bridge appeared in the distance. Feeling feverish himself, he put a hand to his forehead, but of course you really needed someone else for an accurate read. If Joy had been in the seat next to him, and he'd asked, she wouldn't have refused him. He knew that much. But even though nothing in the world would have made him happier right then than the gift of her cool touch, he also knew he wouldn't have asked her. Because even if he did have a temperature, it would feel like trying to elicit sympathy he didn't deserve, his father's son.

A hundred yards from the Bourne, his phone vibrated again. Seeing who it was, he pulled onto the shoulder and answered, just as Joy's SUV climbed up onto the bridge and disappeared from sight.

"I think I found out what Sid had for you," Tommy told him. "You remember Ruben Hand? Ruby?"

The name rang a vague bell, but . . .

"We were going to write that film for him back in the day, but the money went south? Anyway, he's in TV now. He's got this made-for-cable movie thing, some story about a college professor. Sid apparently pitched you."

"You know this how?"

"My guy pitched me. If we could convince Ruby we're right, we could do it together. Take six to eight weeks, ten at the outside. You'd be back grading your grammar exercises by Labor Day. Decent money. Possible series to follow if it works."

"Ruby Hand. The guy I'm remembering was an asshole."

"That's right, a producer."

"I'm in the car right now. How about I talk to Joy and call you back when I get home."

"Not to influence you, but I could use the gig."

"Okay if I ask you a question?"

"Sure."

"Are you still in love with Joy?"

Not even a second's hesitation. "Sure," said his old friend. "Aren't you?"

Such a simple question. Such a simple answer. Yet somehow, sitting there in the shadow of the Bourne Bridge, he'd managed to twist it all around. To make it instead a question of whether Joy still loved him. If she did, he told himself, she'd be waiting for him on the other side. Years ago, finally leaving L.A., they'd made the journey in two cars loaded down with things they didn't trust to the movers. That was before cell phones, of course, but after the first day they had it down to a science, each intuiting when the other was going to need to stop for gas or food or the lavatory. They tried to stay close, within sight of each other, and whoever was in the lead would periodically check the rearview mirror and, if the other car wasn't there, slow down or pull over until it caught up. Would Joy remember? Had she seen him pull over? If so, she'd be waiting for him on the other side. Or, more likely, farther on. By now, he was sure, she'd have checked her mirror, and noticed he wasn't there.

Turning off his cell, he put it back in the cup holder. He didn't want to talk to her on the phone. There'd been too much talk already. He just wanted to see her off on the shoulder, waiting for him, concerned for his well-being. If she pulled over, he'd know that whatever was between them could be worked out.

Carefully pulling out into traffic, he climbed onto the Bourne, passing the sign—DESPERATE?—a group called the Samaritans put there to discourage leapers. From the elevated midpoint of the bridge, he could see a steady stream of cars that reached almost a mile down the highway, but none were off on the shoulder. Half an hour later he switched his cell back on, hoping to see that he'd missed a call, but none had come in.

9

Rehearsal

The rugged Maine coastline was stunning, Griffin had to admit, the light so pure it almost hurt. He couldn't help wondering what would have happened if his parents had fallen in love with this part of the world instead of the Cape. Certainly it would have been more affordable, but that begged an obvious question: would they really have wanted something they could afford? After all, much of the Cape's allure was its shimmering elusiveness, the magical way it receded before them year after year, the stuff of dreams. Coastal Maine, by contrast, seemed not just real but battered by reality. Where Cape Cod somehow managed to give the impression that July lasted all year, Maine reminded you, even in lush late spring, of its long, harsh winters, of snowdrifts that rotted baseboards and splintered latticework, of relentless winds that howled in the eaves and scoured the paint, leaving gutters rusted white with salt. Even the people looked scoured, or so it seemed to Griffin as he drove down the peninsula toward the Hedges, the resort hotel where Laura's wedding would take place tomorrow. *Wouldn't Have It As a Gift*, his mother informed him, in answer to his unspoken question.

Since her death last winter, she'd become even more talkative than when alive, ever anxious to share her opinions with Griffin, especially, but not exclusively, during his long, insomniac nights. Proximity—she now rode in the left wheel well of his rental car— also made her chatty. With any luck this would soon end. The plan was to drive down to the Cape after the wedding, find a resting place for both his parents. He'd had many months to think it over, but he still had no better plan than the one she'd proposed this time last year, to scatter his father on one side and his mother on the other. Maybe that would shut her up. *Fat chance,* she snorted.

All of Joy's family and most of the other guests were staying at the Hedges so they wouldn't be tempted to drive after drinking too much at the reception. Griffin had been offered a room there, too, but given the separation and the fact that he was bringing a guest, he thought it might be better to stay someplace nearby. When he suggested this, neither Joy nor Laura had objected, so he'd booked a room at a small inn half a mile up the peninsula.

It hadn't started out as a separation, at least not in the legal sense. After Wellfleet, they'd agreed that Griffin would go to L.A. for the summer and write the made-for-cable movie with Tommy, who had a spare room in his condo and was glad to have someone to help with expenses for a couple months. The time apart would do him and Joy good. Absence had been known to make other hearts grow fonder, so why not theirs? Though in truth they barely discussed what was happening, Wellfleet having drained them of words. When they got home, he'd simply gone online and booked a flight to L.A.

"And I tell our daughter what?" Joy asked, as he stuffed two large suitcases with what he'd need for the summer.

"Tell her I'll be home as soon as we deliver the script."

"We've never lied to her."

"That's a lie?"

The following morning he'd driven to campus to finish reading the kids' portfolios and put his academic life in some semblance of order. There was a summer program at the college, and his office would probably be used by visiting faculty. He put his father's urn in the locked bottom drawer of his filing cabinet, promising himself he'd deal with it when he returned. Later that same day when he tossed the suitcases into the trunk, Joy noticed the urn was gone. "In your office?" she said when he told her what he'd done. "Why there?" she asked.

"I didn't think it was fair for you to have to look at it every day," he said, registering her sad, defeated smile. He understood—how could he not?—that this sort of "consideration" was at the crux of what was between them, but he was at a loss how to do things differently.

In L.A. the work had not gone well. It was clear from the start that he and Tommy didn't view the material the same way. "Look," his friend said. "You're making too much of this. It's *Welcome Back, Kotter*, except at college. The kids are smarter than their professor. They're educating him. That's where the laughs come from." Never having taught, he seemed not to understand how arbitrary and artificial, how downright contrary to reality, this concept was. In the old days they'd been able to read each other's minds, finish each other's sentences, but more than a decade had passed and they'd lost the knack. Worse, Joy was now between them. Tommy seemed to know that not all was well in their marriage, but not much more. Griffin, who kept expecting to be cross-examined about what the hell was going on, didn't know what to make of it when he wasn't. It could mean Tommy didn't have to because Joy, when she called him from Wellfleet, had already explained the situation in detail, but the opposite inference—that his friend was mostly in the dark but was respecting their privacy—was just as likely. To find out Griffin would have to ask, and this he refused to do.

After he'd been in L.A. for a couple weeks, Tommy finally said, "So, you're not going to call her?"

"She knows how to reach me," Griffin responded, both surprised and genuinely appalled by the bitterness and childish petulance in his voice. He'd been telling himself he hadn't called her because he had no idea what to say. But the truth was uglier. What he was waiting for, he realized, was for Joy to blink, and with each passing day it became increasingly apparent that she wasn't going to. In Wellfleet she'd told him as much, that his unhappiness had exhausted her, that it would be a relief not to have to deal with it anymore. Okay, if that was what she wanted.

Except for the proscribed subject of Griffin's marriage and not being able to hit their work stride, he and Tommy did all right. They both by nature were respectful, so they seldom crowded each other, and their mutual affection hadn't waned. After that one remark about not calling Joy, Tommy made it a point to mind his own business, and Griffin returned the favor. His friend started drinking around five in the afternoon, just a glass of wine, no hard stuff anymore, but didn't stop until he called it a night and went to bed. His color wasn't good, and his paunch, while not large, was oddly asymmetrical, like it might contain a large fibroid cyst. For his part Tommy pretended not to notice that Griffin seldom slept for more than three or four hours. He himself got up to pee half a dozen times every night and sometimes poked his head into the living room, where Griffin would be watching television with the sound down. They were, that is, careful, as if consideration and not honesty was the bedrock of true friendship.

In this fashion the summer limped along. When Griffin arrived, they'd moved Tommy's desktop from the guest bedroom to the dining room, and it was here they convened each morning. Tommy always brought in a pot of coffee from the kitchen, and Griffin would print out two sets of the last couple of days' worth of work, which for continuity's sake they always read over before beginning a new scene. One morning Griffin looked up from his pages to see Tommy studying him with a mixture of sadness and irritation. "Griff," he said, "do us both a favor. Go home."

"Another week and a half and we'll have a draft."

"Fuck the draft. You're miserable. And you're hurting that woman."

"You don't know that."

"I know *her*. And what about your daughter?"

Laura, in fact, was not taking it well. She'd called him twice in L.A., wanting to know what was going on. What she'd worried about most of her life was finally happening, even as she and Andy were planning their own wedding. He'd tried to comfort her, saying that he and her mother hadn't decided anything yet, but the only thing that would really comfort her was for him to go home and resume his old life, to pretend nothing had happened in Wellfleet.

Two weeks later, in mid-August, he and Tommy turned the draft in to Ruby Hand. They both thought it stank but were of different minds about what was wrong with it, agreeing only about two things: that the script was unlikely to get better without additional input and that their producer was an even bigger dickhead than they remembered. Good luck getting valuable notes from him. He was prompt, though, give him that. He called the very next day, when Tommy was out. He'd read the script and thought it was definitely "a step in the right direction." How about they all think about it for a few days and exchange notes later in the week?

"That's that, then," Tommy said when Griffin told him about the conversation.

"What do you mean?"

"God, have you really been gone that long? That 'step in the right direction' jazz is code."

"You think we're fired?"

"No, I know we're fired."

He'd always had an almost preternatural gift for knowing when the ax was about to fall, but in this instance Griffin wasn't sure he agreed. "Our contract calls for a polish."

"He's going to eat the polish, Griff. Trust me, we're shitcanned. You might as well pack your bags."

Griffin decided to come clean. "I called the college last week," he said, "and they're granting me a year's leave."

Tommy nodded, then shook his head. "Joy knows about this?"

"Possibly. There aren't many secrets in small colleges."

"But *you* haven't told her."

"Not yet, though it won't be a surprise. She predicted it, in fact. Also, I might've found an apartment."

Tommy just sighed.

"I've stayed too long," Griffin said. "If we land another gig, maybe we could rent a small office."

Later that week, both their cells rang at the same moment. Griffin's said MOM CALLING, so he took it outside onto the patio. He'd been in L.A. a week before remembering his promise to visit and bring her the books and journals she wanted. "Maybe I can find what you need out here," he'd offered, after telling her where he was and why, or at least the small part he wanted her to know. "August is soon enough," she'd told him, confirming his earlier suspicion that she didn't need them to begin with. Their conversation had been short, suspiciously so, he thought. It was almost as if she was relieved he wouldn't be coming to see her as planned. Nor had she called him since, which was stranger still. For her, summer was open season for pestering.

"Mom," he said now, "how are you?"

But it wasn't his mother. The woman identified herself as Gladys, her next-door neighbor. She'd become concerned when Mary didn't answer her knock that morning. They were on the buddy system, Gladys explained, which meant they each had a key to the other's apartment, in case she locked herself out or something else happened. This was something else. She'd found Griffin's mother in bed, still in her nightgown, the curtains drawn and the room dark in the middle of the day. She was staring at nothing and gasping for breath, barely conscious, unresponsive. A heart attack, the emergency people thought. They'd given her oxygen and just minutes ago taken her to the hospital. "She keeps your number on the refrigerator," Gladys said. "I hope she won't be upset with me for using her phone to call. I could've used my own, I suppose, but I didn't think."

Griffin told her he was sure it would be okay.

"She hasn't been feeling good," Gladys said.

"I didn't know that."

"She didn't like to say anything."

Since when? Griffin thought. Were they talking about the same woman?

"We aren't really buddies," Gladys admitted. "That's just what we call it. The buddy system. When you're all alone, you need someone close by." Hearing this, Griffin swallowed hard. "I'm not sure your mother even likes me very much, but I didn't mind buddying with her. She could be very nice when she wanted to."

Griffin thanked her and said he'd be on the first flight he could catch, then hung up and just stood there on the balcony until Tommy poked his head out to check on him. "That sucks," his friend said when Griffin told him what was up, that he had to fly to Indiana.

Tommy insisted on driving him to LAX. At the curb they parted awkwardly, like a married couple in the middle of a spat.

"Okay if I call Joy about this?"

"I'd rather you didn't."

"I might anyway."

Griffin saw no reason to argue. "I'll let you know what's up once I get the lay of the land."

They shook hands.

"I never told you I found *my* mother."

"No kidding."

He nodded.

"And?"

"And you were right."

The Hedges occupied the tip of the peninsula, surrounded on three sides by water. The main building was a grand old structure with a huge porch bordered by eight-foot-tall yew trees that were painstakingly sculpted into a massive hedge. Farther down the sloping lawn, more hedges formed what Griffin guessed was a labyrinth. When he pulled into the gravel lot, he saw Joy's sister June emerge from an opening in the hedge with a crying child in tow. They were quite a ways off, but it was incredibly quiet, especially after L.A., and he could hear her say, "Poor sweetie pie, did you get lost? Didn't Grammy tell you that might happen?"

It was still an hour before the rehearsal dinner was scheduled to begin. Griffin thought it would be good to arrive early, but now he wished he hadn't. There were a couple dozen cars clustered near to the hotel. The lot was huge, though, big enough to handle a convention, so he parked in a remote spot. Joy's family probably would regard this, too, as standoffish, but during his year in L.A. he'd had two minor but costly auto mishaps—one on the freeway, not really his fault, the other in a mall parking lot, entirely his fault—and his insurance premiums were again on the rise. (Interesting, he thought, that his late mother yapped at him incessantly, whereas his dead father was content to communicate via crumpled bumpers and detached side-view mirrors.)

The evening was cool, with a nice breeze off the water, so he decided to just sit in the car for a few minutes and gather himself for what promised to be an ordeal. But Joy must have had an eye out for him, because right after turning off the ignition he caught a glimpse of her in the rearview mirror, coming down the porch steps. On the dashboard was the literary magazine that featured "The Summer of the Brownings." He'd brought a copy along with the idea of giving it to Joy, but he now realized the timing was wrong and left it where it was. *All is vanity,* his mother said, quoting whom? Shakespeare? Thackeray? The Old Testament? *Google it,* she suggested. Lord, Griffin thought. Last year, based on slender evidence, Joy had been convinced that his father was haunting him. What would she make of him losing arguments with his deceased mother? Not that he had any intention of telling her.

"Joy," he said, getting out of the car and giving her the best smile he could muster, "you look terrific."

Which she did. She'd lost some weight, which showed most flatteringly on her face. Her eyes, though, revealed the strain of the last year, and a wave of guilt washed over him, its undertow jellying his knees. He could tell she was registering the physical changes in him as well, and these, he knew, were even more pronounced. What he'd been wondering since leaving the inn was whether they would embrace. He didn't want to presume anything and reminded himself to react, not initiate, though now the moment arrived and his wife of thirty-five years was in his arms before he *could* react. Then just as quickly she stepped back before he could even evaluate what kind of hug it had been. This, he told himself, was probably how the next twenty-four hours would go. One moment moving on to the next with a terrible efficiency, before it could be really taken in. Dear God, how would he ever get through it?

"You look tired," Joy told him. "Was it a rough flight?"

"Not particularly," he said. "The sleeping thing's gotten worse." He actually hadn't meant to tell her that, but three decades' worth of intimacy was a hard habit to break. Was he trying to elicit sympathy?

"I'm sorry to hear it."

"It's been a little better the last couple weeks," he lied. Actually it was worse, but having received the sympathy he'd elicited he now felt unworthy of it.

"Have you seen a doctor?"

"I've got an appointment as soon as I get back," he said, another lie. How many more would he have to tell to balance out the first true statement?

"It's been a rough year," she said, quickly adding, "Your mother, I mean," lest he conclude she meant their being apart.

That first heart attack, back in August, had done serious damage, and the surgery necessary to repair it, the heart specialist had explained, was not without risk, especially for a woman her age. Without the operation she'd have only a year or two, maybe as little as six months. The upside of the surgery, assuming she didn't suffer a stroke on the operating table, was significant. Years, they were talking, maybe a decade. "That idiot must think I'm enjoying my life, if he imagines I want another decade," she told Griffin when they were alone. He tried to speak, but couldn't. "That's that, then," she said after a moment's silence, meeting his eye with what looked for all the world like satisfaction, as if this were the very news he'd been hoping for.

"It's okay," he said now, trying to help Joy out. "I knew what you meant."

"Where's . . . ?"

"In the trunk," Griffin admitted, feeling himself flush.

Only when Joy regarded him as if he'd lost his mind did he realize she wasn't asking about the whereabouts of his mother's ashes. "Oh, you mean . . . sorry," he said, flushing even deeper now. "She's back at the inn."

"You could've brought her to the dinner, Jack."

And, incredibly, he again thought she was talking about his mother. Jesus! Was it going to be like this all night? Would he misread everything anybody said? "She thought it'd be easier on everybody if she skipped the rehearsal."

Joy regarded him doubtfully. "Are you going to be all right?"

"Sure," he said, feeling anything but.

"A couple of things, before we go in," she said.

"Okay."

"Daddy's in a wheelchair now."

"I didn't know that."

"He fell last month. He says it's temporary, but Dot says no."

"Dot?"

"Jack. He remarried. You know that."

"I forgot, I guess." Though it all came back to him now. Joy's sisters had been furious. Marriage? At their father's advanced age? It was beyond ridiculous. Joy had had to talk them out of boycotting the wedding.

"Also, he doesn't make sense all the time."

"That's okay, neither do I," Griffin said. Obviously.

"He does all right in familiar surroundings, but—"

"I'll be aware."

"Just so you know—regarding us?—I've warned everybody to be on their best behavior. They've all agreed to be civil."

Back in the fall, when Joy's family found out they'd separated and were probably headed for divorce, emotions had run high. Her twin brothers, Jared and Jason, had promised to do Griffin bodily harm when next they met. One of them (their voices, too, were identical) had somehow gotten his cell number and called him up, drunk, in the middle of the night. "I always knew you were a fucking asshole," he said without bothering to identify himself.

"Jeez," said Griffin, who at three in the morning was watching an old movie. By this time he wasn't living with Tommy anymore but rather in his own tiny efficiency apartment. Most nights he didn't even pull the bed out of the sofa. "Always? I wish you'd said something."

"You better hope I never see you again," the caller continued, music and barroom laughter in the background.

Griffin knew it had to be either Jared or Jason, but which? "Oh, I do, Jason," he said, taking a flier.

"It's not Jason, it's Jared."

"Yeah, but same deal."

The other man was quiet for a minute. "What did my sister ever do to you? Why are you treating her like this?"

"Listen, Jared—"

"Because you don't fucking deserve her."

"I agree."

"Yeah, well . . . you just better hope I never see you again," he repeated. Griffin's ready concurrence had apparently thrown him off track, and he was now trying to get back on as best he could.

"Where are you these days? Just so I know where not to go."

"I'm stationed in Honolulu."

"Okay, then. That's easy enough."

"I got a leave coming up, though. How about I fly to L.A. and kick your ass?"

"I'm going to hang up now, Jared."

"You're probably thinking I don't know where you live, but I can find out. Don't think I can't."

"I live on Bellwood Terrace. The Caprice. Apartment E-217."

"I have my ways."

"Good night, Jared."

He hadn't heard from either twin since, but was happy to hear they'd agreed to a truce during the wedding.

"I told them if they didn't chill, they couldn't come, and they both promised," Joy went on. "I just hope you can tell them apart when you see them, because it pisses them both off when people get it wrong. Especially now that Jason's out of the service and has some hair."

"I'll try to remember."

"There'll be lots of kids. Try not to look like you hate them."

Yes, by all means, his mother chimed in, startling him. *Pretend. Shut up, Mom.*

"And you know about the ceremony, right? That there's a minister? Nothing in your face, but God will be invoked."

"Which?"

The Protestant one. The god of gated communities and domino theories. Jesus. With a J, like the rest of them.

Best to ignore her, Griffin decided. Telling her to shut up had never worked in life, either. "You don't have to worry about me, Joy. I'll behave."

"I know you will," she said. "I just . . ."

"What?"

"Well, I guess I wish we could've found a way to . . ."

"Keep it together one more year?"

"But we didn't, did we?"

"My fault, not yours."

She looked off into the distance, her eyes filling, then gathered herself. "There's one question I have to ask."

"Shoot."

She took his hand lightly. "Are you going to be able to write these checks? Tonight and tomorrow?"

"I said I would." Though in truth he was a little worried. He'd taken twenty-five K out of his retirement, hoping that would do the trick and trying not to panic as the guest list grew. Last week he'd taken out another ten just to be sure.

"You also said you weren't working."

What he'd actually said was that writing assignments had been few and far between since he and Tommy had been fired off the cable picture, and of course there was his mother. After the first heart attack, he'd returned to Indiana several times, trying to make his visits coincide with her major transitions—from the hospital to a rehab facility, then back home with hospice volunteers and, finally, to the hospice wing of the hospital and full nursing care.

In January he'd picked up a couple of film-school classes, adjunct status, so the pay was for shit, but it was something. He had a new agent, Tommy's, but all she'd come up with was a quickie dialogue rewrite. This he'd done on his own. Since he'd moved out of Tommy's place, they'd seen little of each other. They occasionally met for a drink, but Tommy always made some excuse to call it an early night. Griffin knew his old friend was at a loss to understand why Griffin didn't just tuck his tail between his legs and go home and beg Joy's forgiveness, as husbands in his circumstance invariably did, if they had any brains. "You *want* to end up alone?" he asked one night. "Is that it?" No, it wasn't, but Griffin was hard-pressed to articulate what it was, exactly.

"I just don't want any embarrassment for Laura," Joy was saying. "I can help if—"

"No, I should be fine," he told her. "Mom actually left some money." Though this wasn't true, either, really. Her insurance had just about covered the hospital and nursing-home expenses, the cost of cremation. He'd sold a few of her books and given the rest away. Her laptop and printer and a few pieces of furniture had netted a couple grand. His father had left the world in about the same financial condition. Not much to show for a life, he couldn't help thinking, though Thoreau would have been pleased. Simplicity, simplicity, simplicity.

"Were you able to get Dad's ashes from my office?"

"Yes, but can we do that later?"

"Of course."

Laura was waiting for them in the hotel foyer, her eyes full,

Andy at her side. The expression on the young man's face was frank puzzlement, and Griffin couldn't imagine why until it dawned on him that halfway across the parking lot, without realizing it, he'd taken Joy's hand.

"*Daddy*," his daughter said, choking on the word, and Griffin was glad he could think of nothing to say because he was incapable of the slightest utterance.

"I don't have a doubt in the world about that boy," Laura assured him as they entered the maze.

She and Andy had just parted as if it would be an eternity before they saw each other again, and she now turned to wave goodbye one last time before her fiancé and her mother disappeared from sight. His daughter's idea that the two of them go for a stroll in the maze seemed to surprise neither Joy nor Andy, and that made Griffin apprehensive. Had they all thought further about Griffin's presence at the wedding and decided against it? Did Laura plan to explain this to him among the tall yews, far from witnesses, in case he objected or broke down in tears? But of course he knew better than that, so he took a deep breath and told himself to relax. Laura's need for a private, father-daughter moment wasn't about him or the myriad ways he'd failed her and her mother since Kelsey's wedding. She was just a bride, and fatherly reassurance was part of the program. Enjoy it. Who knew how long it would be before his presence was deemed necessary again?

"Andy's terrific, darlin'," he said, putting his arm around her shoulder and feeling a wave of gratitude when she allowed herself to be drawn toward him. "It's hard to imagine anyone more smitten, except for your old man, of course." He meant this to elicit a smile, but it seemed to make his daughter even more thoughtful, and for a time they were quiet, turning first left, then right, then left again among the hedges, until he was good and lost.

"I guess the one I worry about is me," she finally said. "What if I end up hurting him?"

"Why would you do that?" he said, feeling another wave of guilt. Would his daughter have harbored such self-doubt this time last year, or was it his doing?

A park bench had been thoughtfully placed near what Griffin guessed must be the far end, and here they took a seat. It was darker in the maze, very little of the remaining daylight penetrating its black branches, and Griffin was visited by a childish, irrational fear that they wouldn't be able to find their way out. Laura would miss her wedding and that, too, would be his doing. He took her hand, unsure whether he meant to dispense comfort or receive it.

"Do you ever feel like you're not who people think you are?" she said. "Like you're pretending to be this person that people like? And the worst part is they all believe you?"

"Only every day," he admitted. "Unless I'm mistaken, that feeling's what people mean by original sin. Only sociopaths are spared. Trouble is, if you take it to heart you'll never do anything, never pursue any happiness, for fear of hurting people."

"I should ignore it?"

"Everybody else does."

She seemed only partially convinced. "I've been thinking a lot about Grandma lately," she said.

That surprised him, and he paused before responding, half expecting his mother, who was, after all, right over the hedge, in easy shouting distance, to offer her own two cents' worth. Perhaps the maze had confounded her. "Any idea why?"

She shrugged. "Seeing her like that last December, I guess. All the tubes and the oxygen. She looked so tiny and all wasted away."

How well he remembered. It had been December when she visited, just a couple weeks from the end. By then, mentally and emotionally exhausted, Griffin had checked into an extended-stay motel near the hospital. The doctors had warned him that patients like his mother sometimes lived on for months after being put on morphine, but it seemed to him that his mother was dying as she'd lived, on the academic calendar. He doubted she'd begin another semester.

The day of Laura's unexpected visit had been a particularly difficult one. Several times during the night his mother had been awakened by nurses taking her vitals and talking noisily in the corridor outside her room. As a result she'd been irritable all morning, convinced she'd not been given her morphine, though both the duty nurse and her chart testified otherwise. At midday Griffin had gone back to his motel to shower and eat something. When he returned, he discovered that his mother had a visitor, her first, not counting himself. A woman was sitting on the edge of the narrow bed, her back to the doorway, holding his mother's hand. Joy, he thought, and felt some ice dam in his heart break apart at the possibility. Back in November she'd called him in L.A. to say she had to fly to Sacramento the following week. She could stop in Indiana going or coming back if he needed her to. He'd wanted desperately to say yes, but he heard himself say no, he had things under control. When he asked if everything was okay in California, she said yes, that it was just some family stuff she had to attend to. And not his family anymore, was her clear implication, which he had to admit he had coming.

His first thought was she'd decided to come anyway, but of course this couldn't be Joy. His mother never would have allowed her daughter-in-law to hold her hand. "Look who's here," she said. Only when Laura turned to face him did Griffin recognize her. "Would you mind absenting yourself from felicity awhile?" his mother said after he and his daughter had embraced. "My granddaughter has come a long way to see me, and she can only stay an hour."

"It's okay, Daddy," Laura told him when he tried to object.

"Yes, do run along," his mother said triumphantly, pleased, he could tell, both by his reluctance and the fact that he would have prevented this visit if he could've.

They'd had very little contact when Laura was a child. His mother had visited a couple months after Laura was born, "to help out," but when Joy handed her the baby, she'd grasped her as gingerly as you would something unclean. Laura had regarded her grandmother with interest, smiled, then projected a stream of sour yellow milk onto her. Quickly handing the baby back to Joy, his mother had spent the next fifteen minutes at the sink, scrubbing her blouse with a dishcloth. She'd planned to stay for a week, but after two days, during which she never changed a single diaper, she made a flimsy excuse and flew back to Indiana. "Who changed *your* diapers, I wonder?" Joy said, finding the whole episode amusing, whereas Griffin had been homicidal.

The two thousand miles separating them had been an adequate buffer during Laura's childhood, but even after they moved to Connecticut, things didn't change much. Only when Laura was a junior in high school and thinking about where to apply to college did her grandmother begin to show much interest. She thought Laura should go to Yale, of course, and turned up her nose at the small liberal arts colleges her granddaughter was most keen on, the same ones where she and Griffin's father had once hoped to secure jobs. "Safety schools" was how she now regarded them. "Dear God, not Williams," she told Laura. "Do you know the kind of people who send their progeny to Williams? Rich. Privileged. White. Republican. Or, even worse, people who aspire to all that." Not so unlike your other grandparents, she meant. "Their kids aren't smart enough to get into an Ivy but have to go somewhere, so God created Williams." Griffin couldn't imagine why, but Laura actually seemed to enjoy talking about all this with her grandmother (who called it brainstorming), and sometimes their phone conversations went on for forty-five minutes or an hour. It probably served him right that these all took place behind the closed door of his daughter's bedroom. "Your grandmother has a lot of opinions," Griffin told her. "That doesn't mean they should carry much weight." What he was doing, of course, was fishing, curious as to just how many and which opinions she was sharing with his daughter. "Oh, I don't know," Laura had responded noncommittally. "She has some good ideas." But she didn't say what they were.

Joy warned him not to press the issue. Laura was old and smart enough to sift ideas, and his mother needn't be treated like a venomous snake. He'd reluctantly given in, but when his mother suggested she be the one to accompany Laura on the Yale-Columbia-Cornell swing of what they all referred to as the Great American College Tour, he put his foot down. "I'm sorry, Mom," he said, managing, with great effort, not to raise his voice, but failing to keep the anger out of it, "but you don't get to infect my daughter with your snobbery and bitterness. All that ends here, with me."

It had been a horrible thing to say, full of the very bitterness he was accusing her of. He regretted the words as soon as they were spoken, but there was no taking them back, nor could he quite bring himself to apologize.

"You have to call her back," Joy said when he confessed what he'd done.

But he hadn't. Nor did he soften and allow her to take Laura on that trip, managing it all by himself. They never referred to the matter again, but he knew his mother too well to imagine she'd forgotten. She no doubt saw her granddaughter's hospital visit as a kind of revenge, or so it had seemed to him, banished to the nurses' lounge, where he willed the big clock on the wall to move, damn it. At the end of the hour, Laura seemed fine, and he felt relieved that nothing too terrible had transpired, but as soon as they were in the car Laura broke down and sobbed all the way to the airport. Though it probably shouldn't have, the intensity of her grief had surprised Griffin. No doubt she was coming to terms with the likelihood that she'd never see her grandmother again, but there seemed to be more to it, as if she was also mourning that someone who should've been important to her had remained a stranger. And whose fault was that? His mother's, for being completely disinterested until so late in the game? It was tempting to lay the full blame on her, but deep down Griffin knew that if she'd shown interest in Laura any earlier, he would have just stepped between them that much sooner. He'd behaved as if she were a serpent because, God help him, he believed her to be one.

"I thought she'd want to know all about the man I was going to marry," Laura told him now, her eyes filling at the memory of that hour in the hospital, indeed their last visit, "but when I tried to tell her about him . . ."

Griffin waited, but when his daughter seemed unable to continue, he completed her thought. "She wasn't very curious?"

"I don't know," she admitted, wiping her eyes on her wrist. "When I talk about Andy, all my friends say their gag reflex kicks in. They say we're nauseatingly in love."

"Happiness sucks as a spectator sport, darlin'."

"I guess. Anyway, after I told Grandma a few things about Andy, she interrupted, saying, 'You need to get tougher.' When I asked her why, she said marriage is combat. Somebody hurts, somebody gets hurt. One does, the other gets done to."

"You know she was on morphine, right?"

"It wasn't so much what she said that got under my skin. It was the funny way she was looking at me, like she could see deep down and knew I had it in me to be cruel. That if somebody had to get hurt, it'd be Andy, not me."

"Sweetie, you say she was looking at you, looking *into* you, but I doubt it. Your grandmother was a narcissist, and they don't really look outward. To them the world just reflects their own inner reality. She saw love as a trap. Therefore, you should, too."

She sat up straight now. "All I know is I don't ever want to break his heart."

"You won't."

"Promise?"

"Absolutely."

Had he been writing this scene in a script, the conversation wouldn't have ended there. His fictional daughter would have asked the obvious questions. How could he possibly promise that she wouldn't do the very thing he was doing? Wasn't she his daughter? But it wasn't a script, and his real-life daughter was too kind to say what she was thinking, maybe even too kind to think it.

"What I've been wondering is whether you'll ever forgive me."

"Oh, I already have," she said, shouldering him hard but playfully, then getting to her feet. Apparently the father-daughter segment of the program was drawing to a close. "I'm still pretty mad at you, though," she admitted.

"I know," he said, rising as well. "Me too."

When they emerged from the maze, she said, "Grandma told me one other thing, actually. About you."

"What's that?" he asked, though he wasn't sure he wanted to know.

"She said you'd never admit it, but you're just like her."

Damn right you are, his mother said, agreeing with herself.

Everyone did seem to be on their best behavior, just as Joy had promised. He'd no sooner gotten himself a glass of wine than Jared—at least he was pretty sure it was Jared, given the shaved skull—came over and extended his hand, which Griffin saw no reason not to take. Whichever brother he was shaking hands with looked like what he was, a career marine: lantern jawed, thick necked, improbably muscled. "So," he said, pumping Griffin's hand in his crushing grip, "no hard feelings?"

Jared, then. Note to self: Jared, skull; Jason, hair. Griffin said no, there were no hard feelings.

The twins were a family enigma, born nearly a decade after Joy (Jane and June were older, the girls all spaced in two-year intervals) and completely different in temperament. As boys they'd worried Harve and Jill by fighting constantly and ferociously, neither ever seeking parental redress or justice. They fought until they bled, then fought some more. But suddenly all of that was over. Instead of wanting to kill each other, they had each other's backs. With the leftover energy they took to bodybuilding and making gentle, sometimes not so gentle, fun of their father, first behind his back, later to his face. Neither had married. Now in their forties, they still liked heavy-metal music, strip clubs and the kind of women one met there.

"Two sides to every story, I guess," Jared said, a worm squiggling under the skin of one temple, evidence how costly, for him, such magnanimity actually was. "Push comes to shove, I have to side with my sister, but . . ."

"I'm kind of on her side myself," Griffin told him, because it was true, but also because it seemed like a good idea to suggest to Jared that pushing really needn't come to shoving. Or punching, or stomping, or castration. All of which had apparently been on the table at one point. Brother Jason (not hair so much as stubble, really) was watching them from across the room, Griffin noticed, his expression, well, *murderous* was probably too strong a word. "I hear your brother left the service," Griffin ventured, genuinely curious that either twin should do something so brazenly individualistic.

Jared snorted, glancing over his shoulder at his brother and raising his voice enough to be sure he could hear him. "Yeah, well, Jason always was a pussy."

"We'll see, J.J.," his brother called back. This was short for Jared the Jarhead, the nickname he'd immediately picked up when he joined the marines. As if there weren't enough *J*'s in the family already. "You wait."

Joy's father was indeed in a wheelchair along the far wall. A tall, angular woman who Griffin assumed must be Dot stood sentry at his elbow, and when he approached, she bent at the waist to whisper, like a handler to a pol, in Harve's ear. To remind him who Griffin was? That he and Joy had separated?

"What?" Harve barked at her, and then, when she repeated whatever she'd told him, said, "Hell, I know who it is." He extended a feeble, palsied hand, and Griffin felt an unexpected surge of pity. His father-in-law had always been a robust man, but no more. His pale blue eyes were watery, their lids outlined in bright red, as if with a cosmetic pencil.

"Jack," he said, "are you keeping your head down?"

"Look up and all you'll see is a bad shot," Griffin replied. "It's good to see you, Harve."

The man nodded. "You know my wife died?"

"Yes," said Griffin. He'd attended Jill's funeral, of course, and thought about reminding Harve of this but decided not to. "Yes."

"He knows," said Dot, unhelpfully.

"Hell of a thing," Harve said, unwilling to let go of the subject. "I hope you never have to go through it."

"Me too," Griffin said, realizing that despite Joy's warning he'd given him far too much cognitive credit. If he knew about their separation, he'd clearly forgotten. Either that or someone had informed him that Griffin was bringing a guest to the wedding, and it was this woman he was hoping wouldn't die on him.

"Hope you never have to walk into a room and find your wife in a heap on the floor."

"Harvey," Dot said, "you're going to upset yourself."

"Because that's no fun, let me tell you," he went on, ignoring her completely. "No replacing a woman like that."

Dot sighed and looked off into the middle distance. She'd clearly heard this sentiment expressed many times before.

"You probably didn't know, but she was writing a pistolary when she died."

Griffin glanced at Dot, who rolled her eyes. "A Western?" Griffin asked.

"No, a pistolary. You don't know what that is?"

He confessed he didn't.

"Well, she was writing one of those," he said. "Your Joy's a lot like her mother."

Ah, Griffin thought, Joy was still his. At least as far as her demented father was concerned.

"All three girls take after their mother, of course, but Joy's the most like Jilly. Always was."

"And Laura's like her mother," Griffin added, hoping he might take comfort in further feminine continuity.

But Harve just blinked at this, clearly unsure who this Laura might be.

"Laura's the bride," Dot informed him under her breath. "We're here for her wedding."

"Well of course we are," Harve said. "You think I don't know my own granddaughter?" Then, to Griffin, "She thinks I forget things, but I don't. Like you. I remember perfectly well you could never keep your damn head down. You still don't, I bet."

"You're right, Harve, I still look up."

Harve nodded sadly, as if to admit that human beings were frail creatures indeed. Impossible to teach most of them the rudiments of anything, much less a complex activity like golf. "You look up," he said, looking up, his watery blue eyes fixing on Griffin, "all you'll ever see is a bad shot."

Then he looked away again, and Griffin could tell he was following the errant shot's trajectory in his mind as it sliced off into the dark woods, out of sight, where he could hear it thocking among the trees.

"I know this really isn't the time or place," said Brian Fynch, dean of admissions and Joy's boss. The rehearsal dinner was over, and people had been encouraged to reconfigure over dessert. Griffin had been seated with Andy's family, a smaller group, all of whom seemed a bit cowed by the size and sheer decibel level of Joy's family (Jane and June were both shriekers). For his part, Griffin had been grateful to be seated with them.

Fynch was a tall man, and his suit was well tailored and expensive looking. He seemed comfortable in it, as men who wear suits every day often are. His haircut was early Beatles, sweeping bangs at the eyebrow line, ridiculous, Griffin couldn't help thinking, for someone his age, a few years younger than Joy, and Griffin immediately dubbed him "Ringo." Joy had introduced him as her "friend" (the very word Laura had used on the phone when she told him her mother would also be bringing someone to the wedding). "Jack" was how he himself had been introduced to Fynch, as in *Jack, of whom you've often heard me speak and weep and curse.* He chided himself: *But come on, Griffin, get a grip.* Joy had probably said nothing of the sort. *In fact, be grateful.* She'd have been well within her rights to introduce him as her soon-to-be ex, which would have been worse. He didn't realize he'd been half hoping she'd introduce him as her husband (which he still *was,* after all) until she didn't.

At any rate, he and this "friend" had been chatting amiably for the last ten minutes. Ringo claimed they'd actually been introduced last spring ("No reason for you to remember") when he came on board. *Came on board?* his mother snorted. *What is he, a pirate?* (Silent when he and Laura were in the maze and also during dinner, she was feeling gabby again and seemed to have even less use for Brian Fynch than her son did. Normally her opinion wouldn't have mattered, but she did know her academics.) Ringo loved the college, he went on, as if someone had been spreading vicious rumors to the contrary, and he hoped it would be the last stop on what he termed his "long academic journey." *Long and pointless, perhaps, but hardly academic.* It was a wonderful opportunity, really, the kind that came along once in a lifetime. His "team" in admissions was first-rate, though its star, "just between us," was Joy. (*Oh, you smarmy bastard*, both son and mother concluded in the same instant.) In fact, Ringo wished he had a half dozen more just like her. This fairly ambiguous remark he delivered with such convincing innocence that Griffin wondered if maybe he and Joy *were* just friends. He'd been attentive and solicitous to her all evening, but there was certainly nothing to suggest any intimacy between them, though of course she wouldn't have permitted such a display at her daughter's wedding.

"I wouldn't bring it up, believe me, but Dean Zabian heard I was going to be seeing you this weekend, and I promised I'd ask if your situation for the coming academic year had clarified itself."

It was possible, Griffin supposed, that things had come about just as Fynch claimed. The dean of faculty might well have asked him to inquire. But the far more likely scenario was that Fynch was a sly meddler, an insinuator who'd sought out the dean, not vice versa. Zabian could be forgiven for growing impatient for Griffin to make up his mind, but he more likely would have asked this favor of Joy rather than Ringo. And of course if he *really* wanted to know, the person to ask was Griffin himself.

"Of course everyone's hoping you'll be returning in the fall," Fynch was saying, "but if you can't—"

"I understand," Griffin said. "Tell Carroll I won't hang him up much longer."

"It's not like your replacement's a washout or anything," Fynch continued, oblivious that he'd been given full permission to discontinue this particular conversation. "The department could probably limp along for another semester or two, but as Dean Zabian put it, 'She's no Jack Griffin in the classroom.'"

Griffin smiled, now certain that he (and his mother) were right about Ringo's character. The implied omniscience, the overfamiliarity, the flattery . . . what a putz. He thought of the elderly woman he'd spoken to in Truro this time last year who'd been looking for the right occasion to use *fart-hammer*. Well, here it was.

With relief, he noticed that a young man wearing a blazer with the hotel's insignia on the pocket was conferring with Joy, who turned to point him out. "If you'll excuse me," he said, making a show of taking out his checkbook. At this Ringo turned on his heel and fled, apparently convinced he could provide no further service.

"Mr. Griffin?" said the young man, who appeared to be holding an invoice. "Maybe we should go someplace more private?"

He nodded agreeably and let the checkbook slide back into his jacket pocket. "What are we going to do?"

Turning bright purple, the fellow looked even younger and, Griffin realized too late, clearly gay.

By the time he'd settled up and returned to the private dining room, the mostly teenaged waitstaff was busy clearing away the last of the dessert dishes and tossing stained tablecloths into portable hampers with more energy and enthusiasm than they'd exhibited earlier in the evening. They probably had a party to go to, Griffin supposed. Hard to believe that Laura herself was past all that now, the anticipation of a young night and its many possibilities. The rehearsal guests had all gone out onto the porch, below which, on the lawn, a drunken game of volleyball was under way, with just enough light from the porch to play by. Andy's family, many of whom had traveled a long way that day, had evidently decided to call it a night, so it was just Joy's that remained.

Harve, looking tired and agitated, sat at the far end of the porch, near the top of the long, sloping wheelchair ramp. He'd nodded off during the later stages of the dinner, though he refused to admit it, even after snorting violently awake, which caused Jared and Jason to reenact the event for the edification of the children at the designated kids' table, after which they were all snorting awake and falling out of their chairs. The old man was now struggling to get up out of his chair, apparently determined not to be wheeled down the ramp past the volleyballers. Griffin sympathized, though Dot apparently didn't. With an assist from Joy's sister Jane, she pushed him back into his seat and told him, unless Griffin was mistaken, to behave. Whatever Harve said back caused her to spin on her heel and head indoors in the general direction of the ladies' restroom, leaving Jane to reason with her father.

Joy was at the far end of the porch, talking to her other sister, June, and June's husband, but Griffin could tell she was monitoring the situation. According to Laura, the whole family—Harve and Dot, her mother, Jane and June and their families, Jason and Jared—was sharing the large cottage at the water's edge apart from the main hotel. Its dark outline was visible against the night sky, its windows glowing warmly yellow. No doubt it would remind Joy of the house they'd rented when she was a girl. Jane and June had probably remembered to bring board games, and after Harve and the smaller children were put to bed, the rest of them would stay up late playing Monopoly and Clue, swapping all the old nostalgic family stories. Griffin, who'd heard these too many times, nevertheless felt a twinge of regret (admit it) at being suddenly outside the family circle. Would Ringo, ridiculous oaf that he was, be invited to the table tonight and given Griffin's Professor Plum game piece, his silver thimble? He'd made a point of telling Griffin that he was staying in the hotel proper, but that might just be for appearances. He now joined Joy and her sister and brother-in-law, and when Griffin saw him rest his hand lightly on the small of her back, it occurred to him that having just discharged his primary responsibility of the evening, he could slip away unnoticed and probably not be missed.

Why didn't he want to? He was standing in the porch doorway trying to figure that out when his mother said, *You know who you remind me of, don't you?* Which Griffin took to be a rhetorical question. *I thought you told Laura I was just like you,* he fired back, and the shot must have landed, because she shut up. Off to the right he noticed a small alcove from which he could see, without being observed himself, both the porch and the game on the lawn below. A coffee urn had been set up on a sideboard, and that, he decided, was probably a good idea before he drove back up the peninsula. He poured himself a cup and closed the door, lest someone notice him and decide he needed company.

With the exception of pregnant Kelsey, the whole wedding party, as well as some of the teenaged guests, had been recruited to play volleyball. The little kids wanted to play, too, and were running around with their arms up, though the game was taking place well above them. Laura and Andy were on the back line, and when they stopped to kiss, the ball landed right at their feet, causing their teammates to groan. Jared and Jason had positioned themselves on opposite sides of the net and were shoving each other back whenever one of them violated the neutral zone. "Coming right down your throat, J.J.," Jason warned, and when the ball came over the net he spiked it hard, clearly aiming at his brother, but the shot careened away and narrowly missed Kelsey, who was watching, one hand under her belly, from what she'd wrongly imagined was a safe distance.

"Hey, hey, easy! Watch out for the little ones!" June called from the porch, and was promptly ignored.

I hope you aren't going to tell me you enjoy these people, his mother said. He'd been hoping she'd been shut out when he closed the door behind him, but no such luck. *You forget how well I know you,* she continued. *Pretend otherwise all you want, but you've always wanted to be done of these people, and now you are. This sentimental mood you're in doesn't become you.*

I'm ignoring you, Mom, he told her, focusing his attention on a small boy who was acting out below. Furious at being ignored, he'd sat down right in the middle of the court, his lower lip sticking out, his face a thundercloud.

A little monster, that one, his mother observed.

No, Mom, he's a child, Griffin said, though she might be right.

Andy, apparently fearing the boy might get trampled, picked him up and set him on his shoulders and, when the ball came over the net, managed to position himself so the kid could hit it. The ball went directly into the net, but his face was aglow with importance, and he raised his arms in triumph, as he'd clearly seen some athlete do on TV, and was given a round of applause.

You don't like children, you don't like volleyball and you don't suffer fools gladly.

Maybe you don't know me as well as you think, Mom.

Fine. Be that way.

Let's talk about something else, shall we?

We can discuss whatever you like. The weather, if you prefer. Remember how it snowed that last two weeks?

Did he ever. Giant drifts of powder banked two-thirds of the way up the hospital window. Laura's flight out had been one of the last before the airport closed, and it hadn't reopened until Christmas Eve. Twice Griffin had to walk a good mile from the hospital to his motel, the roads impassable, his car plowed in.

In the days following Laura's surprise visit, his mother became increasingly agitated. The morphine calmed her breathing, but something was clearly troubling her that had to do with her granddaughter, Griffin suspected, though he had no idea what. "She's so . . . ," she began several times, her thought always trailing off, as if she were trying to articulate something just beyond her grasp. The oxygen made her mouth dry, so Griffin gave her some ice chips to suck on, thinking that might help, but they didn't. "She's so . . ."

"She's so what, Mom?"

She fell asleep, still struggling, and Griffin drifted off as well, awaking to the sound of her voice.

"She's so . . . *kind*, isn't she?"

Kind? *That* was the word she'd been straining to locate? It was as if the concept were fabulously exotic, one she'd read about but hadn't personally encountered until now. Either that or she'd done a quick genetic scan, looking for and not finding a familial antecedent.

"Yes," he said, feeling his throat constrict with pride. "She is that."

"She makes me almost"—she was struggling again now, and Griffin guessed that another unfamiliar concept was groping blindly toward articulation—"ashamed."

The next day, however, she was more herself. "She's not brilliant, though, is she?" she said, staring off into space. They'd been sitting quietly for the last hour, each in private thought. "I doubt she'll go back to school."

"Actually, she's smart as hell," Griffin told her, instantly angry. "More important, she's *happy*, Mom. She's going to marry someone she loves and who loves her."

"Happy," she repeated, catching his eyes and locking in. "Only very stupid people are happy."

A few short hours, Griffin remembered thinking. That's all it had taken for her to reflect upon kindness in general and her granddaughter's in particular, then to discard it as a cardinal virtue.

They didn't discuss Laura after that, but he continued to feel the ghostly residue of her visit, and unless he was mistaken, his mother did, too. Her decline seemed more rapid now, though over the long days that followed she rallied several more times, much as the doctors had predicted. The peaks weren't nearly so high, however, and the valleys were lower. The morphine necessary for her breathing, in ever larger doses, made things weird, then weirder. Each time a dose was administered, her breathing became less labored and she was calmer, but not, somehow, any more at peace.

"She's battling something," one of the nurses remarked. "That's not unusual at this stage. We may never know what it's about."

When she let him, he read to her or they watched television listlessly until the morphine took her under. He'd brought "The Summer of the Brownings" with him from L.A., and he worked on it while she slept. Something about his mother's frail condition, together with the small, rhythmic sounds of the hospital room, made the story accessible in a way it hadn't been the summer before on the Cape. At one point, though, his mother had awakened unexpectedly and asked what he was working on so intently. "Oh, them," she sniffed when he told her, clearly disappointed by his choice of subject matter. Thinking it might please her, he said she'd been helpful. "You told me last June that it was asthma the little Browning girl suffered from, and about Peter eventually dying in Vietnam." But she claimed to have no memory of the conversation. "How would I know what happened to those people?" she said when pressed. He couldn't figure out what to make of it. His mother's usual MO was to feign knowledge she didn't have, not to confess ignorance.

As Christmas bore down on them, his exhaustion, fueled by sleepless nights and cafeteria food, began to take its toll, and Griffin felt his tenuous grip on reality begin to fray, as if he, too, were being dosed with morphine. He found himself sleeping when she did, dreaming fitfully, the Browning story in his lap. More than once he awoke with his mother's eyes on him, an enigmatic smile playing on her lips. "You aren't the only one with a story to tell, you know," she said one afternoon.

"I'm sure that's true," he replied. He had exactly no desire to be the beneficiary of any morphine-fueled revelations, and the nurses had warned him to try to steer clear of upsetting topics. He hoped she'd let the subject drop, but a few minutes later, she said, "I bet you didn't know your father and I were lovers right to the end."

That, as it turned out, was the opening salvo, a warning shot across his bow, the beginning of what over the next few days he'd come to think of as his mother's Morphine Narrative. Chronically short of breath now, she delivered it the only way she could, in short installments, like an old Saturday matinee serial. After each segment she closed her eyes and slept, or pretended to, leaving him to digest and puzzle over what she'd told him.

The real reason Claudia had abandoned his father, his mother now explained, was that she'd discovered they were still sexually involved. She'd visited him off and on that whole period, telling Bartleby—who was easy to lie to, since he preferred not knowing anyway—that she was attending conferences. She claimed Griffin himself had nearly found them out when he visited his father in Amherst. She'd meant to leave well before he arrived, but her car, parked in plain sight in the driveway, wouldn't start. The engine had turned over just in the nick of time. They'd actually driven past each other on his father's street, but he'd been off in his own world and hadn't noticed her. The first installment had ended here, and when Griffin asked why she was telling him these things at such great cost, she said, "So you'll know. You think you know all about your father and me, but you don't."

"Why is that so important?" he asked, but she just smiled, her eyes drooping toward sleep. Did she mean to imply that he was wasting his time writing about the Brownings when instead he could've been writing about them? That a writer with real imagination wouldn't have been "off in his own world" when he could have been off in theirs?

The sex, she told him with a sly smile (of invention or memory?), was better than it had ever been when they were married. Cheating *with* rather than *on* each other had added another whole layer of excitement. Later, after his father and Claudia returned to the university, they'd just kept on. In the end the fat cow had given his father an ultimatum—herself or his ex-wife—never dreaming what his choice would be (that sly smile broadening now).

Each time she dozed, Griffin was certain she'd either forget the story she was telling him or, upon awakening, not have the strength to continue, but he was wrong. The tale seemed to satisfy some need as fundamental as breathing. "Let her tell it," the nurse advised.

"But it's not even true. She's exhausting herself spinning a ridiculous yarn that neither one of us believes. It's complete bullshit."

Which got him a stern look. "Not to her. Your mother was a professor, right? She's professing. She'll stop when she's ready, or when she can't go on."

Whenever she resumed the story, he felt his heart plunge, thinking, *Here we go again,* but gradually, as the snow outside drifted higher and higher up the hospital window, he became intrigued and eventually fascinated by the tale that struggled to be born even as its teller slipped away.

At some point one of Bartleby's grown children had tumbled to what was going on between them, which explained why, when their father died, the siblings were united in their determination that she not inherit a farthing, the little shits. Not that she really cared. Bartleby never had anything she really wanted (yet another sly smile here, to let Griffin know she wasn't just talking about worldly goods). She even claimed she'd continued to visit his father, though less frequently, at his subsequent academic postings. Indeed, they'd remained lovers for as long as he was physically able, and they hadn't entirely broken off the relationship even then.

Could *any* of this be true? Griffin couldn't decide. The story didn't really track, or rather it tracked for a while, then jumped the tracks, then somehow climbed back on again. In an attempt to reconcile them, he made a mental point-by-point comparison of the Morphine Narrative and the earlier one. At least one detail of the morphine version was factually untrue. Griffin had never visited his father in Amherst, so either his mother was confused in her recollection of who'd almost caught them when her car wouldn't start (Claudia, returning from Charleston?) or she'd invented the entire episode. The problem was there were relatively few flagrant discrepancies, and resolving the ones there were wasn't terribly helpful. The skeleton of the two tales was pretty much the same, so it came down to plausibility, to each story's interior logic.

Griffin hated to admit it, but in one respect the Morphine Narrative was marginally more credible. In the original, when his mother informed him, with great satisfaction, about his father's disastrous year at Amherst, he—the veteran of a thousand sets of studio notes—had objected there was no way she could know everything she claimed to. His father was in one place and she in another, and even with a vast network of academic spies, the story she was pitching would have been, of necessity, a patchwork quilt of secondhand testimony. What his father had been thinking as he first outlined Claudia's dissertation, and later as he composed an introduction and, finally, throwing caution to the wind, wrote the whole thing, was something only he could testify to, and he certainly wouldn't have told her. But if there was any truth to the Morphine Narrative, then of course his mother had *been* there in Amherst, an off-and-on eyewitness. If they really were lovers, the story *wasn't* secondhand but rather based on her own observations, however sporadic. His intimate revelations to her during this period therefore made a kind of sense. But if she'd been a regular visitor, his father couldn't have been lonely; and if he wasn't lonely, then missing Claudia hadn't unhinged him; and if he wasn't unhinged, why had he written her dissertation? *Had* he, in fact, written it?

In almost all respects, though, his mother's original saga was far more credible. Its general thrust—*Look how far your father has fallen without me to look after him*—was completely in character. It wasn't just how *she* would feel, but indeed any woman similarly horse-traded. Its logic was consistent, and the visual evidence corroborated it. Griffin hadn't visited him during his year at Amherst, but he'd seen him shortly after his return and vividly recalled his physical and emotional state, his health ruined, his nervous system shattered. Emaciated, ill, exhausted, he'd *looked* like a desperately lonely man who'd come unglued. That's what his mother's gleeful account had prepared Griffin to see, granted, but still. If he credited the Morphine Narrative and his parents had instead been having the best sex of their lives, then his haggard, distraught appearance afterward was due to what, carpal fatigue? And if he and Griffin's mother were still passionately involved, why would he have surrendered a cushy full professorship for crappier jobs? And why keep such a secret from his son?

But that, of course, was the whole point of the latter version. *You never knew us. You thought you did, but how wrong you were. Our lives were a glorious secret, even from you.* And this was also the problem in a nutshell. The most compelling thing about the Morphine Narrative was his mother's need to tell it. At a stage of life when most people wanted to unburden themselves, why had she so desperately needed to lie? With so little time left, why use your last ounce of strength to invent such an elaborate falsehood? What difference could it possibly make to her what he thought about their marriage? No, the whole thing was nonsense, and the clincher was this: if the Morphine Narrative was true, in whole or part, then why, before falling ill, had his mother been so adamant that his father's ashes be scattered on one side of the Cape, her own on the other? If their lives were intertwined right to the end, wouldn't she want their ashes to commingle?

Still, the nearer she got to the end—of her Morphine Narrative, of her life—the more he found himself wanting the story to be true, or if not true at least not completely false, not completely morphine. He kept hoping for a load-bearing detail strong enough to support the weight of its creaky structure, to fortify the too-often-chimerical motives of its characters. If she'd told him, for instance, that she'd been with his father when he died at that rest stop on the Mass Pike, that they'd decided to make one last trip to the Cape together, maybe hoping to find a little bungalow there, he'd have believed her, and not just because he'd never told her the details of how his father had been discovered in the passenger seat, never shared his suspicion that a woman had been with him. Okay, there'd still have been cause for doubt (if his mother was the mystery driver, why had she run off?), but also reason, at least a writer's reason, to believe. Because in its own way that ending would have been perfect, symmetrical, implied in its beginning. A love story.

Perhaps the oddest thing of all was how satisfied his mother had been when she finally finished telling it. Whatever urgency had driven the story evaporated when she finally let her voice fall. She no longer seemed to care whether he believed her or not, and shortly thereafter she'd lapsed into virtual silence for the three days that remained to her. "When is Christmas?" she wondered at one point, and he had to think. He'd been measuring time by her narration and by the snow, which by then had nearly covered the window, darkening the room in the middle of the day.

"The day after tomorrow," he told her.

"You'll be going home then," she said.

"No, I'll be spending Christmas here," he told her. "Did you really think I meant to leave you alone?"

"How," she asked, matter-of-factly, "does having you sit there day after day make me any less alone?"

He then *did* think about leaving, going home, and he might have if he'd known where home was, but he didn't, not anymore, and so he'd stayed. On Christmas morning she asked if he remembered how as a boy he liked to crawl under the tree and look up at the lights. And later that afternoon she said, "So . . . your marriage is ruined," and he said yes, he supposed it was. After that, he remembered her saying only one other thing. "He'd be here," she assured him, smiling, "if he wasn't dead."

Unlike so many of her smiles, this one was neither sly nor lewd. Beatific was more like it. And for that reason he said, "I know, Mom. I know."

She was right about one thing: the fucking kid was a monster.

Tired of trying to play volleyball with a kid on his shoulders, Andy returned him to his oblivious mother, but the little brat was having none of that. He clearly enjoyed being the center of attention and liked the applause even more, so he followed Andy right back onto the court, his arms raised, demanding to be restored to Andy's shoulders. By this time all the other kids had been coaxed away by parents who were calling it a night. Several of the little ones had fallen asleep, and others were rubbing their eyes.

Seeing the kid had followed him back into the fray, Andy took him by the wrist and tried to pull him gently back to the sideline, but no dice. Wrenching his hand free, the little bastard balled it into a fist and punched the groom in the groin.

Witnessing this, his mother, instead of marching onto the court and removing the brat by force, went down on one knee and entreated him. "Come on now, Justin, come to Mommy. Can't you see you're holding up the game? And you *hurt* that nice boy. Come on now, sweetie." But Justin had other thoughts. His original strategy had worked before, and he saw no reason why it shouldn't again. Ignoring his mother, he plopped down on the court and stuck out his lower lip.

Five bucks says she gives up, Griffin's mother said, which was precisely what the woman did, returning to her conversation. *Tell me you wouldn't like to blister his little behind.*

I'm going home now, Mom, he told her. *Why don't you stay here, since you're enjoying yourself so much.*

The game resumed, rather tentatively now, the players trying as best they could to navigate around the pouting boy. Andy was taking deep breaths and leaning on his bride, who seemed to be inquiring, given these new developments, what their prospects now were for a successful prewedding night. By the time Griffin emerged onto the porch, parents were calling their teenagers off the court, and the game began to break up. His sulk pointless now, the brat got to his feet and ran crying toward his mother. Griffin saw what was going to happen next before it did. Stationary, the kid had been relatively safe, in full view of the players in the back line, as well as those dancing around the net. But now the ball was in the air, and the kid wasn't where he was supposed to be. Jason, no doubt hoping for one last hard spike at his brother, lunged a step to his right and leapt, his knee catching the boy under the chin and snapping his head back. The next instant the kid lay flat on his back, motionless, and before Griffin could prevent her from weighing in, his mother said, *Good.* Or possibly, face it, the sentiment so succinctly expressed was his own.

Jane and June let out simultaneous, identical yelps, and everyone on the porch hurried down onto the lawn, where a circle formed around the fallen child, his mouth now open and working like a fish's, though no sound came out. Griffin, alone on the porch and ashamed of himself (or his mother), caught a quick glimpse of the little shit's bloody face. Finally able to catch his breath, he began to wail, and his mother, gathering him to her ample bosom, joined in. "Oh, poor sweetie! Poor, *poor* sweetie! What happened? Did the big people play too rough?"

Jason looked like he might object to this characterization, but being responsible for the kid's injuries, he decided on a different tactic. "He's all right, aren't you, sport," he said, tousling his hair. "He's a tough guy." Whereupon the brat broke free of his mother's grasp and tried to punch Jason where he'd punched Andy. This time, though, he was trying to punch a marine, whose crack training allowed him to deftly parry assaults from even the most malicious seven-year-olds. But the kid's intent couldn't have been clearer, the groining strategy apparently his default mode.

"Justin!" his mother barked, taking him by the shoulders and spinning him around to face her. "What did Mommy say about hitting people there? Didn't she tell you it's *not nice*?" Whereupon he punched her in the same place.

It had been Griffin's intention to say a quick goodbye to Joy and Laura, but they were now at the center of the commotion on the lawn, and he decided against it. The entrance to the wheelchair ramp was close at hand, and with everyone distracted he'd be able to slip away unnoticed, using the yew hedge for cover all the way to the parking lot. Even as he planned this, something tugged at his short-term memory like a continuity problem in a movie (hadn't the main character's shirt been unbuttoned in the previous frame?), though only when he started down the incline and saw the splintered railing right where the ramp made a ninety-degree turn did he realize what it was: that just a few moments ago an impatient Harve had been sitting here.

When Griffin got close, he could hear him groaning. The railing was rotten—he could see that much—and had snapped on impact. Due to the severe slope of the lawn, the porch was at this point a good ten feet above it, the top of the hedge a couple feet below. The yew was still quivering when he peered over the side. "Harve?" Griffin said. "You okay?"

The voice that answered sounded more like a child's than a grown man's. "Won't . . . *go*," it said.

It wasn't difficult to piece together what must have happened. His father-in-law, abandoned by his daughter when the brat got clobbered, and too impatient to wait for assistance, had tried to navigate the ramp on his own and lost control of his chair. He was now planted headfirst in the hedge, his chair on top of him, its wheels up and still spinning. Actually, no, that last part couldn't be right. The wheels were turning, all right, but that was because Harve, invisible beneath the chair but apparently still in the saddle, was pushing on them like mad, trying to power himself out of this predicament, apparently unaware that he was capsized in the yew's branches, suspended eight feet in the air.

Griffin kneeled, leaned over and reached down as far as he could; the nearest spinning wheel was just beyond his fingertips. From somewhere behind and above there came a shriek, and he didn't have to turn to know that Dot had returned, no doubt expecting to find her husband where she'd left him. For a woman her age, she had a hell of a set of pipes on her. "*Nooo!*" she wailed. "Is he *deaaad*?"

"Harve," he told his father-in-law, "stop spinning the damn wheels." Poised as precariously as he was—a large man, with the additional weight of the chair on top of him—he easily could snap one of the branches, Griffin feared, and impale himself on it.

"*Won't . . . go, goddammit*," the unseen Harve grunted, still fully committed to his impossible exit strategy.

Now, in addition to Dot's wailing, Griffin heard the thunder of feet pounding up the porch steps and then down the narrow ramp. "*Daddy!*" screamed a frantic voice that he first identified as Joy's, then realized, no, it must be one of her sisters'.

He reluctantly rose to his feet. The chair, alas, was out of his reach, and it probably wasn't a great idea to grab on to the wheels anyway. The thing to do—he should've realized this from the start—was to extract him from below. But the urge to peer over the side into the palsied hedge was irresistible, as the crowd now gathered at the busted railing attested.

Jared was among the first to arrive and immediately dropped to his knees and leaned forward to grab hold, though the chair was just beyond his reach as well.

"That's not going to work," Griffin said, placing a hand on his brother-in-law's shoulder. "Maybe you and Jason and I can pull him out from below."

For a moment Jared appeared to consider this suggestion. But then, getting to his feet, he seemed to really take in who'd just spoken to him, and his expression instantly morphed from thoughtfulness to rage. That would have been perplexing enough, even if Jason hadn't been standing right next to him with the same identical fucking look on his face.

Honestly, Griffin's mother said. *Would you* look *at these two morons?*

It was as if they could hear her.

"You son of a bitch," Jared said, that worm wriggling again beneath his temple, and before Griffin could object, a fist (Jared's or Jason's?), foreshortened, suddenly caught him flush on the cheekbone, and he felt himself lift off the ramp, his body describing a parabola in the air above the hedge. He could sense the ground coming up to meet him, but before it did he heard, or thought he heard, a loud splintering sound and a chorus of screams. *What the . . . ?* he managed to think, but that was as far as he got.

Say good night, his mother advised, just as the screen went black.

10

Pistolary

The splintering sound Griffin heard as he went airborne was the wheelchair ramp collapsing under the weight of fifty well-fed celebrants. Those closest to the broken railing went into the yew, several landing on top of Harve and driving him deeper into its dark interior, where he bellowed piteously. When Joy fell, the middle finger of her right hand got caught in the spokes of her father's chair, the digit snapping like a twig. She should have been among the first to be rushed to the emergency room—most of the other injuries were only cuts and abrasions—but she refused to leave with her father still trapped in the hedge. The remaining guests gathered in a semicircle to watch Jason and Jared try to shake him loose. The hedge was far too thick, however, and its branches seemed naturally designed to funnel human victims straight down into its dark, dense center. Though they were slow to realize it, the twins' efforts actually made matters worse by snapping some of the interior branches that were supporting their father, their fresh, sharp ends probing his soft flesh and making him howl in pain until he grew hoarse and then, finally, silent. The hotel manager urged patience while they looked for the head groundskeeper, who apparently had the only key to the locked shed where the chain saw was kept.

For a time nobody noticed Griffin, who lay unconscious beneath the hedge, with only his feet sticking out, or else they concluded he was conversing with Harve in the yew above. He came to in stages, as if from a long, luxurious nap, his senses returning one at a time, beginning with smell. He lay on his back, on soil that smelled richly of fertilizer, recently applied. His eyes were open, but there was nothing to see. Wait, that wasn't quite true. What he was looking at, when he squinted, resembled a pen-and-ink drawing, except that its intricate lines wouldn't stay still and were encased, at the edges, in dense fog. Wellfleet, he thought. Somehow he'd been transported back to the fog capital of the world, where no doubt he'd be expected to scatter his father's ashes and this time do it right. But he didn't have the ashes, Joy did, and had promised to give them back, though here he was in Wellfleet without them. Then, finally, there was a sound track, played through a crackling, blown speaker, nearby voices, lots of them, all talking and shouting at once. Why couldn't he see who they belonged to? He was trying to sort out these complexities when he felt someone grab him by the ankles and pull him back into the world.

And what a world! For the next ten minutes he stood (swayed, actually) by himself, trying to make sense of it by going over in his mind what he believed to be true, allowing what he hoped were hard facts to surface, like gaseous bubbles through mud, into his wobbly consciousness. He wasn't in Wellfleet, he was in Maine. He'd come here with a woman not his wife to attend his daughter's wedding. To this same wedding his wife had also come, accompanied by a man who was not Griffin. His left eye was swollen tightly shut as a result of his being sucker punched (why?) by one of his brothers-in-law (which?). His father-in-law had, like a character in a fairy tale, got trapped in a tree. Highly improbable—all of it— and yet evidently true. It wasn't someone's opinion; no alternative theory had been advanced. He would have liked to talk it over with someone, but even his mother seemed to have abandoned him.

But hold on, he'd spoken to somebody after being yanked from under the hedge, hadn't he? Who, though? And what had they talked about? It couldn't have happened more than five minutes ago, but the memory was gone. He thought about joining the others over at the hedge where Harve was still imprisoned. Joy and Laura were over there, but so were Andy and Ringo, which made him super . . . what was the word? Unnecessary. The twins were there, too, and if he joined them without invitation, they might punch him again. He doubted this would actually happen, but couldn't be sure. He still didn't understand why they punched him the first time, and whatever their reason, it might still pertain. Super . . . ?

Gradually, the dense Wellfleet fog in his brain began to lift, and then he noticed a woman sitting all by herself on a bench facing the ocean. Her scowl, together with how defiantly her arms were crossed over her chest, suggested that neither the hedge nor the crowd fixated on it was of the slightest interest to her. Griffin was aware he should know who this woman was, so he concentrated on her identity until it finally revealed itself. She was Dot, Harve's second wife. Pleased with himself for recognizing her and anxious to test the coherence of his speech, he decided to join her. When he sat down, though, she said, "Go away," without even glancing in his direction to see who it was.

Having only just arrived and feeling woozy from his journey, he was unwilling to depart quite yet, not until he'd discovered what she was doing all by herself, glowering at the unoffending ocean, when her husband had just been swallowed by a tree. An idea occurred to him that might explain it, so he said, "They can be tough . . ." He meant to go on but didn't, his voice sounding remote in the echo chamber of his head.

She did turn to regard him now, her eyes narrowing. She

seemed to be trying to decide if his sympathy was something she wanted, or if her misery was company enough. "*That*," she said, pointing at his eye with her index finger, its tip sculpted to a frighteningly lethal point, "is what I feel like when I'm around those people. Like I'm being . . . pummeled. Bludgeoned. Battered. Cudgeled."

That seemed to Griffin a tad overstated, but he knew what she meant, and having just struggled to construct a four-word sentence fragment, he envied her ability to summon so many impressive, violent synonyms. Clearly nobody'd punched *her* lights out recently. Together they swiveled on the bench to afford themselves a better view of what was transpiring at the hedge. People seemed to be taking turns talking to it. Had the bush been burning, the whole thing would have been biblical.

"All he ever talks about is that woman," Dot said, as if she were able to see Harve at the center of the yew. "I want to scream, '*She's dead, she's dead, she's dead.*'" When she said this, the volume in Griffin's head went down, back up, back down again, a wire loose somewhere.

"They were married a long time," he ventured, benignly, he thought.

But she turned quickly and glared at him. "Then why marry *me*?" she demanded.

For the life of him Griffin couldn't think of a reason for Harve or anyone else to marry her, and she must have seen this register on his face, because she was suddenly standing over him with her fists clenched. Good Lord, he thought, was she going to punch him, too? He barely knew her. "Superfluous," he said, the word he'd needed earlier suddenly coming to him.

"Why don't you just . . ."

When she paused, Griffin's mind raced ahead, supplying the words *fuck off,* though of course women in their late sixties didn't say that.

". . . fuck off," she concluded, and strode away in the general direction of the parking lot.

He watched her go, then glanced at the spot where she'd been sitting, trying to decide if the woman had really been there, if the conversation had actually taken place. A couple minutes later his daughter, looking exhausted and despondent, sank down next to him on the bench and rested her head on his shoulder. Which was nice. "Where's Andy?" he said, hoping that wherever he was he'd stay there for a while.

"He's gone to get the car," she told him, or at least that's what he thought she said. She was sitting right next to him, but he could barely hear her. "You ready to go?"

"Where?"

She lifted her head to regard him. "The hospital?"

"Shouldn't we wait until they extra . . . extratake . . ."

"Extricate?"

". . . Harve from the hedge?"

"Dad," she said, her mother's sternness creeping into her voice, "we've already had this conversation."

"When?"

"Ten minutes ago. You were supposed to wait for me by the tree."

He was?

"Look at me," she said, taking him by the chin. The sensation wasn't nearly as pleasurable as having her rest her head on his shoulder. "Your eyes are dilated. Did you land on your head?"

He had no memory of landing at all, but the last thing he wanted was for her to be worried about him. "I'm fine," he assured her. "People need to quit punching me and telling me to fuck off, but otherwise . . ." Unable to complete the sentence, he considered the word count impressive, nonetheless.

Behind them a chain saw roared to life, and its sheer volume reconnected something in Griffin's cranial circuitry. The world's many varied sounds were again playing at their normal volume. Also, the earlier conversation with his daughter, the one in which he'd promised to wait by the tree, was suddenly there in its entirety. It was she and Andy who'd pulled him from beneath the hedge, he now recalled.

"I must be allergic to yew," Laura said, scratching at her fore-arms.

"To me?"

She stopped scratching and looked at him.

"Oh. *Yew*. Gotcha." Now that he looked at them, her arms were grotesquely swollen.

"You're definitely coming to the hospital," she said. "You're concussed."

"They'll have Benadryl," he assured her, still a beat behind but catching up fast.

"Yeah, right," she said with a sweeping gesture that took in the whole resort. "Benadryl's going to make all this fine."

"Hey, it could've been worse," he said.

She waited patiently for him to explain how, which took a minute. Then another. Among the crowd at the hedge was a preg-nant young woman. He knew her, just not her name. Then sud-denly that was there, too. "Kelsey could have fallen in with the others," he said, pleased with himself for saying something that might, if closely examined, actually be valid. "The shock could've sent her into labor."

"You know, I never thought of that," his daughter said in a golly-gee voice. "*Or* a disgruntled hotel employee could've laced our dinners with arsenic, in which case we'd all be dead instead of just hideously maimed."

"Sorry," he said. "I was trying to cheer you up."

Staring at her Popeye forearms, he finally realized she was weeping.

"Dad," she said, "tomorrow's my wedding day, and I'm going to be ugly."

Over at the hedge, the chain saw sputtered and died. Taking advantage of the silence, he quietly said, "No, you're going to be beautiful. Everything's going to be fine."

Andy pulled up then, and they climbed in, Laura next to her fiancé, Griffin into the back. The car was identical to his rental, right down to the color and features. It even had a copy of the same literary magazine on the dash. He patted his pants pocket, but felt no keys. Unless that was them dangling in the ignition. "So this is my car?" he asked, and they both turned around to stare at him.

"Yes, Dad. This is your car. You gave Andy the keys. You're scaring me."

Before driving off, they were treated to one last bizarre sight: Jared and Jason, shaking what remained of the mutilated hedge like madmen, until finally it surrendered from its dark center an elderly man in a wheelchair. Out Harve tumbled, somehow landing wheels down on the lawn, to wild cheers.

"He's out," Andy said, taking his bride's hand. "See? Everything's going to be fine."

And she smiled, believing him, Griffin could tell. He'd just told her the same thing, but of course he was no longer the person from whom his daughter needed such reassurances. Which meant there was nothing to do but relax in the backseat, which was where you put people you don't have to listen to, even when it's *their* car.

The tiny regional hospital was really more of a clinic, and its usually sleepy, preseason emergency room had been overwhelmed by the first wave of injured wedding guests, not all of whom had been seen to by the time Laura, Andy and Griffin arrived, moments ahead of the ambulance bearing Joy and her father, which in turn was closely followed by a small flotilla of cars. Harve, finally pried loose from his chair, was wheeled in on a gurney. Griffin caught a glimpse of him as he rolled by, surrounded by EMTs. His cheeks were a grid of angry scratches, and a nasty-looking abrasion ran from his neck down his shoulder. Otherwise, he looked to be in reasonably good condition. He'd been wearing a baseball cap, and its bill had protected his eyes. Jane and June, on opposite sides of the gurney, having reluctantly given their father over to the professionals, now provided narration as they sped past the front desk: "See, Daddy? We're at the hospital already. Look at all the nurses. You *like* nurses, remember? They'll fix *all* your scratches . . ."

Harve was able to sum up his circumstance in a single, hoarse croak. "Hurt," he said.

Curious to see how bad his own injuries were, Griffin located a men's room off the main corridor. What he saw in the wall-length mirror shocked him. His swollen eye looked hideous, as if the eyeball had been removed from its socket, a tennis ball inserted in its place and the skin stretched over it and sewn shut. There was also a trail of dried blood beneath his left nostril, a deep scratch on his forehead and bits of hedge in his hair. Dear God, was he really going to walk his daughter down the aisle tomorrow looking like this? Would sunglasses, assuming he could find a pair, even fit over something that size? He could feel other urgent questions forming in his still-addled brain, but before he was able to resolve any of them the door to the men's room swung open and one of the twins walked in. The stubbled one. Which was . . .

Unzipping, whichever twin it was stepped in front of the single wall urinal. "Okay," he said, studying Griffin in the mirror, his urine hitting the porcelain with enough force to make Griffin envious. "Settle an argument. Jared says our family's fucked up. I say no."

Griffin, making a mental note that unless he was speaking of himself in the third person this was Jason, pointed to his grotesque, swollen eye.

"You shouldn't have called us morons," he said.

"I didn't." Hadn't his mother offered that observation, in the privacy of his own brain?

"We both heard you. We were standing right there."

"Huh," Griffin said, reluctantly entertaining the possibility that a dead woman had, albeit briefly, taken control of his larynx.

"Also, we thought you'd pushed our father into the hedge."

"Why would I do that, Jason?" Griffin said.

"You've never liked any of us," he said, as if stating a well-known fact. "Plus you were the only one who *could* have done it. Standing just where he'd been with that shit-eating grin on your face. Same one you've got now."

Griffin turned to examine his face in the mirror. What he saw there was a grimace, not a grin. A well-earned grimace, come to that.

"Like you were enjoying the whole thing," Jason continued. "Jared thought the same thing."

"Jason," Griffin said, "you and your brother arriving at the same conclusion isn't really a test of its validity. Seek some genetic variety would be my advice." Griffin half expected this observation to provoke further hostility, but it didn't.

"It's true," the other man chuckled. "We sort of share a brain, don't we? Always did. No reason to call us morons, though." Finished, he gave it a shake, zipped up and came over to the sink.

Griffin stepped aside so Jason could wash his hands. His forearms were striped with angry yew scratches, but they weren't swollen like Laura's. "I apologize if I called you a moron."

"What do you mean *if*?"

"And I wasn't enjoying it," he told him, to set the record straight.

"I'm just saying it's how you looked. Call it a misunderstanding, I guess. Anyway, nobody died, and tomorrow's a new day," he said, vigorously washing his hands of the old one and yanking a paper towel from the dispenser. "You think this *wedding's* fucked up, you should try Iraq."

"Yeah, sure, but New England weddings aren't supposed to invite that kind of comparison," Griffin said, pleased that he was again capable of making such subtle distinctions, more or less effortlessly.

"I'm only saying," Jason shrugged, tossing his wadded-up towel into the bin. He apparently saw no need to elaborate further on what, exactly, he was only saying.

"Tell your brother all families are fucked up," Griffin said. "It's not an argument either of you can win."

"That's truly warped," Jason said. "You know how you end up if you go through life thinking like that?"

"No, how?"

"You end up like you. One working eye, with twigs and shit in your hair."

Griffin couldn't help smiling, though it literally hurt to.

"I'm sorry I punched you, though," Jason admitted thoughtfully. "I've been thinking about it, and I realize now it probably wasn't just because you called me a name and pushed Pop into the hedge. The way I'm figuring it, subconsciously?" Here he pointed at his forehead, perhaps to suggest where such delicate, refined "figuring" took place. "Subconsciously, I was still pissed at you for being such a prick to my sister. You think that's possible?"

Griffin did, consciously.

At the nurses' station he was told his wife was in examination room 2B, where he was treated to an unexpected sight: Brian Fynch, glassy-eyed, being wheeled out of the room on a gurney. On his forehead, a knot the size of an egg pushed up through his Ringo bangs. Griffin was pretty sure he hadn't been one of those hurt when the ramp collapsed, so . . . what? He'd been injured at the *hospital*?

Inside the room, Joy, dressed for some reason in a pale blue Johnnie, was seated on the examination table, looking shell-shocked. "What happened to . . ." He'd been about to say *Ringo*, but caught himself.

His wife sighed deeply. "I warned him not to keep looking at it." She showed him her finger, which lay at an almost anatomically impossible angle. "But I guess he couldn't help it. He got really pale, and then . . ." She pointed at the wall, specifically at an indentation in the plaster that looked to be about the same size as a college dean's forehead. Griffin had to look away lest she observe one of those vintage shit-eating grins Jason had accused him of wearing earlier. When he finally turned back, though, he saw that Joy herself was smiling. A grudging, guilty smile, but still definitely a smile. "You know the wet sound a ripe cantaloupe makes when you drop it on the kitchen floor? That's what he sounded like."

"Jesus," Griffin said, feeling genuine sympathy for the man. His wife's finger was a truly gruesome sight, enough to make a squeamish man light-headed, and he was, like his father before him, a squeamish man.

"Don't you faint, too," she said, slipping the hand under her Johnnie.

Back in the men's room, after washing his face, Griffin had congratulated himself that the abstraction and confusion he'd felt after being pulled from under the hedge had mostly dissipated, but now, studying his wife, he wasn't so sure. "I guess my question would be, why did you have to get undressed for them to set your finger?" Also, how in the world had she *gotten* undressed with her finger bent back like that?

"We discovered something else." She pulled the Johnnie forward, exposing her left side and part of her breast, beneath which there was a three-inch gash. It hadn't bled much, but it looked deep. "I'm going to need stitches."

Okay, it had been a bizarre day, Griffin thought, with its mazes and man-eating hedges and collapsing wheelchair ramps and dead ventriloquist parents, but *this* had to be the strangest thing yet. Think about it. He'd spent most of his adult life with this woman. He'd forfeited the right to admire her body, though it was even now—admit it—capable of stirring lust. How perfectly, ludicrously insane not to be able to take this same woman in his arms and at least try to comfort her, comfort them both. Why shouldn't he? What possible reason could there be? Well, he could think of a couple. For one, another woman was waiting patiently for him back at the B and B. Maybe he wasn't in love with her, but he did feel— okay, admit this too—great fondness, which meant he should not be drawing his Johnnie-clad wife into his not entirely innocent embrace. And there was knot-headed Ringo, who would appreciate neither the comfort he meant to provide Joy with nor its accompanying erection.

"You might as well tell me what you think of him," Joy said, as though she'd read his thought. Something in her tone suggested she had her own misgivings about the man, reservations his fainting had confirmed.

Griffin shrugged. "He seems amiable enough," he said. "Bit of a booster, maybe."

"That's his job," Joy said, and he knew immediately he'd said the exact wrong thing. "He sells the college. It helps to have an upbeat personality."

"Nice change of pace, too," he added, sounding more bitter than he meant to, more the "congenitally unhappy" man she'd accused him of being last summer.

"It has been, actually."

Feeling the wind go out of his sails and his earlier wooziness return, Griffin slumped into a folding chair. "I know it's crazy," he said, "but I can't shake the feeling that all this is my fault." Meaning, he supposed, not just his behavior on the Cape last summer and their subsequent separation but also tonight's fiasco, most of which—the rotten railing; Harve's injuries, whatever they turned out to be; Joy's broken finger; the grade-A jumbo egg on Ringo's noggin; his daughter's swollen Popeye forearms—no reasonable person could have held him responsible for. Nor did it stop there. Whatever happened from this point forward would be his fault as well. When a big string of dominoes falls, you don't blame the ones in the middle.

From somewhere down the hall Harve, who'd apparently gotten his voice back, bellowed "No!" and a moment later, "No, goddammit!" as if he'd somehow been privy to his son-in-law's confession and felt compelled, like a Greek chorus, to register strenuous objection. Griffin found himself smiling weakly, grateful for even the appearance of someone being on his side.

"In fact, it's not that crazy," Joy said.

"You think?" he said, genuinely surprised. He'd been willing, as an exercise in self-pity, to take full responsibility for the evening's events, but he certainly hadn't expected his wife to agree with him.

"Where's Dot?" Harve shouted. "Where is she?"

"*Our* fault, I meant," his wife clarified. "It wasn't just you."

"Well," he said, "I guess it doesn't do much good to say I'm sorry, but I am. And . . ." He paused, not sure he could say the next part, though simple justice demanded it be said.

"And?"

"And if this Brian Fynch makes you happy—"

"No!" Harve bellowed again, refusing to countenance any such suggestion. "I want Dot, damn it!"

Dot damn it?

Griffin looked over at Joy and saw that she, too, was on the verge of cracking up, and his heart leapt in recognition of the old mischievousness he'd so loved about her back when they were first married, all but extinguished now so many long years later. Could he himself be the one who'd put it out?

"Either of you seen Dot?" said a voice, startling both of them. Jared's shaved head was framed in the doorway.

They told him they hadn't.

"He wants Dot, damn it!" he said, his mimicry spot-on, as always. "So what's this about, then?" Meaning, presumably, their being so intimately sequestered.

"Nothing," they said in unison.

He nodded, registering their denial, but continued to study them curiously, his mouth open one notch on its hinge. It occurred to Griffin that as a military cop he had to ask people all sorts of questions—*How much have you had to drink tonight? You the one that gave this young lady the shiner?*—and this was the look he gave people he suspected weren't being entirely candid in their responses. "Jason," he called over his shoulder, and then there were two heads framed in the doorway, or rather the same head twice, the second stubbled. "They say there's nothin' going on in here. This look like nothin' to you?"

Jason didn't answer immediately, his jaw dropping that same single notch. "No."

"Jared." Joy sighed. "Jason."

"It definitely looks like *some*thing," Jason said, squinting, as if to bring the two of them into clearer focus.

"Yeah, but what?"

"Don't know," Jason said finally. "Don't care. You guys seen Dot?"

"They haven't," Jared answered for them.

"He wants Dot, damn it."

"They know that."

"Then let's go find the bitch."

When the doorway was empty, Joy let her chin fall to her chest.

"Does it make any sense that this whole year, whenever I've been with my family, *that's* when I've missed you?"

"Not really," he admitted. Why would she miss his snarky, all-too-predictable comments about her loved ones?

"Brian actually thinks they're all terrific," she told him, and for the life of him Griffin couldn't tell whether this mitigated in the other man's favor or not. "Last December," she continued, "that's when I missed you most."

He tried hard to hear in this statement his wife's undying affection but had to suspect she was trying to express something very different, maybe even the opposite. She was talking about when she'd *needed* him most. When he should have been there and wasn't. "Back then you mentioned there was some family stuff going on."

She nodded, looking down at her lap as if she could see her broken finger through the Johnnie. "It was horrible. Dot found them."

Griffin waited for her to continue, not at all sure she would.

"She was helping Daddy go through some of Mom's things. Getting annoyed with him because he didn't want to get rid of anything. Anyway, there was a locked box."

"Which she opened."

"It held a bundle of letters." She met Griffin's eyes now, her own spilling over.

"An affair?"

She nodded.

"And she showed the letters to Harve."

"He called me up wanting to know what they meant." She paused to wipe her eyes. "I told him they didn't mean anything."

"Good for you."

"But he knew, Jack. He didn't want to, but oh, God, he was sobbing. My father. The whole time I was growing up, I never saw him cry. He kept saying 'Jilly-Billy,' over and over. 'Jilly-Billy.' And it made me so . . . angry. I wanted to yell at him to stop, please, please *stop* calling her by that stupid, stupid name. There was my father, calling me up in the middle of the night, brokenhearted, wanting to cry on my shoulder, and all I wanted to do was to scream at him, to tell him whatever Mom did was his fault for being so . . . for being such a . . ." She stopped, unable to continue, until finally she said, "I was glad. Glad she found somebody."

"And you had an urge to tell him."

She shook her head, trying to rid it of the memory. "What kind of person . . ."

"Joy. Stop. It was a perfectly natural reaction."

"You'll never guess who saved the day. June. Princess Grace of Morocco. She told him Mom was writing an epistolary novel. That the letters were part of that. Her pistolary book, he calls it."

"Ah," Griffin said, now understanding the reference. "He mentioned it, actually."

"You always said we were messed up. All of us."

"Not you," he corrected, but she wasn't really listening.

"And now look. We've come together here and totaled our daughter's wedding. The part *we* hadn't already totaled."

"It's not totaled," he told her.

"What would you call it—a fender bender?"

"Tomorrow will be fine."

He said this with as much conviction as he could muster, but of course a more convincing argument to the contrary was his grotesque appearance, which she now seemed to be taking in for the first time. "You know what I'm doing?" she said. "I'm imagining the wedding pictures."

"I've looked better? Is that what you're saying?"

"You look like you're about to drop."

"I am," he admitted, his limbs suddenly deadweight, his head impossibly heavy on his neck. But he didn't want this conversation, this time, to end, not just yet.

"Are you going to get that eye looked at?"

"No, I just need some sleep. That and a handful of I-be-hurtin's." Their joke term for ibuprofen. It had slipped out naturally, unconsciously, like taking her hand earlier in the evening.

When he rose to leave, Joy said, "I guess I'm trying to say I owe you an apology."

"What on earth for?"

"Your mother," she said. "I never should've let you do that alone. I told myself it was the way you wanted it, that it was just you going back into that room of yours, the one where I've never been allowed, and closing the door behind you. I told myself I'd come if you asked, but not until. That was wrong. And, just so you know, you aren't the only one your daughter's mad at."

"I'll speak to her."

"There's no need. She loves us both. I think she tried not to for a while, but it didn't work."

"She's her mother's daughter."

"Before you go," she said, handing him her purse, "open that, will you?" When he did, she fished around with her good hand until she located her keys. "Your father's urn is on the backseat. Just leave the keys in the cup holder."

Griffin took them.

When he reached the door, she said, "You wanted to know if Brian makes me happy?"

He wasn't sure he did, but nodded anyway.

She started to say something, then stopped, and when she finally spoke he had the distinct impression it wasn't what she'd started to say. "He doesn't make me *un*happy."

"Well," he said, his heart sinking, "that's something, I guess."

Did she call after him as the door swung shut? He paused in the corridor but heard no further sound from inside the room. In fact, in that instant the whole world was still.

Down the hall Laura and Andy came out of another examination room and told him they didn't want him driving anywhere, but he said he was fine, just exhausted, and offered to take them back to the Hedges, but Laura said they'd wait for her mother. Outside, he took the urn from Joy's SUV and left the keys in the cup holder as instructed. After popping the trunk of his rental car, he paused, half expecting his mother to object, but it had been a long day and apparently even ghosts slept, so he slipped his father's urn into the wheel well opposite hers. Then he got into the car, rolled the window down and just sat there. The magazine with "The Summer of the Brownings" was still on the dashboard. The evening hadn't provided the right moment to give it to Joy, and he doubted tomorrow would either. He could leave it in her SUV, he supposed, but then decided not to. He was suddenly just too tired to walk back across the hospital lot.

The night air was rich with the sea, and he breathed it in deeply, thinking how good it would feel to fall asleep right here. Again it occurred to him how different Maine was from the Cape. What would've happened if he and Joy had honeymooned here, as she'd wanted to, instead of Truro? Would they have drawn up a different accord? He was nodding off when he heard shouts coming from the direction of the hospital. *Lord,* he thought, *what now?* But it was just the idiot twins, Jared and Jason, expanding the search for their stepmother. In the voice of the man they still imagined to be their father, they shouted in marine unison, "Dot! Where are you, dot damn it!"

By the time he got back to the B and B, the clock on the nightstand said 12:07. He undressed in the dark, as quietly as possible, and slipped between the sheets in stages so as not to wake the woman who now shared his bed. They'd been together for several months, but it still felt strange—and never more so than tonight—to be with a woman who wasn't Joy. When she stirred he expected her to ask how things had gone at the rehearsal, if she'd missed anything good, but she didn't and her breathing quickly became regular again. A minute later he was asleep himself.

Then he was wide awake again and listening, for what he wasn't sure. According to the clock it was just after one. The window closest to the bed had been cracked open a couple inches, and in the unnaturally still Maine night he heard the thunk of a car trunk below. Someone stealing his urns was his first, lunatic thought.

Struggling out of bed, he padded barefoot over to the window and saw a taxi idling in the circular drive. Its driver pulled a suitcase from the trunk and handed it to his fare, a well-dressed young man who gave him some money. Apparently surprised by his generosity, the driver said, "Hey, thanks, pal," and when the young man turned toward the inn, Griffin smiled, realizing it was Sunny Kim who'd just arrived.

There was stirring behind him now. "Jack? Is everything okay?" Her husky voice was low and intimate in the dark.

Yes, he told her. Everything was fine.

"Good," said Marguerite.

Plumb Some

The night of his daughter's wedding Griffin had a particularly vivid (no doubt alcohol- and anxiety-induced) dream in which he was driving over the Sagamore Bridge in a pouring rain that made the surface slick and treacherous. The bridge went on forever, and his was the only vehicle on it. Harve, for some reason, was in the backseat, instructing him. *You're never too old to learn to drive,* he was saying, in the same tone of voice he used when telling Griffin how to play golf. *You just have to keep both hands on the wheel and both eyes on the road.*

Griffin explained that he already knew how to drive, but Harve paid no attention.

It's not complicated, he went on. *Just the two things to remember: hands on the wheel, eyes on the road. Hell, I taught my three daughters to drive, then both my sons. If those two can learn, so can you.*

Harve, Griffin said, *listen to me. I already—*

Car! his father-in-law shouted, pointing in alarm, and Griffin hit the brake. Immediately the car's rear end lost traction and came around, which meant, according to the dream's curious logic, that he was now facing Harve, who was sitting in the backseat and saying, *Both hands on the wheel*. Griffin braced for impact against one of the bridge's stone buttresses, but when it came, it was surprisingly gentle, like a boat nosing into a dock.

I just wanted to test your reflexes, Harve explained. *Without good reflexes you're just an accident waiting to happen*.

When Griffin got out to inspect the damage, he saw that the trunk had popped open and both his parents' urns had ruptured. The trunk was full of their mingled ash, about a hundred urns' worth, it looked like, and the rain was turning it all to mud.

Now you've done it, said Harve, who'd materialized at his elbow. *How you going to figure out who's who?*

Rather than contemplate the problem, Griffin woke up.

It was raining out, less hard than in his dream but definitely coming down. The soft dream-collision had been occasioned in the real world by Marguerite getting out of bed. Not quite ready to face a new day, he closed his eyes and pretended to be asleep. Marguerite adored weddings and after yesterday's she would be, he feared, in one of her best and brightest moods, and he wasn't sure he could confront either it or her just yet. He sensed her standing there, observing him, probably suspicious, but eventually he heard the bathroom door open and close, and when the shower rumbled on moments later he realized he'd been holding his breath.

"Well, *I* think it was a lovely wedding," she told him fifteen minutes later, her first words of the day, as if he'd expressed a contrarian view in his sleep. She was toweling off unself-consciously at the foot of the bed. It was amazing, really, how different she was from Joy, how confident and secure she was in her own naked, glistening skin. Even fully dressed, she always managed to convey that she was patiently waiting for someone to suggest a skinny-dip. Maybe her body wasn't what it once was, but she remained confident there were men around who desired it and probably would be for quite some time. "Are you going to shower," she said, "or did you have something else in mind?" That was the other thing. Marguerite loved sex, as fervently as you loved something you'd been denied when you were young and which you were now making up for.

"Shower," he said, because they had a long drive ahead of them and a task at the end of it—the scattering, finally, of his parents' ashes—that was unpleasant enough to have wormed its way into his dreams. "How about tonight?"

She was right, though, Griffin thought as he stepped under the burst of hot water. The wedding had been lovely—and, like all events that involved months of intricate planning, over surprisingly quickly. It had gone off without further melodrama, a well-earned blessing, all agreed, after the catastrophic rehearsal. Despite the scratches on her forearms, Laura had been, just as he'd promised her, a heartbreakingly beautiful bride. Drawing on some reserve of optimism that hadn't been there the night before, she'd given herself over fully to richly deserved joy. Only once, just minutes before the ceremony was to commence, did she allow herself to express any fear. The bridesmaids and groomsmen were lining up at the end of the corridor for the procession, and she and Griffin were cloistered in a small anteroom. He'd told her how lovely she was and how proud he and Joy were of her, and she'd told him he looked very L.A. (he'd found a pair of very dark glasses to cover his still-hideous but not-quite-so-swollen left eye). But when Pachelbel's Canon leaked into the room, she took a deep breath, looped her arm through his and said, "I don't want you and Mom to get old."

It was, of course, her familiar fear—that he and her mother would divorce—now mutated. Either that or, after yesterday, Harve and the various humiliations of old age were on her mind.

After much discussion her grandfather, battered but unbowed, had been allowed to attend the wedding. His doctors were understandably reluctant. Harve's physical injuries were relatively minor, but the trauma he'd suffered in the hedge wasn't insignificant, especially for someone his age. At the hospital he'd exhibited signs of confusion and agitation, though the former, according to his children, was normal and the latter occasioned by the possibility he wouldn't get his way. The physicians finally gave in, on the condition that someone would attend him at all times.

That someone was the redoubtable Dot (damn it!), who'd finally been located down in Portland, where she'd checked into an airport motel with every intention of catching the first flight back to California in the morning. But the family, one sibling after another, had pleaded for her return, and then finally Harve himself got on the phone and told her that she was indispensable to the day's proceedings, a fairly transparent lie, it seemed to Griffin, but apparently the very one she wanted to hear, and so the twins had been dispatched to Portland to fetch her back up the coast. At the ceremony she seemed to be in reasonably good spirits, and Griffin kept expecting her to come over and apologize for telling him to fuck off, especially since he was the only one in the family who'd showed her the slightest kindness or consideration during what he'd already come to think of as the Ordeal of the Hedge, but she rather pointedly kept her distance, as if to suggest that by correctly diagnosing and sympathizing with her plight he'd assumed responsibility for it.

The ceremony had been performed by a Unitarian minister, a friend of Andy's family, and Joy needn't have worried about there being too many religious overtones, because this fellow seemed utterly unencumbered by liturgical obligation. He clearly fancied himself a comedian, though, and used those parts of the service that might otherwise have been given over to prayer to relive the more memorable moments of the rehearsal dinner, which he himself had not attended but obviously had been briefed on. While the smattering of nervous laughter that his attempts at humor occasioned couldn't have been terribly gratifying, he'd soldiered on, his faith in his own comic talent apparently as deep and unshakable as his belief in the Almighty. When he described for the edification of those who'd been present that the bride's grandfather had had to be removed from a Venus-flytrap hedge by means of a chain saw, Harve, hearing himself alluded to, loudly asked, his voice still raspy from yesterday's bellowing, "Who the hell *is* this guy?"

Griffin's fatherly duties kept him centered and focused during the ceremony itself, though the reception, which made fewer demands on his time, proved more of a challenge. Laura had chosen "Teach Your Children Well," he hoped unironically, for their father-daughter dance. They were joined by Andy and his mother, who seemed not to have anticipated this tradition and were rigid with fear during its execution. Before long the floor was crowded with dancers, a statistically improbable percentage sporting gauzy bandages. As the wine began to flow and everyone began to relax and have a good time, Griffin felt increasingly adrift. He and Joy had agreed beforehand they wouldn't dance together, fearing their daughter might break down at the sight of them. Joy, her middle finger made obscene by a large, gleaming metal splint, had already excused herself, saying the stitches in her side hurt, but Griffin suspected she felt it inappropriate to dance with Ringo at her daughter's wedding. Perhaps there was more. Something about their body language was different today, and he wondered if they'd had words. That possibility would have cheered him had he not sensed there was a greater distance between Joy and him as well, as if their brief, unguarded intimacy at the emergency room had frightened her enough that she was determined not to risk it again.

That morning he'd suggested to Marguerite that they shouldn't be too much of a couple, either. Knowing how much she loved to dance, he allowed that it would probably be okay if they boogied to a couple of fast numbers, but no slow, clingy stuff. If he worried about cramping her style, he needn't have. Recognizing Sunny Kim from last year's leftover table with a squeal of delight, she immediately dragged him out there and didn't let him go until they'd hoofed it through three long tracks. After that she danced with Andy, with all of his groomsmen and even with Ringo, who sported an impressive hematoma on his forehead and moved, Griffin was pleased to see, like a man in a truss. When she'd exhausted all these partners, she set upon the Unitarian comic, whose expression suggested he'd become a man of the cloth as a hedge against precisely this sort of social necessity. On the dance floor he looked everywhere but at Marguerite's chest, unintentionally providing the very comedy that had eluded him during the wedding ceremony. When she wasn't dancing, Marguerite took refuge at the table presided over by Kelsey and her husband ("Aunt Rita? What're *you* doing here?"), getting a recap of the couple's first year of wedded bliss.

Her defection left Griffin—who had it coming, of course—too often alone at the long head table. Laura (he could tell) coerced her bridesmaids to dance with him, and out of a similar sense of duty he'd asked Andy's mother, who said, no, no, she really couldn't't, as if the single dance ticket she'd been issued at the door had already been redeemed by her son. Joy's sisters had their husbands to deal with and they didn't like him besides, so he steered clear there. Joy herself was going from table to table, making sure people had what they needed and were enjoying themselves, a duty he begrudged her until it occurred to him that it was his as well, so he started at the other end of the room and did the same thing, as slowly as possible, lest he be forced to return to the nearly abandoned head table.

His sense that something wasn't right intensified as the evening wore on, though he had no idea what the hell might be wrong. Everybody seemed to be having a good time, especially the young people, Laura and Andy's college friends, which was as it should be. The only person more disconnected to the proceedings was poor Harve. After successfully lobbying to attend, he dozed through the exchange of vows and then much of the reception, though at one point he struggled to his feet and gyrated his hips with the prettiest of Laura's bridesmaids, occasioning thunderous applause from everyone but Dot, who thrust him forcefully back into his chair. The boy who'd punched Andy (and his own mother) in the groin the night before—Griffin still had no idea who the little fucker was—recognized Jason and once again attempted his signature move, but the MP saw it coming and put the palm of his hand on the kid's forehead and let him swing away, and this, too, everyone seemed to think was funny.

Gradually Griffin came to understand that he was waiting for another moment of grace, like the one at last year's wedding when Laura pulled Sunny Kim onto the dance floor. The night before, in the emergency room with Joy, he'd sensed the proximity of just such a moment, but the twins had interrupted and it was lost, though at the time it hadn't worried him. If he didn't force it, he told himself, the moment would come of its own volition, probably at some point during the wedding. Maybe even heralded by that old Bon Jovi song. What was it called? "Livin' on a Prayer"? He checked with the DJ, who said it was definitely on the playlist, but it didn't play, and still didn't, and when some of the guests with small children began to gather them up and bid farewell to the bride and groom, he realized it wasn't going to.

Feeling his emotions come untethered and rise dangerously toward the surface, he left the wedding tent, whispering to Marguerite that he needed to visit the gents. Inside the hotel he found Sunny Kim sitting alone in the small, dark bar, drinking in the only place where the booze wasn't free.

"Do you enjoy single-malt scotch?" he asked when Griffin slid onto the bar stool next to him.

Even in the dim light, he could see the young man's eyes were full. "I do," he admitted, although hard liquor was probably the last thing he needed right then.

Sunny ordered him a very expensive one. "I love fine scotch," he said, "but I can't drink it without remembering my father." Was this, Griffin wondered, to explain his liquid eyes? "What would he have thought about such extravagance? He didn't believe in excess."

"Are you sure?" Griffin said. "Not being able to afford something isn't the same as disapproving of it."

"True," Sunny admitted. "It's also true that I never really knew him."

"He'd have been proud of you," Griffin assured him, because he hadn't meant to suggest any such thing. "Hell, we're not even related and I'm proud of you."

Which clearly pleased the young man, though his smile vanished as quickly as it appeared, replaced by confusion. "Laura's uncles? Jason and . . . Jared?"

Griffin chuckled. Back in the tent he'd noticed the twins had taken a shine to Sunny, introducing him to all the pretty girls, most of whom they hadn't been introduced to themselves.

"They mock their father," he said.

Sunny hadn't been at the rehearsal, of course, but Griffin suspected that even if he'd witnessed the collapse of the wheelchair ramp and the ensuing Ordeal of the Hedge, none of that would've been as profoundly inexplicable and unsettling to him as their treatment of Harve. "It's hard for them to express love," he explained. "Being men. And idiots."

Sunny nodded seriously.

"Otherwise they aren't bad fellows," Griffin said. "They'd be good to have on your side in a fight. Of course"—he pointed to his eye—"if you're with them there's a much better chance there'll *be* a fight."

"I made the mistake of telling them I don't have to be back in Washington until Monday. They want me to go with them to Bar Harbor tomorrow. Do you think I shouldn't?"

"No, I wouldn't say that. Just remember they act first, think later, and then neither clearly nor deeply. Have you ever thought of getting a tattoo, Sunny?"

"I'm sorry?"

"I ask because if you go drinking with them, you could wake up with one." And it would say *Laura*.

Sunny must have been thinking along these same lines, because after a moment, he said, "I'm getting married myself later this year."

"No kidding? Congratulations." They clumsily clinked glasses. "You want to tell me about her?"

"Yes." But then, for a long moment, he didn't. "She's Korean," he finally said. "From a fine family. She's been very patient waiting for me to ask for her hand."

"Will the wedding be here?"

"No, in Seoul. I've invited Laura and . . . Andrew, but of course I'll understand if they can't come. It's a long trip and very expensive. I'm hoping we'll get together later. Andrew's never been to Washington."

"You'll live in the U.S., then?"

"Yes, of course. My mother's here, my brothers, and my work's important, too."

"Yes, it is."

He seemed pleased to be given this vote of confidence, but troubled, too. "Why does a rich country like ours blame people who have nothing for its problems?"

"Good question. It's a problem that predates Lou Dobbs, and it's probably not just us in the States."

"No, but we're not responsible for other countries."

"Are we responsible for this one, as individuals? Isn't that a lot to ask?"

"Yes. But I do believe we are responsible."

Griffin nodded, surprised to discover that despite raising the question he agreed with Sunny's response. Also that he'd finished his scotch.

"She's very happy," Sunny said, as if this leap from political and philosophical discussion to deeply personal were perfectly natural.

Love, Griffin thought, smiling. Only love made such a leap possible. Only love related one thing to all other things, putting all your eggs into a single basket—that dumbest yet most courageous and thrilling of economic and emotional strategies. "I think she is," he said, almost apologetically. His daughter was happy and deserved to be. Yet, sitting here in the dark, quiet bar with Sunny Kim, Griffin couldn't help wondering if the worm might already be in the apple. A decade from now, or a decade after that, would Laura suddenly see Sunny differently? Griffin knew no finer, truer heart than Laura's, but even the best hearts, as her mother could testify, were notoriously unruly. Would some good, unexpected thing happen in his daughter's life, something that caused her very soul to swell with pride and joy, whereupon she'd realize that the man she wanted to tell first and most wasn't who she'd married today but the one who'd loved her since they were kids and who once, in the middle of the night, had trusted her enough to share his family's shame? Would she understand that such trust and intimacy do not—indeed cannot—exist apart from consequence and obligation? Would she understand then what she didn't yet suspect, that remembering Sunny Kim at the moment of her own great happiness at Kelsey's wedding last year had been kind and generous, yes, of course, but also an unwitting acknowledgment of something yet hidden from her?

And what of Andy? Would he one day come upon his wife unawares, her good heart broken, and just *know,* as Griffin had, even though he'd tried not to, that there was someone else? Sensing the power of jealousy to wound deeply and maybe even destroy, would Andy bury that knowledge, as Griffin had, even before he knew for sure what it was? And later, after Laura at great cost had done all any woman could do to rule what was by nature unrulable, would her husband then resent her because the wound to his own heart, neither acknowledged nor treated, hadn't healed?

Griffin did not want to believe that any of this would come to pass. In fact, he refused to.

"Thank you," Sunny said, finishing his own scotch.

"What for?"

"For the honest conversation. A rare thing."

"And thank you, for the drink. A rare scotch."

"It's not my business," Sunny said, "but will you and Mrs. Griffin try again?"

Griffin could tell from Sunny's worried, almost frightened expression that he wasn't asking out of curiosity, or probably even affection, though of course these, too, were present. Until that moment, it hadn't occurred to Griffin that his daughter wasn't the only one who'd played an important part in Sunny's life. He and Joy also had. Sure, Sunny'd gone to Stanford and then to Georgetown, but before that he'd crossed Shoreham Drive from his parents' immigrant neighborhood to where the Griffins and Kelsey and her parents lived. Just a few blocks if you were talking real estate, but much farther in all other respects. Griffin could see him at thirteen, all dressed up for Laura's party, waiting at the Shoreham Drive intersection for the light to change. And at their "lovely home," he'd fallen in love (if he wasn't already) with Laura, yes, but also with her parents, who didn't unduly burden their child with obligations, who laughed and looked at each other in a way that his own parents never did. Was it Kelsey who'd observed back then that it was clear Laura's parents still had sex? Sunny would've sensed that, too. Hell, he'd have seen it with his own hungry, adolescent eyes. Joy had never been more beautiful than she was then, in her late thirties, and when Sunny compared Laura's parents with his rigid little mother and chronically ill father, he would've felt envy and shame in equal measure. He'd fallen in love with them, Griffin realized, much as Griffin had fallen in love with the Brownings on Cape Cod: thoroughly, uncritically. Had the nation itself been part of his seduction? America, like the Cape, that finer place, with its myriad implicit promises and gifts, chief among them the permission to dream? Who better than Sunny Kim to ask why America blamed its ills on the most recent of its dreamers, whether legal or illegal? By now, Griffin thought, Sunny must be coming to the reluctant understanding that such dreams embodied a paradox, that they, like love itself, were at once real and chimerical.

"I don't know if we will or not," he at last said, embarrassed by Sunny's personal stake in their marriage and by the larger questions that any marriage—a public institution, after all—in fact begged, no matter the circumstances. And even more embarrassed by his own passivity. Having squandered last year's moment of grace, he'd waited today for another and felt cheated when it didn't come. "I don't know if she wants to, or even how to ask her," he said. "She's done pretty well this year without me."

"Do you mind if I ask if this is self-pity?"

"Almost certainly," Griffin admitted, a little taken aback by Sunny's forthrightness, though it was impossible to take offense when you were so well understood. "I'm prone to it. Not to mention nostalgia and some other bogus emotions."

"Allow me to say that things will work out for the best."

This made Griffin chuckle. "We've known each other a long time, Sunny," he said, rising from his bar stool, "and that's the first dumb thing I've ever heard you say."

Hauling his and Marguerite's bags out to their rental car and getting soaked in the process, Griffin discovered that yesterday's inertia, which Sunny had correctly diagnosed as self-pity, had returned, along with a terrible understanding. Part of the reason he'd been so passive at his daughter's wedding was his profound sense that something was *supposed* to happen there; all he had to do was be patient and recognize the moment when it arrived. Today, though, he knew better. The only things that were supposed to happen were things you *made* happen. The intimate, bittersweet moment he'd shared with Joy at the hospital had seemed to promise more, but he saw now that it was all he was going to get, probably because it was all he deserved. The events that had culminated in his daughter's wedding and the eventual dissolution of his own marriage were on parallel tracks, both set in motion this time last year, and over the long months they'd gained sufficient momentum to be virtually unstoppable. Even the fiasco of the rehearsal dinner hadn't derailed the wedding, and he was grateful for that, but apparently the sundering of marriage was subject to the same immutable law of motion. It was like the third act—the final twenty minutes—of a well-constructed screenplay, during which there was no more choosing, no more deciding, just the juggernaut of action and consequence.

Was Joy, too, feeling the same dispiriting sense of inevitability? Was that why she'd kept her distance at the reception? He wished he could ask her. Sliding in behind the wheel, Griffin again noticed the "Summer of the Brownings" magazine on the dashboard. He'd wanted her to see the story because he was proud of it, but also, he now realized, because it constituted evidence of—what? That he'd been trying for a long time to understand and resolve his almost pathological resentment toward his deceased parents? That perhaps he'd made some progress? The facts on the ground suggested rather the opposite. This time last year he was driving around with one parent in the trunk of his car, whereas now he had both. Far from resolving anything, the Browning story probably just explained how he'd come to be the husband and father he was instead of the one he meant to be. It was also possible he wanted to show Joy the story for even more selfish reasons. Tommy, puzzled by the story in its earlier incarnation, had been both surprised and impressed by the new version. "Jesus, Griff," he said. "This is really . . . there's fucking *truth* in here." Maybe all he wanted from Joy was more praise.

He studied the cover, where his name was listed along with eight or ten other writers, none of them household names, and felt the smallness of his accomplishment. Sure, he could use the story as an excuse to drive back down to the Hedges. Once there, if he screwed up his courage, he could ask Joy if this really was the end, if that's what she truly wanted, but he already knew the answer, didn't he? She'd told him at the hospital that Brian Fynch didn't make her *un*happy, and for her, given the last few years of their marriage, this was probably a step in the right direction. Besides which, he thought, tossing the magazine onto the backseat, he'd have to explain to Marguerite why driving back down the peninsula made more sense than just mailing the issue once they got back to L.A.

But what the hell was taking her so long to check out, he wondered. He supposed he might go find out, but decided instead to stay where it was dry. After all, there wasn't any hurry. No doubt the vague sense of urgency he was feeling was just residue from the wedding, which was now over. Laura and Andy were already in a limo headed for Boston, where they'd catch their flight to Paris. Had they agreed on that destination for their honeymoon? he wondered. Laura had spent her junior year in France and talked about returning ever since. But had Paris been Andy's first choice, too, or had he been persuaded, the first tiny burr of resentment under the marriage saddle? Griffin banished the thought. They'd make their own marriage, not repeat his.

Lord, it was raining hard, he thought. Would it let up by the time they got to the Cape or would the deluge intensify, preventing the ash-scattering yet again? Was that what he was hoping for, another excuse? What did it mean that he had so little access to something as straightforward as what he really wanted? He considered turning the key in the ignition so he could at least use the wipers and the defroster, then decided to just sit there in his watery cave, rain streaming down the windows in solid sheets. When his cell phone rang and he saw HEDGES on the screen, he felt his heart leap, thinking it must be Joy calling to suggest he stop by for a quick debriefing, a well-by-golly-we-did-it-despite-difficult-circumstances moment, just the two of them, Ringo and Marguerite off someplace. They were owed that much, right?

Apparently not. It was only the manager calling to express his fond hope that the wedding had met or (yes!) even exceeded Mr. Griffin's expectations. The resort had incurred a few additional expenses above and beyond the charges covered by the checks he'd already written (the mutilated yew?) but he didn't feel it was right to pass these on. No, they were pleased to absorb any additional costs. He personally felt terrible about the collapse of the wheelchair ramp and the injuries it had caused. He hoped Mr. Griffin understood that such structures weren't designed to accommodate so many people at once, all of them moving in the same direction, but still, he couldn't help but feel responsible, if not in the *legal* sense, then in some other. "Moral?" Griffin helpfully suggested. Well, yes, something like that. Griffin told him that of course he couldn't speak for the other guests, but he knew most of the people involved and doubted there'd be any litigation.

He hung up, and a moment later Marguerite thudded into the passenger seat beside him, soaked to the skin but otherwise as happy as a schoolgirl.

"What took so long?"

"I was saying goodbye to Sunny. He's in the breakfast room. Do you want to go in? I think you should. It'll only take a minute."

"We said our goodbyes last night," Griffin said. He liked Sunny a lot but had no desire to see him this morning, to yet again come face-to-face with his courage and optimism. He started the car, put the heater on defrost and waited for the windshield to clear, feeling Marguerite's eyes on him. But when he finally turned to look at her, she was peering out the small patch of windshield that had defogged. "*I* think it's going to clear," she said.

Ambiguous pronoun reference, his mother piped up from the back, her first critical observation of the new day. *Is she talking about the weather or the windshield?*

"That's not what the Weather Channel's calling for," Griffin said.

Marguerite leaned over and kissed his cheek. "It's what I'm calling for."

Oh, honestly, his mother said.

Griffin turned on the radio, which sometimes silenced her, just as a car careened into the drive and rocked to a halt in front of the B and B. Jared and Jason, oblivious to the downpour, leapt out and began chanting up at the second-floor windows, "Suh-*nee,* Suh-*nee,* Suh-*nee!*"

Griffin put the car in gear before they were noticed.

"Can you see?" Marguerite said.

"Well enough," he told her.

Go! his mother urged him, as if they'd just robbed a bank and he was driving the getaway car. *Go, go, go!*

He turned up the radio.

His mother chattered to the rhythm of the wipers all the way to New Hampshire, where the rain stopped as abruptly as if a spigot had just been turned off. Twenty minutes later, when they crossed into Massachusetts, the skies cleared. "Voilà," said Marguerite, as if she'd just performed a nifty parlor trick.

Oh, my, Griffin's mother said, *she's bilingual.*

Having fled the twins earlier, he now almost wished they were around. Maybe he could get one of them to punch him in the head again and knock his mother out. And if he had to be knocked out himself, so be it.

Marguerite switched off the radio. "Okay," she said, "tell me about your mother," as if she'd also been listening to her running commentary all the way down the coast and decided it was high time to acknowledge the bitch. "I want to know all about your father, too."

What she had in mind was to create personality profiles for each of them, so she'd know the right spot on the Cape when she saw it—a silly idea, Griffin thought, but he indulged her. After all, it wasn't like he was wedded to a plan of his own. Moreover, when she'd proposed the idea the trunk fell silent, as if his mother (maybe his father, too?) was curious what he'd have to say about them. So, Marguerite began. What was her favorite color? Green. His? Blue. Where were they born? Buffalo (Dad). Rochester (Mom). And their favorite foods? Him, king crab legs; her, double-cut broiled lamb chops. Any hobbies? He collected P. G. Wodehouse first editions, vintage campaign buttons and Victorian pornography; she, after retiring from teaching, did thousand-piece mono-chromatic jigsaw puzzles and swore colorfully at the television whenever George W. Bush appeared.

Marguerite's curiosity was so benign and well meaning that Griffin gradually became more expansive. What were their favorite times of the day? Well, his father had been a morning person, he told her, up hours before he and his mother, especially on their vacations. He liked to go out for pastries and the newspaper. "You missed a great sunrise," he'd inform his wife when she finally shuffled out onto the deck, midmorning, for a breakfast with Al Fresco. ("Al Fresco? Who was he?") "Like hell I did," she always replied. His mother's favorite time of day was cocktail hour. She loved the sound of ice cubes in glasses, of jazz and gin-induced laughter, of lots of people talking all at once. So much better, to her way of thinking, than eavesdropping on smaller conversations where you could actually hear whatever stupid opinions people held. He told Marguerite about his father's propensity for sudden, violent, rear-end collisions in parking lots, about his mother's speech at her retirement dinner, even a little about the Morphine Narrative. And when she asked him, apropos of nothing, for a Christmas memory, he told her about their search, each December, for the perfect tree.

Though they professed to hate the season for its hypocrisy, for all that trumped-up seasonal "goodwill toward men" crap, his parents demanded big, full Christmas trees. Finding one that passed muster took days, sometimes weeks. They had to visit every lot within a ten-mile radius and carefully examine all trees over seven feet. The lot attendants went from smiling and helpful to frowning and exasperated and homicidal. Other tree shoppers queued up and then gave up while every tall tree on the lot was hauled out, stood up, vigorously shaken and twirled for a full inspection. Sometimes, just as it seemed a sale was imminent, Griffin's mother would sigh and say, "No, there's a hole," and his father would ask where, and she'd point and he'd cock his head and say, "Oh, right." Most attendants, not knowing his parents, would sensibly suggest that the "hole" she saw might face in toward the wall, whereupon she'd sigh again and say, "Let's keep looking." Griffin remembered one old guy who said, after his parents had rejected a dozen trees, "Lady, maybe there's something you don't understand. Those holes you keep seeing's the space between the goddamn branches. Wasn't for the spaces, the tree would be solid fuckin' wood." He made a sweeping gesture that included the entire lot. "Every one of these trees got holes. It's the holes that *makes* 'em trees. Now, you want one or not?"

Other attendants, equally tired and frustrated, tried reason. "What kinda ceiling we looking at here?" Griffin remembered one asking, hoping at least to narrow the search. Of course his parents had no idea. A high ceiling was one of their requirements every year when they rented a new house or apartment, but as professional humanists it wouldn't have occurred to them to actually *measure*. "Doesn't matter," his father would say. "We can cut a little off the top if we need to." To which the man responded, "Look kind of funny, wouldn't it?" At which point his mother might take the tip of a branch between her thumb and forefinger, give it a good tug and, if needles came off, complain, "When was this tree cut? Last August?"

Griffin came to understand that the perfect Christmas tree was a lot like the perfect house on the Cape, first because it didn't exist in the real world, and second because all the imperfect trees fell into two categories. The first was the all-too-familiar Wouldn't Have It As a Gift, and the second applied to just one tree: Well, I Guess It'll Have to Do. He couldn't remember ever voicing an opinion about the tree his parents finally agreed would have to do. The search over at last, his father would hand the lucky attendant a length of gray, weathered clothesline so the tree could be hoisted onto the roof of their car and secured through its open windows. Sometimes the clothesline would snap when they rounded a corner, sending the tree into the gutter. One year they didn't even make it out of the lot. Griffin's father, leaning forward so he could keep an eye on the tree strapped to the roof, backed into a parked pickup, and their tree leapt as if by wizardry into its bed.

Back home, they invariably discovered, by trying to stand the tree up, that it was indeed too tall, and with a curse his father would lay it back down on the floor. Some years the tree lay there in the middle of the living room for days while he canvassed his English department colleagues for a saw he could borrow. What he actually meant, they understood all too well, was a saw he could *have*, since he never once returned a tool. (The saw he'd borrowed the previous Christmas was no doubt hanging from a nail in the garage of last year's rental.) Eventually, though, someone would come through, and that was when the real magic began.

The first cut never took quite enough off—here again, no measuring for the Griffins—and the second usually didn't, either. The third would be off by a mere half inch, close enough if you forced matters (they always did), and the freshly cut top of the tree would leave a moist, six-inch, greenish-brown streak on the white ceiling, which no doubt puzzled the owners when they returned home from their sabbatical. The broken toaster oven, the missing eighth chair from the dining room set, the red wine stains on the shag carpet—these things could happen, but how on earth had the Griffins managed to scar the fucking *ceiling*? And of course the tree *did* look funny with its top sawed off. Their Christmas trees always looked to Griffin like they'd grown right through the ceiling, as if what you were looking at was just the bottom two-thirds, and if you went upstairs, the top third would be growing right out of the hardwood floor.

Once the tree was upright, Griffin's father would pick the lock on the closet where the owners stored the stuff they didn't want ruined or broken, see what they had by way of Christmas decorations and berate their bad taste. His mother thought the prettiest trees were decorated all in white, with maybe a little silver for contrast, but Griffin himself liked all the blues and greens and reds and was grateful for other people's lack of refinement. She claimed garlands were especially tacky, but he liked those, too. He was allowed to help decorate, of course, but he couldn't remember ever hanging an ornament or icicle that his mother didn't adjust later. Once the tree was finished, his favorite thing was to crawl beneath it, lie on his back and peer up through the branches, imagining other worlds, himself miniaturized and climbing ever upward, from branch to branch, among all the blinking lights and shiny ornaments, until the whole world lay below him.

One year—he must have been seven or eight—he'd crawled under the tree during his parents' annual boozy Christmas party and watched the drunken kaleidoscopic proceedings from there. Over the course of the evening, two or three of their guests noticed him back there and asked his parents if he was okay, and they responded that yes, he was fine. He remembered *feeling* fine. His father had spiked the eggnog that afternoon, forgetting to reserve some for Griffin. His mother said he couldn't have any of the spiked, but his father felt guilty about forgetting him and let him have a big glass before anyone arrived. During the party he kept wishing somebody would slide him a plate of Christmas cookies, but otherwise he felt warm and happy and tipsy tucked into his own private little corner. He'd fallen asleep there, staring up into the magical branches, and eventually one of his parents must have pulled him out because the next morning he woke up in his bed, the sheets full of pine needles. Which one of them had remembered him? he'd wondered at the time.

"It's okay," Marguerite said, taking his hand, and only then did he realize there were tears running down his cheeks. He was pretty sure he'd never told that story to anyone before, not even Joy. He might have expected all manner of comment from the trunk, but there wasn't a peep.

After he'd gathered himself, he said, "Okay, enough about me. Tell me about *your* parents," but Marguerite shook her head. "Let's just say that if you knew them you'd understand how I ended up with a man like Harold."

It was the first bitter thing he could remember hearing her say, and it begged an obvious question, one he didn't want to ask but did anyway. "And a man like me?"

"Nobody's ever been nicer to me than you," she said, squeezing his hand. He appreciated the vote of confidence, he really did, until she added, "I'm going to miss that."

He started to ask her what she meant when her cell rang. It was Beth, the woman she'd left in charge of the flower shop back in L.A., with a question about inventory. By the time Marguerite hung up, they were rumbling up onto the Sagamore Bridge. "What's that you're humming?" she wanted to know.

He'd been *humming*?

They scattered his father in a cove near Barnstable. It was serene there, with views of a marsh redolent of bluish-purple wildflowers and the sunrise. For his mother they chose a tidal inlet on the Atlantic side, mid-Cape. Across the water, a quarter mile away, sat a posh restaurant with a huge deck from which the breezes carried the sounds of moneyed voices and the occasional pop of a champagne cork and, when the wind shifted, the sound of surf. An older couple, strolling past when he was emptying his mother's urn, saw what he was doing and came over to Marguerite, who was quietly weeping (as she'd done for his father), and offered her their condolences. "You take good care of her," the woman told dry-eyed Griffin, as if she'd taken his measure at a glance and doubted he was up to the task.

Back in the car, Marguerite said, "Okay, I'll tell you this much. My father hanged himself when I was a little girl."

Now it was Griffin's turn to take her hand. "That's terrible. I'm sorry."

"It's okay. I don't really even remember that much about him. Only what my mother said to me."

Griffin didn't want to ask, but there was no way not to.

"She said, 'There. Happy now?' "

When he suggested they splurge on a fancy restaurant in Chatham, Marguerite again scrunched up her shoulders and said, "I have a better idea. Let's go back to that restaurant where we met."

Griffin couldn't imagine why she'd want to return to the Olde Cape Lounge—when he'd left her there with Harold last year, she'd been in tears—but if that's what she wanted it was fine with him. Spending the evening around there made sense, making the morning's drive to Logan and their flight back to L.A. that much easier.

Because he wasn't sure he'd be able to find it again, they decided to look for the restaurant first, then book a room nearby. He meant to avoid the B and B where he and Joy had stayed, which he remembered (correctly) as being about half a mile down the road from the restaurant, but thought (incorrectly) there'd be someplace to turn back onto Route 28 before he got there. "Oooh, that looks nice," Marguerite said when they passed the B and B, so Griffin, unwilling to explain why he'd have preferred anywhere else, turned around and went back. The same woman who'd checked him in last summer did so again, though if she recognized him as repeat business—no reason she should, given his massive dark glasses—she gave no sign. When she showed them to the same room he and Joy had occupied, he considered asking for a different one but decided not to. Late middle age, he was coming to understand, was a time of life when everything was predictable and yet somehow you failed to see any of it coming.

Exhausted by the day's emotion and the long drive down from Maine, they took a nap before dinner. Marguerite awoke from hers refreshed and buoyant, while Griffin was slow and groggy, his already low spirits having ebbed even further. And why, for God's sake? His daughter was successfully married and halfway to Paris by now. The checks he'd written weren't going to bounce and, thanks to Marguerite, his parents were finally at rest. By rights he should've been ready to celebrate. Was he coming down with something? That would make sense. Like his parents before him, he often got sick whenever he could afford to, like at the end of the academic term. Back when he was writing movies with Tommy, he'd hand a just-finished script to their producer and sneeze in the same motion. So maybe.

In any event, for Marguerite's sake, he meant to soldier through whatever this was. In the bathroom he swallowed a couple of ibuprofen (vowing not to call them I-be-hurtin's anymore, even to himself) for the headache he felt gathering behind his eyes, and took a shower, hoping it might wake him up.

"Let's dress up," Marguerite suggested when he emerged.

"It's not a very fancy place," Griffin reminded her.

"Us," she replied. "We'll be fancy."

And Griffin, knowing she was about to scrunch up her shoulders again, purposely looked away.

"Oh, good," she said twenty minutes later when they slipped onto bar stools. "They've still got that funny sign."

The Olde Cape Lounge was as mobbed as before, and the hostess had warned them it would be a good hour before they got a table. Marguerite seemed to enjoy being overdressed. Her outfit wasn't one Griffin had seen before, but it was very Marguerite, showing plenty of skin, the kind designed to make Unitarian comedians perspire.

"How does it go again?" she said, squinting at the sign.

"Drink a couple of these and it'll make sense," the bartender said, setting down her cosmo and Griffin's martini. A communal joke, apparently, since this was a different bartender from the one last year. "You know there's a law against spouse abuse in this state," he told her and nodded at Griffin, who'd slid his dark glasses down his nose so he could look at the sign.

"But he's not my husband," she said.

"My mistake," the man said. "In that case, do whatever you want."

"I can't remember how you're supposed to read it," Marguerite said when the bartender was gone.

At just such a juncture Griffin's mother would usually chime in, wanting to know where this bimbo had done her graduate work, but she was mum. In fact, now that he thought about it, she hadn't voiced a single opinion since they'd left Chatham. Was it possible that by scattering her ashes they'd silenced her? For*ever*? That possibility, while remote, should have raised his spirits, but somehow it didn't.

"Ignore the spaces," he told her, putting his hand on the small of her back, where the skin was warm, almost feverish. "Let the words form themselves." He was more determined than ever to show this generous woman the good time she'd earned. It wasn't like she was hard to make happy. All she wanted was a little fun. "Where do you *find* such good-hearted women?" was how Tommy put it after they'd met, and he was right. Even after being married to Harold, Marguerite didn't understand unkindness as an option, its myriad perverse satisfactions as foreign to her as the sign she was now laboriously translating ("Here . . . stop . . . and") from English into, well, English. Next year, if they were still together and they were back at the Olde Cape Lounge, he'd have to teach her how to read the sign all over again, this despite the fact that the gist of it was her own personal philosophy of life in a nutshell.

But tomorrow she'd get him over the Sagamore Bridge and onto a plane and back to L.A. and . . . then what? When he tried imagining what would come next for them he couldn't, though of course that had less to do with her than himself. It was his own future, with or without Marguerite, that refused to take shape. With the help of his new agent he could continue chasing low-end screenwriting assignments, teach a night class or two and cobble together a kind of living. But that hardly amounted to a future, or for that matter a life. The only good work he'd done in L.A. was "The Summer of the Brownings," and he'd been paid for that in contributor's copies. Not even a check there, never mind a future. *Quit*, he told himself. *Stop thinking. Get through tonight without moping.*

"Be . . . just . . . and . . . kind . . . and . . . devil . . ."

"And evil," he corrected her.

"Oh, right," she said, taking his hand and squeezing it. "Speak of no one."

None, Griffin started to say, then stopped himself. "Words to live by."

"And that old poop Harold said it didn't mean anything." She gave Griffin a kiss on the cheek, a kiss that might have been Harold's, the gesture seemed to imply, if only he'd played his cards right. Marguerite enjoyed public displays of affection almost as much as the affection itself. Yet another contrast with Joy, who after their wedding had never kissed him except in private. He still recalled the keen disappointment he'd felt early in their marriage when it became obvious she wasn't about to kiss or embrace him in front of her parents. Marguerite felt no such compunctions. She'd have kissed him (or Harold before him) in front of the pope, and the kiss would have been long and full of tongue. "Why do I feel guilty about being here and not calling him?"

"Harold? Now that *is* a mystery."

She shrugged and went back to studying the sign, as if her translation had not unearthed all its secrets. "Imagine that boy figuring it out all by himself," she said, then turned to face him. "It's a shame he's so in love with her."

Griffin was pretty sure he'd never mentioned Sunny Kim's lifelong devotion to Laura, which meant Marguerite had done some figuring out of her own. "He'll be fine," he said, draining the last of his martini and trying to sound more certain on this score than he felt. He considered telling her about Sunny's own marriage plans but decided not to, afraid that in the telling he'd betray his own misgivings.

"I know. He's smart and good-looking and he's a lawyer," she said. "It's just a shame you can't say yes to one person without saying no to another."

She was talking about Laura, Griffin thought. Of course she

was. Except that her expression was unfamiliar to him, a strange combination of sadness and foreknowledge that made him desperately want to change the subject and head off whatever she meant to say next. "I've been wondering what you meant earlier," he said. "About how you were going to miss me being nice to you. Do you think I'm going to turn into that old poop Harold or something?"

"No," she said. "I just meant I'm going to miss that when it's over."

"When what's over?" But of course he knew, just as he knew that he hadn't really changed the subject.

"Us," she said, causing his heart to sink. "When you and I are over." She scrunched her shoulders then, her signature gesture of delight, though he'd never before seen her do it in anticipation of anything but pleasure. "It's okay," she said, her eyes spilling over. "Really. I've known from the start."

"No," he said, shaking his head stubbornly like a child being told something he didn't want to hear. Because if he accepted her conclusion, it meant that he'd failed yet again to accomplish a simple task, to get through the evening without making this woman cry and in so doing to outperform Harold. Was it possible to set the bar any lower? This was beyond demoralizing. Taking Marguerite's face in his hands, he kissed her forehead, thinking as he did of that day so long ago, the first of the Browning summer, when he'd watched from the window under the eaves as his father drew his mother to him and told her that other women in his life meant nothing. Given their history of infidelity, Griffin had always assumed he was simply lying, but he saw now that in order to lie to his mother, he'd first had to lie to himself. How badly he must have wanted what he was telling her to be true. After all, his mother deserved that much, and if he could somehow *make* it true, that would prove he was a better man than he knew himself to be.

"Look," he told Marguerite, another woman who deserved this much and more, "it's been a rough trip. I couldn't have done it without you. Any of it." By which he meant not just today, not just yesterday, but indeed the long months since his mother's death. "We're going to have a nice time tonight, and tomorrow we're going to get on a plane and fly back home to L.A."

Home to L.A. He'd meant to say something simple, clear and true, but a minor falsehood had somehow slipped in, because of course L.A. wasn't home. "You and me, okay?" he continued, a nameless panic rising. "No discussion."

Though here his voice faltered, because he knew as well as she did what came next, what *words* came next. If he could speak them, he might even convince her they were true, as his father had convinced his mother that Browning summer. It was the worst lie there was, imprisoning and ultimately embittering the hearer, playing upon her terrible need to believe. He could feel the *I love you* forming on his lips. Would he have said it if she hadn't interrupted?

"See?" she said, wiping away her tears with the back of her hand and smearing her makeup. "Right there. *That's* what I'm going to miss."

He slept. It was after nine the next morning when he finally woke up, and perhaps because the last time he'd slept so long and so well it was in this same bed almost exactly a year ago, his first drowsy thought was that the preceding twelve months had been a dream. The door to the balcony was partly open, just as it had been the morning after Kelsey's wedding, and on the other side of it a woman was talking on a cell phone, her voice low. Joy, he thought sleepily, talking to their daughter about her engagement to Andy, discussing the possibility of a wedding next spring. Later in the morning—there was no hurry—they'd drive to Truro and see if they could find the inn where they'd honeymooned. Which in turn meant that his mother was still alive in Indiana and that he'd *not* spent the last nine months in L.A. It meant he was a happily married man, that his wife had never accused him of being otherwise, that she'd never been other than happy herself. It was a fine narrative, plausible and coherent. He found himself smiling.

He heard her say goodbye outside, heard the cell phone's cover slap shut, saw the door to the balcony swing inward. In another split second Joy would appear, and he'd beckon her back to their bed. But of course it was Marguerite who stepped into the room, trailing cruel reality in her wake. Sitting on the edge of the bed, she touched his forehead with the back of her fingers. "Your hair's always funny after you sleep," she informed him. He was about to ask whom she'd been talking to when she said, "Tommy says thanks for being so predictable."

"Tommy," he repeated. Why was it that every time a woman who was supposedly with him made a secret phone call, it was always to the same guy? "Predictable how?"

She was now running her fingers through his hair like a comb, apparently trying to make it look less ridiculous. "We had a friendly wager. I had this dumb idea we'd be stopping off in Vegas to get married. He bet you'd end up back with your wife."

"What does he win?"

She smiled ruefully. "He gets to take me out to dinner. He said the way he looked at it, he'd come out of this with a good woman no matter what. He just wasn't sure which one."

"Tell him I said he doesn't deserve a good woman." As if any man ever did.

"I also called the airline and got them to change my flight."

"Why?" Griffin said, suddenly alarmed. Had he hallucinated the proposal he'd reluctantly agreed to last night in the Olde Cape Lounge after it became clear that Marguerite's mind was made up? They'd have a leisurely breakfast at the B and B, after which he'd drive her to Logan in plenty of time for her flight back to L.A. After that he'd drive down to Connecticut, to what had once been home and might be again. There, if possible, he'd reconcile with the woman he apparently still loved. If he failed, if it was too late to fix the mess he'd made, he still had his plane ticket.

"Well, the next few days are supposed to be beautiful here," Marguerite explained, "and Beth says the store will survive a couple more days without me, so . . ."

"Uh—"

"Oh, don't look so mortified. None of this involves you."

"I don't get it."

"I made one other call, too."

Griffin nodded, finally understanding. No need to ask who the other call was to.

"I better not hear you been mean to her," Harold warned him an hour later. He was studying Griffin's still-swollen, now-yellow-green eye with interest. "If I do, I'll make it so that's your *good* eye."

He'd pulled into the B and B's driveway just as they emerged with their luggage.

"Harold," Marguerite said, handing him her suitcase before Griffin could say a word in his own defense. "Quit. He wasn't mean to me. Pay no attention," she added to Griffin, who these days was paying close attention when anyone offered violence.

"Because this woman and I go back a long way," Harold went on.

"On his worst day," Marguerite elaborated, "he was nicer to me than you were on your best."

"And when her mouth's not running like a whip-poor-will's ass, I have strong, serious feelings for her."

"Go put the suitcase in the trunk, Harold, so we can say our goodbyes. Now, there's a good man."

He consulted his watch. "Will these goodbyes be concluded in a timely manner?"

"Are we on a schedule?"

"Yeah, after here, we're driving down to Westerly," he told her, forgetting Griffin entirely. "I've invested in a condo on the water there. *Practically* on the water. I thought you might like to see. There's a couple of spots we could skinny-dip and nobody would mind. Take some dirty pictures with our cell phones. Plus they got good fried calamari with hot peppers."

"Okay, fine, but go away for a minute."

Harold reluctantly did as he was told, but, remembering Griffin, he stopped halfway to his car. "Did I mention I better not hear you were mean to her?"

"Ignore him," Marguerite advised when Harold's car door shut behind him. "It's just how he is." After she scrunched up her shoulders, they embraced one last time. "Write a movie with a girl like me in it sometime," she suggested when they separated. "With Susan Sarandon. She'd make a good me."

In Falmouth he gassed up at a 7-Eleven and he bought himself a sticky bun and a coffee for the road. He'd had no appetite back at the B and B, but after saying goodbye to Marguerite he was suddenly hungry and ate the pastry right there in the parking lot. It was ten-thirty, and normally it would've made the most sense to head straight up Route 28, cross the canal at the Bourne Bridge, then shoot across 195 to 95, but if he left now he'd almost certainly get home before Joy. The last of her family was flying out of Portland this morning, and there was no way she'd head back to Connecticut before they all were airborne. If he arrived before she did, he'd have an unpleasant decision to make: sit in his own driveway and wait for her or just use his key and go inside. The former would make him feel like the fool he was, but having walked away from that house last June he really had no right to enter it now without invitation.

He needed to kill an hour or two and was too antsy to just sit around. If he got going now and crossed the canal at the Sagamore instead of the Bourne, he could head up Route 3 toward Boston for a while, then loop back down I-95. The idea of crossing the bridge of his unhappy childhood one last time was appealing. Now that he'd finally scattered his parents' ashes, he doubted he'd be returning to the Cape again. He felt finished with both the place and its false promises. Also, on the Sagamore he'd likely find out if his mother was really through haunting him or was just waiting for Marguerite, his guardian angel, to depart. When he knew for certain that she was at rest, he'd be able to think about what he'd say when he arrived home without fear of her sarcastic comments.

Wiping his fingers on a napkin, he adjusted the mirror, turned the key in the ignition and shifted into reverse. He'd have to apologize, of course, for everything he'd allowed to happen, but he knew it wasn't really apologies Joy cared about. She'd been right all along that his parents, not hers, had intruded on their marriage with such disastrous consequences, which meant that he had to figure out how to convince her that all that was finally over, that they could begin again with a clean slate.

Clean slate. Those were the exact words in his head at the moment of impact. The sound was explosive: the initial boom, then the shattering of glass and the shriek of metal on metal, as the back of Griffin's head hit the padded rest. "Ow!" he said, rubbing his neck, just as he'd always done as a kid after one of his father's rear-enders, all of which had occurred just like this one, completely without warning. *Ow.* A child's word, and he'd spoken it in a child's voice, full of grievance and resentment. He half expected to see a child's startled, betrayed eyes, not his father's knowing, sad ones, staring back at him from the rearview.

The driver of the other car, a teenaged boy with an acne-ravaged face, appeared at his window. "You okay?" he said.

Griffin couldn't tell whether the boy was asking if he was hurt or why on earth he was laughing. Griffin rolled down his window and told him he was fine, just surprised.

"I don't see what's so funny," the kid said tentatively, as if, given the difference in their ages, he wasn't sure he was entitled to this opinion.

"Wait a few years," Griffin told him, unlatching his seat belt and getting out.

The other vehicle was a late-model BMW. The boy had also been backing out. Griffin identified the parking space he'd just vacated, saw in his mind's eye the perfect arc in space and time that had resulted in their violent meeting, each blind to the other's existence until the instant of collision. Both trunks had sprung and were standing up at perfect right angles. Griffin tried to close his, but the lock mechanism wasn't properly aligned anymore, and it popped right up again. Both sets of taillights were smashed, both bumpers crumpled. It was the kind of wreck that would've cost his father a few hundred bucks to repair, but today would run into thousands. Otherwise, the vehicles looked drivable. "I guess we should exchange insurance information," he said.

At this the boy visibly wilted, as if the necessity were tantamount to admitting that, yes, they'd just had an accident, something he still hoped might be avoided.

Griffin got a pen and a piece of paper from the car and handed them to him.

The boy said, "Couldn't we just . . . ," then lapsed into silence.

The cops would have to be called, of course, but when Griffin went back to the car he saw that the cup holder where his cell had been sitting was now empty. He finally located the phone on the floor under the rear seat. Its screen was black, and when he pressed the space bar it stayed black. He pressed several other keys and was about to give up when the screen suddenly leapt to life with a message: CALLING JOY. Before he could hit the button to disconnect, he heard his wife answer, her voice sounding tinny and far away.

"Joy," he said. He was about to explain that he hadn't meant to call when he realized that this might just be the moment of grace he'd been waiting for yesterday and had given up on. "Is this a bad time?"

"I'm in the car," she admitted. "I'm surprised to hear your voice. I guess I thought you'd be halfway back to L.A."

He decided on a jaunty tone. "No, I'm on the Cape. I called to tell you it's official. I've become my father. I just backed my rental car into a brand-new BMW. We scattered his ashes yesterday, and I think this might be his way of telling me I won't be rid of him so easily." When she didn't immediately respond, he realized just how forced the jauntiness must have sounded. "We did Mom, too," he continued more seriously. "Near Chatham. Her favorite part of the Cape."

"Are you okay? Was anyone injured?"

"No." To both questions.

Silence again. *So why tell me about it?* was what she must have been thinking.

"And here's the really weird part," he said, unsure whether he was just talking to keep her on the line or, in some roundabout fashion, finally coming to the point. "Since yesterday, maybe for a while before that, I've been wondering . . ." He stopped here, unsure how to continue, though what he'd been wondering couldn't have been simpler. "I've been wondering if maybe I loved them. It's crazy, I know, but . . . do you think that's possible?"

"Oh, Jack," Joy said, as if she would've liked to ask where in the world he'd done his graduate work. "Of course you did. What do you think I've been trying to tell you?"

In the rearview mirror Griffin could see the boy, pen in hand, staring blankly at the piece of paper, as if he'd forgotten his very identity.

"Jack?"

"I'm here," he told her, then, a moment later, heard himself ask, "Is there anything left, Joy, or did I kill it all?"

She didn't answer immediately, and he understood that the

long, painful beat of silence was what he'd been dreading far more than the final verdict. "You came close," she finally admitted, sniffling. "But no. You killed only the part that could be killed."

They talked for another minute or two, though only about logistics. She offered to drive down to Falmouth, but he told her that wouldn't be necessary. In a town this size he shouldn't have any trouble finding a bungee cord to secure the trunk, his father's time-honored solution and good enough for now. It'd probably take him an hour or so with the cops, after which, if the car was drivable, he'd be back on the road. They left it that they'd meet just over the Sagamore. They could have some lunch around there, call the rental-car company and find out what they wanted him to do with the wreck, then drive home together.

When he hung up, his mother said, *There, was that so difficult?*

Yeah, he told her, *it was.*

He expected a smart-assed retort but it didn't come, and when it didn't he became aware of an unfamiliar but extremely pleasurable feeling. How to describe it? Plumb. He was feeling plumb. Okay, maybe not completely, but no more than a half bubble off. Plumb some. As good as could be expected. He wondered if *plumb* might be another word for happy.

I think maybe I'm going to be okay, Mom, he ventured. Still no response. *I guess what I'm saying is it's okay for you to be dead now. Both of you. In fact,* he added, afraid he'd given them too much leeway, *I insist.*

The boy was kicking impotently at the brightly colored shards of taillight glass when Griffin returned. He'd somehow written down all the necessary information, and his name was Tony Loveli. He was sixteen. "My father's on his way," he said. "He's going to kill me. I just got my license last week."

"Don't worry, Tony," Griffin said. "We'll tell him it was my fault."

The kid shook his head morosely. "You don't understand.

That's not going to matter. He's a divorce attorney. A complete and total fucking asshole."

"Not complete," Griffin said, though of course he'd never met the man, who might well be an asshole. "Not total."

A fat gull circling overhead screeched a loud objection. Griffin watched it warily, but it was just a stupid bird, and after a moment, no harm done, it flew away.

Acknowledgments

Okay, I admit it. I had help. Many thanks to my agents, Nat Sobel, Judith Weber and Joel Gotler; to my editors, Gary Fisketjon and Alison Samuel; to Emily Milder, Gabrielle Brooks, Meghan Wilson, Russell Perreault, Kate Runde, Victoria Gerken and all the other good folks at Knopf/Vintage who sell my books; to my daughters, Emily and Kate, whose weddings inspired all manner of imagined catastrophe; to my wife, Barbara, who knows enough about marriage to write her own book but read mine several times without complaint. Thanks also to The Silver Lounge on Cape Cod for the use of their sign. And, finally, my gratitude to my mother, whose recent passing caused me to reflect more deeply on inheritance and all that the word implies. Not to mention love.

A NOTE ON THE TYPE

This book was set in Minion, a typeface produced by the Adobe Corporation specifically for the Macintosh personal computer, and released in 1990. Designed by Robert Slimbach, Minion combines the classic characteristics of old-style faces with the full complement of weights required for modern typesetting.

Designed by Virginia Tan